U0165557

# 華語教學與電腦輔助運用

## CHINESE LANGUAGE TEACHING AND COMPUTER USAGES

總策劃・信世昌

主 編・陳俊光
謝佳玲

五南圖書出版公司 印行

# 總策劃序

　　本書是基於「第八屆全球華文網路教育研討會」（僑務委員會主辦）所發表之部分論文，再經過徵選及雙向匿名審查而編輯完成。

　　運用電腦於華語教學早在1970年代即開始，但直到1990年代中期網際網路及影音多媒體普遍之後，華語文電腦教學才大舉發展，至今不過二十年。回頭看到過去諸多的電腦數位教學研究論文，許多都是基於特定的軟硬體或平台系統，但因科技過時或軟體系統淘汰而再也一無是用。換言之，以電腦技術為本位的論文其價值難以持久，反而是基於語言本體的論文（字詞、語音、語法、篇章等）或是基於語言教學為本位的論文（聽說讀寫及溝通現象）多能歷久彌新，仍具參考價值。因此，從語文內容為本位的電腦數位教學（或學習）的研究才是華語文教學領域最具價值的內涵。

　　本書取名為「華語教學與電腦輔助運用」（Chinese Language Teaching and Computer Usages），其主軸即是基於語文為主而科技為輔的概念，以中文為第二語言之教學為出發點，來探索科技運用的方式。

　　此書的編輯過程要感謝兩位主編陳俊光教授及謝佳玲教授負責審稿安排及編選事宜，而所有細節有賴研究生張閨婷及陳翊綺的細心聯絡與校閱，以及李芸蓁助理在出版方面的協調。此外，更要感謝五南出版社能堅持與尊重華語文領域的專業而出版此類專書。至盼隨著華語界的學者及老師們經過不斷的實務教學與研究探索，日後能持續發表更多的論文專書。

總策劃

信世昌

謹識於台北

# 主編序

　　近年來華語文教學在世界各地蓬勃發展，隨著電腦科技的進步、網路的普及與發達，與雲端資訊結合的教學設計已成為不容小覷的發展領域。為促進華語教學界網路教育的交流，僑務委員會於1999年起，每兩年舉辦一次「全球華文網路教育研討會」，並定期出版會後論文集，提供海內外學者專業發表的空間。

　　本書收錄十一篇論文，每篇皆經過嚴謹的審查過程。論文分為三個主題，依序為「各級華語程度之線上輔助教學」、「漢字及詞彙之數位輔助學習」、「語言技能及文化之數位輔助資源」。「各級華語程度之線上輔助教學」探討不同程度學生的學習模式與其相對應的數位化教學法。線上學習平台是數位化學習可運用的資源之一，不論是初級、中級，甚至是高中教育裡的AP課程，都可將數位學習平台融入至課程設計中。對初級線上課程而言，須以合適的課室經營法則來促進課程中的互動。而對於高中之AP中文教學，除了線上平台以外，雲端科技的應用亦是教師能善用的資源。「漢字及詞彙之數位輔助學習」的論文則將漢字及詞彙的學習與多媒體相結合，並藉由實證研究鞏固嚴謹的教學規劃。最後，「語言技能及文化之數位輔助資源」將學生的輸出技能及跨文化交際能力的學習模式以數位化的方式呈現，訓練學生主動透過網路資源的運用來學習，並呈現自己已習得的語言技能。教師亦能通過電子白板等多媒體工具的輔助，提升師生之間互動合作及溝通學習之成效。

　　本書之得以出版，皆仰賴各位專家學者的踴躍投稿，以及國內外華語文教學界先進的支持。誠摯感謝各論文作者與審查委員，以及協助論文審查的師長和同學。最後也企盼將來有更多同道先進惠賜論文，一同促進華語文網路教育的交流與進步。

陳俊光、謝佳玲
2015年

# 目　錄

# 三、語言技能及文化之數位輔助資源 ················ 161

# 一、各級華語程度之線上輔助教學

# Chinese Online as an Open Educational Resource: Opportunities, Content and Challenges

**Sue-mei Wu**（吳素美）

Carnegie Mellon University

suemei@andrew.cmu.edu

**Mark Haney**（何禮）

Robert Morris University

haney@rmu.edu

**Yi-ching Liu**（呂逸勤）

University of Iowa, USA

yi-ching-liu@uiowa.edu

## Abstract

The Open learning Initiative (OLI) is an open educational resource project at the Carnegie Mellon University (CMU). Funded by the William and Flora Hewlett Foundation, it supports the creation of high-quality online courses that are open and freely available to anyone who wants to learn, and provides a technological platform for developing, delivering, and assessing learning outcomes in those courses.

This paper introduces the Chinese Online curriculum at CMU, which is being developed on the OLI platform to support a two-semester online course in beginning Chinese. The course addresses the four skills of speaking, listening, reading and writing, and also includes culture learning components. While under development the online course is being used by CMU students, but in the future it will be an openly available course in the OLI program, providing an educational resource that anyone can use to learn Chinese at any time, in any place, with or without the benefit of an instructor.

This paper will introduce the features and goals of the online course and discuss the opportunities, issues, and challenges associated with developing it as an open educational resource on the OLI platform. Finally, a walk-through of a typical module in the OLI Chinese online curriculum will be described.

It is hoped that sharing our experience of developing the Chinese online course on the OLI platform can provide some perspectives on the nature of interdisciplinary collaboration in the context of building an open educational resource for language learning.

Keywords: open educational resources, Chinese e-learning, open learning, online Chinese, online curriculum, technology and Chinese learning

## 1.0 Introduction

The Open learning Initiative (OLI; http://oli.cmu.edu) is an open educational resource project at the Carnegie Mellon University (CMU). Funded in 2002 by the William and Flora Hewlett Foundation, the

OLI provides a technological platform for developing, delivering, and assessing learning outcomes in online courses and activities. It supports the creation of high-quality online courses and learning materials that are open and freely available for anyone to use. As students work through an OLI course, real-time data on their interactions with the learning materials is collected. This data may be used by instructors, course developers or researchers to monitor student learning, test theories of learning, or to inform future improvements to the learning materials.

The Chinese online course was originally developed with the support of a grant from the Pittsburgh Science of Learning Center (PSLC; http://learnlab.org). It was developed to serve two purposes: (1) help beginning students of Chinese who need a more flexible approach to language learning develop communicative competence in the four basic skills of listening, speaking, reading, and writing Chinese, as well as competence in Chinese culture, and (2) function as the Chinese LearnLab course for the PSLC, facilitating the collection of rich data on student learning and enabling in vivo research studies of the learning process, which are studies that take place within the context of the regular course curriculum. It has been offered as a course at Carnegie Mellon University for several years now, and has been structured as a hybrid course, with one required class meeting per week and one individual tutor session per week in addition to the online learning exercises. Now, the course is being developed as a fully-online OLI course (Wu, Haney and Liu 2011; Wu 2007). This paper discusses some of the challenges of this process. In doing so it also addresses some of the challenges of creating a fully online version of a hybrid on-ground/online course.

## 2.0 Chinese Online Content

The course content is designed according to the 5 Cs principles of the National Standards for Foreign Language Education for the 21st Century - Communication, Cultures, Comparisons, Connections and Communities (ACTFL 1999; Wu and Haney, 2005). It is designed to be a two-semester course. At CMU the first semester course, Elementary Chinese I online, covers units 1 – 8 of the online content, and the second semester course, Elementary Chinese II online, covers units 9 – 18. Each unit takes from 1.5 to 2 weeks to cover. Table 1 below details the overall scope of the two semesters of Elementary Chinese online.

**Table 1: Chinese online curriculum scope and Sequence**

| Elementary Chinese I Online (Units 1-8; first semester) | Elementary Chinese II Online (Units 9-18; second semester) |
|---|---|
| 1. Pinyin foundation<br>2. Main Vocabulary (181 items)<br>3. Characters (201)<br>4. Text Notes (28 items)<br>5. Grammar Points (32 points)<br>6. Culture Notes (8 items) | 1. Main Vocabulary (352 items)<br>2. Characters (307)<br>3. Text Notes (37 items)<br>4. Grammar Points (30 items)<br>5. Culture Notes (10 items) |

More detailed information on the scope and sequence of the Chinese Online curriculum is included in the appendix 1.

The online content in the course is delivered through a variety of integrated media, including text, audio and video. The student has many options to control the presentation of the content, for example by clicking on a word to hear its pronunciation, by selecting whether to listen to audio at slow or fast speed, or by selecting how many times to play audio and video elements. Interspersed throughout the content presentation are multimedia tutors that can be utilized for student practice, review or for assessment. These tutors, designed using components developed at CMU, provide students with audio, text, or image prompts. Students are then asked to select the correct answer or answers, or to drag components into the correct order. Like the prompts, the answers the students select from also may be presented as text, audio, or images. The tutors provide students with multiple levels of hints, and also provide feedback that can be customized to apply to distinct errors or types of errors. The tutors provide the ability to tie exercises to specific knowledge components (learning goals), and to provide context-dependent hints and immediate, context-dependent feedback. The Knowledge Components in the online course are organized around the grammatical structure of the Chinese language. Student interaction with course elements is logged in a centralized data repository that can be accessed by both instructors and researchers. These logs provide data to help the instructor see how students are performing on various knowledge components, and may also be used to facilitate research studies within the course.

Each unit of the online content, with the exception of Unit 1(the Pinyin unit), is organized in a similar fashion (please see appendix 2 for an outline). Each unit begins with a multimedia presentation of a main text, which is usually a dialogue. The text is presented first as a video. The videos were filmed in China with native-speaker actors and actresses speaking at natural speed. Figure 1 below shows an example of the video presentation.

Video

**Figure 1: An example video from the Chinese online materials**

The video presentation is followed by multiple choice questions to test students' basic understanding of the video. Since the video contains new vocabulary and grammar structures, students need to infer some things from context and language elements they have previously studied in order to answer the questions. The questions are delivered in a tutor format to facilitate hints and logging of student responses in the centralized data repository. This design helps students learn how to pick things they can understand out of a dialogue which also contains elements that they do not understand. Practicing this helps them to feel comfortable engaging language which contains some elements they have not studied yet.

Following the video, the main text is also presented as written text in Chinese characters. This text is accompanied by the video's audio component, spoken at natural speed. There is also a presentation of the main text in Pinyin, with English translation. This Pinyin text with translation is also accompanied by audio, but this version of the audio is at a speed significantly slower than the speed of the video which provides more time for users to repeat after the sound files.

The presentation of the main text is followed by explanatory notes. Chinese words and phrases in the notes have linked audio, so students may click on them to hear their correct pronunciation. Next, new vocabulary is presented. For each vocabulary item traditional and simplified character forms, Pinyin, part of speech, and meaning are all presented. In addition, clicking on the Pinyin for each item will play audio of that item's pronunciation. This integration of multimedia makes it easy for students to control presentation of the content more easily than if they were working with an audiotape or CD. First, vocabulary items can be accessed individually without searching through a tape, CD, or monolithic MP3 file. Second, the student has control over whether or not to play the audio for each item, and how many times to play the audio for each item.

Following the presentation of the new vocabulary items there are some multiple choice tutors testing students' understanding of the main video.

The next section of each online unit focuses on listening skills. Several different types of listening exercises are delivered via multimedia tutors. First, there are Pinyin recognition exercises in which the student must listen to a prompt and select the correct Pinyin representation. Next, there are a variety of exercises in which the prompt, the answer choices, or both are presented as audio. These include both translation exercises and listening comprehension exercises.

The listening skills section of each unit is followed by a grammar section. The grammar section begins with grammar notes presented as English text with Chinese examples. All Chinese in the grammar notes may be clicked on for an audio pronunciation. Each grammar note is followed by several examples, presented in characters and in translation, which can also be clicked on to access audio of the example. The grammar notes are followed by grammar exercises delivered by multimedia tutors that allow students to drag and drop characters or blocks of text into order in response to a text or audio prompt. We use this type of tutor for two types of exercises that allow students to practice character recognition and listening skills, and to reinforce the grammatical structures studied. In one type of exercise the student listens to audio of a sentence pronounced by a native Chinese speaker. The student then drags and drops characters into position to represent the sentence. In the second type of exercise the student is presented with blocks containing phrases or sentences written in Chinese characters. The student must drag the blocks into correct order. Figure 2 below shows an example of the second type of drag and drop tutor.

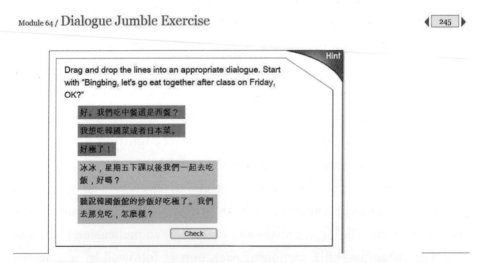

**Figure 2: An example online drag-and-drop tutor**

Grammar exercises are followed by reading comprehension exercises in which students read a text with similar vocabulary and theme to the unit's main text and then answer multiple choice questions. These reading comprehension exercises are followed by consolidation exercises which encapsulate listening skills, character recognition, vocabulary knowledge and grammar skills all in the same tutor exercise. These consolidation exercises present students with an image and then ask them questions related to the image. The questions can be multiple choice or multiple select, and they can include either text or audio prompts and responses. Figure 3 below shows an example of one of these consolidation exercises.

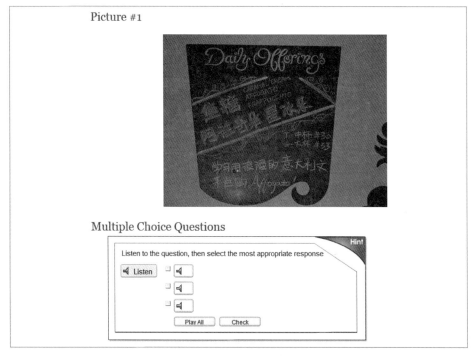

**Figure 3: An example online tutor (picture description)**

The units end with a culture section designed to help learners better understand how phenomena from Chinese society and the

Chinese language reflect Chinese culture. The culture section includes a culturally-related dialogue or reading, multiple-choice exercises based on the dialogue or reading, and explanatory information related to the dialogue or reading. The multiple choice questions are designed to encourage learners to observe, be aware of and compare cultural differences.

## 3.0 Issues and Challenges

Our team has faced several issues and challenges designing and implementing the Chinese online course for the OLI platform. The issues and challenges fall into three categories: moving from a hybrid to a fully online course, developing a course for public use, and technical challenges.

Although the current PSLC Chinese online course is a hybrid course with only one weekly class meeting and one weekly tutorial session, making the transition to a fully online course is still quite challenging. While a hybrid course can take advantage of the strengths and weaknesses of the online and on-ground formats, a fully online course, must make compromises. For example, in the hybrid Chinese course the face-to-face components of the course provide opportunities for real-time interaction in the target language, for feedback and instructions from the instructor, and for assessment opportunities such as tests and quizzes. The classroom environment allows the instructor to efficiently address the class as a group, and facilitates access and evaluation of student-produced language, both written and verbal. The high level of transactional distance in a completely online course, however, makes it difficult to provide the instructor-student dialogue necessary to support the learning process (Moore 1993), and makes it difficult to access and evaluate student-produced language. The tutor components of the online Chinese course are designed to provide students with feedback on their language recognition and understanding, but the online course will have to be revised to provide increased interactivity and assessment opportunities that require students to produce language, either written or oral.

The public nature of the OLI course also provides new challenges. The first challenge will be to augment the course with more clear instructions and documentation. As mentioned above, the online format makes real-time interaction and feedback more difficult. This affects not only interaction and feedback related to target language skills, but also related to how to navigate and use the course features. In a face-to-face classroom setting students can ask questions about how to use the course, and the instructor can give instructions to the class as a group. In the public and fully-online format of an OLI course, however, more students will be using the course and they will not have easy access to the course developers to ask questions. Even if they did, these questions might represent a great demand on the course development team's time. To attempt to address these challenges a course FAQ will be created and maintained, and the instructions provided in the course materials will be audited and revised for clarity.

The public nature of the OLI course also brings with it the challenge of meeting the needs of different institutions and individuals using the course. The PSLC Chinese course was originally developed to meet the needs of CMU students and instructors. Students at other institutions or independent students may have different needs for course content and/or pacing. In order to meet diverse needs as well as possible the OLI Chinese course needs to provide as much flexibility as possible. The units should be modular, and users should be able to choose which units and activities they use. Despite the modular design, course developers should expect at the least an increased communications burden as new users offer suggestions and requests for revisions to the course content.

Funding issues are also a potential problem, as the revisions necessary to adapt the course to the OLI environment require resources. In addition, dealing with the potential increased demand for course revisions and new features will also strain current course development resources.

The OLI platform, while it provides great features, also brings some technical issues. It is a relatively new platform, and its developers make frequent updates. These updates typically bring new capabilities and/or increased usability, but some of them are not fully backward-compatible and they require course developers to make changes to their course materials. Finally, a future technical issue is testing and revising the course to be accessed and used from mobile devices, such as a smartphone, tablet device, or iPod.

## 4.0 Concluding remarks

Open learning educational resources can provide great benefits for both individuals and institutions. They give institutions an alternative to resource-intensive development of their own online courses, helping institutions meet the needs of students who need more flexibility in their time schedules and allowing them to serve a more geographically distributed student pool. They also provide potential as a means of gathering data for learning-related research. For individuals they can provide a semi-structured approach to learning without the costs and restrictions associated with formal enrollment at a college or university.

The PSLC Chinese course has been a successful experiment which has enabled students with tight schedules to pursue Chinese study and achieve positive learning outcomes. Moreover, it has promoted interdisciplinary collaboration among professionals from different fields, such as language instructors, psychologists, psycho-linguists, human-computer interaction specialists, and computer tool developers. This collaboration has endeavored to bring about innovative teaching and robust learning, and to have a positive effect on learning research.

The transition to a fully-online course on the OLI platform, however, brings new challenges. The following course development and revisions are underway or planned to meet these challenges:

1. Assessment/testing center – Since the fully-online course cannot take advantage of testing and assessment in the classroom format, more assessment/testing facilities need to be added to the online course materials. A particular challenge with these testing facilities is that they must have components which require students to produce language in either a written or spoken form. The assessment/testing facilities can serve as learning outcome assessment tools, or as placement tests to help place students into a suitable course level.

2. Character learning center – With the special features of the Chinese pictographic writing system, new content must be added to the online course to help students learn to write Chinese characters, a skill which is covered in the classroom portion of the existing PSLC Chinese hybrid course. To facilitate the learning of Chinese characters in the fully online format online modules focusing on Chinese characters are under development. These online modules feature several interactive activities for improving literacy

in Chinese. They introduce 1,200 commonly used characters. Information on each character is provided, including audio of the character's pronunciation, and an animation demonstrating the stroke order for writing the character. The character information is searchable by several different search keys, and is accompanied by interactive exercises and quizzes, which provide rapid feedback to learners.

By sharing our experience of developing the Chinese online course on the OLI platform, we hope we have provided some useful observations on the nature of the OLI platform, on the benefits of open educational resources, on the challenges of building a course as an open educational resource, and on transitioning from a hybrid on-ground/ online course to a fully online course.

# Acknowledgements

The Chinese online course is one of the LearnLab courses supported by the Pittsburgh Science of Learning Center (PSLC, http:// www.learnlab.org), which is funded by National Science Foundation award number SBE-0836012. We would like to thank them for the support. Sue-mei Wu is the leader of the PSLC Chinese LearnLab course. She is also the PI and coordinator of the PSLC and OLI Chinese online project. Mark Haney is the chief programmer and Yiching Liu is one of the content providers.

**Appendix 1**

SCOPE & SEQUENCE範圍和順序
Unit topics and Communicative Objectives
單元主題，教學目標&交際活動

| | |
|---|---|
| Unit 1: Foundation: Pinyin introduction & basic expressions<br>第一單元：拼音介紹&基本用語 | -Pinyin (Chinese phonetic transliteration system)<br>-structure of Chinese syllable<br>-Chinese tones and pronunciation<br>-basic Chinese expressions |
| Unit 2: Greetings<br>第二單元：問候 | -simple greetings<br>-ask and respond to a Yes/No questions<br>-meet someone for the first time |
| Unit 3: Names<br>第三單元：姓名 | -ask about names<br>-find out who someone is<br>-ask and respond to a simple inquiry |
| Unit 4: Nationality and languages<br>第四單元：國家和語言 | -introduce people<br>-talk about nationality and languages<br>-talk about others |
| Unit 5: Talk about studies<br>第五單元：談學習 | -talk about majors in school<br>-talk about what you like to study<br>-find out what someone has |
| Unit 6: Talk about yourself and your family<br>第六單元：自己和家庭 | -self-introduction<br>-talk about family, occupations<br>-discuss what you want to be in the future |
| Unit 7: Make phone calls<br>第七單元：打電話 | -handle various phone situations<br>-ask/tell what someone is doing<br>-make and respond to a plan |
| Unit 8: Talk about daily schedule<br>第八單元：日常時間表 | -describe a daily schedule<br>-talk about your school life |

| Unit 9: Invitations<br>第九單元：邀請 | -talk about ages and birthdays<br>-make and accept an invitation |
|---|---|
| Unit 10: Requests<br>第十單元：請求 | -make / reply to a request<br>-express one's wishes |
| Unit 11: Order food<br>第十一單元：點菜 | -order food at a restaurant<br>-present/choose from alternatives |
| Unit 12: Shopping<br>第十二單元：買東西 | -talk about price, money and currency<br>-go shopping |
| Unit 13: Locations<br>第十三單元：介紹處所 | -describe where something is located<br>-show people around |
| Unit 14: Hobbies & Sports<br>第十四單元：愛好和運動 | -talk about hobbies<br>-describe how well an action is performed |
| Unit 15: Travel plans<br>第十五單元：旅行計畫 | -describe the four seasons and weather<br>-talk about means of transportation<br>-talk about travel plans |
| Unit 16: Illness<br>第十六單元：生病 | -go to see a doctor<br>-describe something that has happened |
| Unit 17: Rent an apartment<br>第十七單元：租房 | -describe an event and its cause<br>-rent an apartment |
| Unit 18: Future plans & wishes<br>第十八單元：計畫和祝福 | -future plans and expressing wishes |

## Appendix 2

Learning materials: Each Unit (units 2-18) contains the following main content and activities:

I. Main Content

    1. Main video

    2. Video preview questions (multiple choice)

    3. Text and audio of the video (characters, with full-speed audio)

    4. Text translation and Pinyin, with slower audio

    5. Text notes

    6. Vocabulary tables

    7. Video comprehension exercises

II. Listening

    1. Pinyin recognition exercises

    2. True and false exercise (multiple select, with sound prompts)

    3. Translation exercise (select correct English translation of sound prompts)

    4. Listening comprehension exercises

III. Grammar

    1. Grammar notes

    2. Sentence jumble exercise (drag and drop sentence components into correct order)

    3. Dialogue jumble exercise (drag and drop dialogue components into correct order)

IV. Reading Exercises

    1. Reading comprehension (read passage then answer multiple-select questions)

V. Consolidation Exercises

    1. Picture description exercise (answer multiple-select questions

based on an image)

VI. Culture Link

    1. Culture Link dialogue or reading

    2. Multiple choice questions based on the Culture Link

    3. Culture information (explanatory information related to the Culture Link text)

# References

American Council on the Teaching of Foreign Languages (ACTFL). *Standards for Foreign Language Learning in the 21st Century,* 1999.

Moore, M.G. 1993. "Theory of Transactional Distance". In D. Keegan (Ed.), *Theoretical Principles of Distance Education.* New York: Routledge, pp. 22-38.

Wu, Sue-mei, Haney, M and Liu, Y.C. 2011. "A Chinese Online LearnLab Course: Facilitating E-Learning and Research". *ICICE7 Thesis Collection.* pp. 322-330. Edited by J. Chen. Taipei: Overseas Compatriot Affairs Commission. Taiwan, R. O. C.

Wu, Sue-mei 2007. "Chapter 11: Robust language learning for Chinese heritage learners: Technology, motivation and linguistics". In Kimi Kondo-Brown & James Dean Brown (Eds.) *Teaching Chinese, Japanese and Korean Heritage Students: Curriculum, Needs, Materials, and Assessment.* Lawrence Erlbaum Associates, Inc., pp. 271-297.

Wu, Sue-mei, and Haney, M. 2005. "Robust Chinese E-learning: Integrating the 5Cs principles with content and technology". In S. Hsin (Ed.) *Proceedings of The 4th International Conference on Internet Chinese Education* (ICICE 2005). Taipei: Overseas Chinese Affairs Commission (OCAC), pp. 541-548.

# 開放教育資源模式中的中文數位學習：機會、課程內容及挑戰

吳素美（**Sue-mei Wu**）
suemei@andrew.cmu.edu

何禮（**Mark Haney**）
haney@rmu.edu

呂逸勤（**Yi-ching Liu**）
yi-ching-liu@uiowa.edu

## 摘要

　　網上開放學習計畫（OLI）是美國卡內基梅隆大學開放教育資源計畫。本計畫由William and Flora Hewlett基金會贊助，旨在支持創造高品質的網上課程，不限時間地點供大眾免費學習，並提供一個科技平台以開發及傳遞這些網上課程，同時評估其學習成效。

　　本文將介紹美國卡內基梅隆大學在網上開放學習計畫（OLI）平台所開發的網上初級中文課程。此中文網上課程一共為期兩個學期，課程內容包括聽說讀寫四大技巧及文化重點。目前此課程主要使用者為卡內基梅隆大學的學生，未來期望可以提供一個不限時間地點的學習資源，給任何想學習中文的人士自學或搭配老師的指導。

　　本文除了介紹網上課程的特色及目標之外，也同時探討將網上課程開發成網上開放學習計畫（OLI）平台所帶來的機會，議題以及挑戰。文中包括示範網上初級中文課程模板並分享老師及學生的反饋。

　　本文藉由分享開放學習計畫（OLI）平台的網上初級中文課程經驗，期望可以提供跨領域合作的一些想法，以建立一個開放教育資源中的語言學習模式。

關鍵字：開放教育資源、中文數位學習、網上開放學習、網上中
　　　　文、網上課程、科技與漢語教學

# Using Online Classroom Management to Facilitate Collaboration, Interaction, and Communication

**Alice Lee[1], Chin-Chin Tseng[2], Neal Szu-Yen Liang[3]**

[1]Aim for the Top University Plan, Ministry of Education, Taiwan

[2]Department of Chinese as a Second Language,
National Taiwan Normal University

[3]University of Texas at Arlington

alicelee1037@gmail.com   tseng@ntnu.edu.tw   syliang@uta.edu

## Abstract

This paper describes the operation mechanism for classroom management of an online Practice Teaching Program implemented between National Taiwan Normal University and the University of Texas at Arlington. Sixty-eight American college students took an online Chinese course taught by twenty-nine graduate students who major in teaching Chinese as a second language. The teaching graduate students were placed into two to three-person groups and worked together to develop a team-assisted instruction plan. This

[1] This research is partially supported by the "Aim for the Top University Project" of National Taiwan Normal University (NTNU), sponsored by the Ministry of Education, Taiwan, R.O.C.

included curriculum design, lesson planning, preparation of online teaching materials, and problem-based teaching. The mechanism of online classroom management is based on theories of second language acquisition and Chinese teaching pedagogy. Topping (2005) indicated peer learning can be defined as the acquisition of knowledge and skill through active helping and supporting among peers. Teacher education is intended to be "learning by doing". Our goal for the L2 Chinese teacher education was to equip graduate students with the skills needed to nurture desirable qualities such as lifelong learning, self-reflection, critical thinking, and problem solving ability. This paper serves various purposes, including exploring the use of the Adobe Connect teaching platform for synchronous teaching as well as observing performance and effectiveness of the associated Peer Learning, with a focus on collaborative online teaching, interactive online teaching and online teaching reflection and communication.

Keywords: online classroom management, second language acquisition, Chinese teaching pedagogy, peer learning, collaboration, interaction, communication

## 1. Introduction

This program targeted twenty-nine student-teachers in the Chinese Language Teaching Practicum program of National Taiwan Normal University (NTNU). From February to April, 2013, these student-teachers conducted a long-distance learning program with sixty-eight undergraduate university students who study Chinese at the

University of Texas at Arlington (UTA). The Adobe Connect online classroom software was used to conduct a nine-week program. Classes were five days a week with two sessions per day. There were separate classes for beginner, intermediate and advanced students. One hundred and fifty video clips were collected from these sessions. The purpose of this study was to analyze both teacher and student experience using this online learning mechanism and management system, and collect and integrate data and materials. The emphasis was on observing the collaboration in small groups and small group interaction, by looking at both inter and intra-group communication, and from this find support for the effectiveness of online programs.

## 1.1 Foreword

In 2013 Bill Gages gave a Ted Talk where he mentioned that teachers should consider using taped educational content as a tool for reflection (on one's effectiveness) (Ted Talk, May 15, 2013) . Online asynchronous courses are already common in higher education. Prof. Chin-Chin Tseng, former Chair of the Department of Chinese as a Second Language at NTNU has advocated and emphasized the importance of sharing and recording classes to encourage students to observe their peers. Besides being a useful self-assessment tool it can also be useful for giving suggestions to one's peers. UTA's professor Liang Szu-yen wanted to encourage communication between the university's Chinese language students and students in Taiwan, and this coincided with Prof. Tseng's schedule for conducting the Chinese Language Teaching Practicum on virtual classroom learning. Thus, both sides could benefit from observations and learning of both teachers and students via a virtualized classroom educational experience.

## 1.2 Theoretical Foundation

Honebein (1996) pointed out that the Design of Constructivist Learning Environments Model includes three essential parts: fundamental design elements, a collaborative design element, and learning assessment design elements. Topping's (2005) theory, as stated in A Theoretical Model of Peer Learning, was used during this project. The authors strongly agree with his statement that peer learning can be defined as the acquisition of knowledge and skill through active helping and supporting among those equal in status or matched companions. Garrison's (2005) reference to structure and leadership was found to be important for online learners, and this will be discussed later in the paper. In addition, we also refer to Salmon's (2011) E-learning Five-Stage Model and Koohang's (2009) online classroom management model. Self-assessment, team assessment, and facilitator assessment are built into the study design to continuously assess learning outcomes.

## 1.3 Study Areas

The scope of this study focuses on the teacher's peer learning during online teaching management, and is divided into results for the areas of collaboration, interaction, and communication through careful observation of the process of online collaborative teaching situations. The authors will explain how NTNU student-teachers collaborated and cooperated, including how they divided work and responsibilities. Parameters discussed will include content, objectives, curriculum, participants, helping techniques, the coordinator's role, study materials, training, monitoring, student assessment, evaluation, and feedback. Through online interaction between teachers we can observe how teachers deal with hardware and software issues, connectivity issues, and on-going operations. Through these experiences, we hope our student-teachers may become lifelong learners, capable of self-reflection and critical thinking, and have the ability to solve problems. Using Garrison's (2005) methods, we looked at a teacher's ability to lead the classroom, the instructor's supervising, the overall level of interaction, and how the student-teachers reflected on their work. From the results of interaction between teachers, we observed each teachers approach and effectiveness. After a teacher observed his online classroom video recordings, he was expected to take notes on equipment/platform issues, student learning difficulties, teaching strategies, as well as perform self-assessment and peer assessment.

# 1.4 The Importance of the Research

1. The importance of online teaching management

   One no longer needs to travel great distances to study language, but instead can do online synchronous learning. Meredith, S. and B. Newton (2003) stated: "Good pedagogical practice has a theory of learning at its core. No single best-practice e-learning standard has emerged; various pedagogical approaches or learning theories may be considered in designing and interacting with e-learning programs." Honebein (1996) mentioned that the model includes three essential parts: fundamental design elements, a collaborative design element, and learning assessment design elements. This paper explores areas of collaboration, interaction and communication and where they fit into online classroom management.

2. Online teaching to enhance the effectiveness of peer learning

   The main goal of higher education has moved towards supporting students to develop into 'reflective practitioners' who are able to reflect critically upon their own professional practice (Schon, 1987; Falchikov & Boud, 1989; and Kwan & Leung, 1996). For Koohang (2009), E-learning or Distance Education is increasingly being chosen by students in higher education institutions. In the future, online learning will become an irreversible trend. How to manage and improve online peer learning will also be an important research subject in the future. This paper will explore areas of collaboration, interaction and communication among study subjects in order to discover how to improve peer learning.

3. Collect instructional videos, and keywords for analysis of online classroom teaching

　　Under NTNU's Aim for the Top University project, there is a plan to conduct various interviews with important people related to the subject of Chinese teaching. For this purpose, NTNU researchers did a series of recorded interviews. These interviews were transcribed as digital text, and the results assigned keywords to facilitate further research and analysis. We plan to do similar work using the videos from this research project on online teaching between NTNU and UTA.

## 2. Literature

## 2.1 Related Research

　　Our goals for the L2 Chinese teacher education are to equip graduate students to be a person capable of lifelong learning, self-reflection, critical thinking, and have the ability to solve problems. We followed Salmon's a five-stage model for computer-mediated communication (CMC) in education and training (Salmon, 2011). The ability of students to use technology is the first step towards achievement. The second step involves students creating an online identity and finding others with whom to interact; online social interaction is a critical element of the e-learning process in this step. In step three, students share information relevant to the course. Collaborative interaction amongst students is central to step four. Lastly, the fifth step in Salmon's model involves students looking for benefits from the system, but using outside resources to deepen their learning. When NTNU student-teachers start their teaching careers, they will need to be very familiar and competent in managing online classroom operations. This would include: how to resolve issues related to the online platform system and operating that system, cooperating with others, dividing work load appropriately, interacting with other teachers, and improving oneself through frequent reflection. In Salmon's book he also discusses e-learning and e-moderating. For Salmon, the tutor/teacher/lecturer fulfills the role of moderator or e-moderator, acting as a facilitator of student learning.

Broderick (2001) gave a definition of instructional design at www.geocities.com as follows: "Instructional Design is the art and science of creating an instructional environment and materials that will bring the learner from the state of not being able to accomplish certain tasks to the state of being able to accomplish those tasks." (Kanuka, 2006, p. 3) Instructional design has always relied on instructional models, based either on behaviorism, cognitivism, humanism, or constructivism.

According to Honebein (1996), when designing online learning programs, one must consider the use of constructivist learning theory as a necessary component. Honebein advanced a set of goals that aid the design of constructivism in learning settings.

1. "Provide experience with the knowledge construction process;
2. Provide experience in and appreciation for multiple perspectives;
3. Embed learning in realistic and relevant contexts;
4. Encourage ownership and voice in the learning process;
5. Embed learning in social experience;
6. Encourage the use of multiple modes of representation; and
7. Encourage self-awareness in the knowledge construction process."
   (Honebein, 1996 p. 11)

This paper focuses on the influence of online learning with relation to peer-assisted learning. The structure of such peer-assisted learning has been discussed by various experts before. Defazio (2009) wrote about peer-assisted learning in his Theoretical Model of Peer-Assisted Learning of ADDIE (Analysis, Design, Development, Implementation, and Evaluation). Defazio also referenced a subject in Topping's paper A Theoretical Model of Peer Learning- that is, groups of processes influencing effectiveness, where he states that one must first consider organization & engagement, cognitive conflict, scaffolding & error management, communication, and affect; and then continuously refine and correct such processes. Structure and leadership were found to be crucial for online learners to take a deep and meaningful approach to teaching (Garrison, 2005). The writers use Garrison's 2005 research on structure and leadership as a key to guiding interaction principles. Study design had a significant impact on the nature of the interactions, and whether students approached learning in a deep and meaningful manner. At the same time, "a community of inquiry must include various combinations of interaction among various contexts, teachers, and students." (Anderson and Garrison 1997, p.134)

Peer assessment encourages students to take a more active role in cooperative learning, as opposed to competitive learning (Falchikov, 1991). The primary functions of peer assessment are to develop the students own skills of reflection (Somervell, 1993) and to develop their attitudes of responsibility towards other group members (Burnett & Cavaye, 1980). Within the context of a clearly defined and carefully monitored assignment, it can be shown that students do have a realistic perception of their own abilities and can make rational judgments on the achievements of their peers (Stefani, 1994). Assessment is then characterized by a pluralistic approach and by the use of interesting real-life (i.e. authentic) tasks (Segers, 1996). The increasing requirement of lifelong learning in modern society (Sambell & McDowell, 1997) enhances the need for learning throughout one's entire working life. In such an era, traditional testing methods do not fit well with such goals as lifelong learning, reflective thinking, being critical, the capacity to evaluate oneself, and problem-solving (Dochy & Moerkerke, 1997). When peer tutoring or cooperative learning is implemented with thoughtfulness about what form of organization best fits the target purpose, context, and population, and with reasonably high implementation integrity; results are typically very good (Topping, 2001a; Topping & Ehly, 1998). "Peer learning can be defined as the acquisition of knowledge and skill through active helping and supporting among status equals or matched companions." (Topping, 2005, p. 631) "The longest established and most intensively researched forms of peer learning are peer tutoring and cooperative learning." (Topping, 2005, p. 632)

## 2.2 The Relationship between this thesis and other Research

This research is related to other research in various ways, including how it uses learning platforms or learning management systems, online learning theory, the Theoretical Model of Peer-Assisted Learning, and E-Learning and Constructivism.

Koohang (2004) stated appropriate instructional design that includes learning theories and principles is critical to the success of e-learning. And later, Koohang and Harman (2005) stated that "... e-learning is the delivery of education (all activities relevant to instructing, teaching, and learning) through various electronic media." E-learning or Distance Education is increasingly being chosen by students in higher education institutions. "Nearly twenty percent of all U.S. higher education students were taking at least one online course in the fall of 2006." (Koohang 2009, p. 92)

When using online resources for teaching Birenbaum (1996) referred to the key characteristics of peer learning. "The specific competencies that are required of such a person include: (a) cognitive competencies such as problem solving, critical thinking, formulating questions, searching for relevant information, making informed judgments, efficient use of information, conducting observations, investigations, inventing and creating new things, analyzing data, presenting data communicatively, oral and written expression; (b) metacognitive competencies such as self-reflection and self-evaluation; (c) social competencies such as leading discussions and conversations, persuading, co-operating, working in groups, etc. and (d) affective dispositions such as for instance perseverance, internal motivation, responsibility, self-efficacy, independence, flexibility, or coping with frustrating situations." (Dochy, Segers, & Sluijsmans, 1999, p. 332)

# 3. Research Design

## 3.1 Goal of the study

The main goal of this research is to investigate online learning and program management with a concentration on student-teacher peer learning. With the research results achieved, the authors hope to achieve Chinese teaching goals while leveraging modern methods and long-distance learning tools. Our goal for the L2 Chinese teacher education program is to equip graduate students to become people who are lifelong learners, capable of self-reflection and critical thinking, and have the ability to solve problems. Through curriculum and instructional planning to establish a course framework, real-time online teaching via Adobe Connect, teacher reflection, and a three peer assessment process via observation of recommended teaching goals; we will collect data related to online collaborative teaching, interactive online teaching and online teaching reflection and communication.

Chart 1: Online Classroom Management Research Design

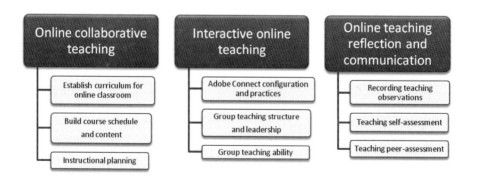

## 3.2 Research method

The methodology of this research included employment of methods previously referenced, such as the following:

1. Topping (2005): A Theoretical Model of Peer Learning
2. Salmon (2011): E-learning Five-Stage Model, which breaks verbal communication into four parts
3. Topping (2001a): When planning peer learning twelve aspects of organization need to be considered, such as analyzing the class enrollment and makeup, the curriculum and the teaching programs.
4. Dochy (1999): He analyzed and put together seven key elements of peer assessment.

In our research we used four digital education platforms. In preparing this program, we used the Moodle platform from NTNU, allowing student-teachers to upload their plans and designs, to help establish courses and teaching plans. We Used Adobe Connect virtual classroom for online teaching to create a real-time classroom teaching experience. After teaching, when reflecting and reviewing, we used the functionality of Google Drive to record each group's self-assessment and peer-assessments, and to incorporate suggestions of others. The data from observations and reflections from peer assessment were uploaded to Google Drive for convenient access. Participants could then periodically look at this material to do analysis, and dig deeper into the peer learning information collected during the nine-week period of instruction. At the end, we assembled all relevant materials into a Google Site for collaboration. In this way, we were able to look at three aspects of every participant's input at a glance - teacher planning, online teaching and after-class study interactions.

# 3.3 Data Collection

## 3.3.1 Online Collaborative Teaching

1. Establish curriculum for online classroom

Before establishing this online language program, twenty-nine student-teachers were divided into groups of two or three students per group. There were sixty-eight UTA students from three grades, which also corresponded to their level of Chinese study. The first and lowest level contained the most students. These students were broken up into groups of no more than four per group. The second year student (intermediate level) groups had at most three students per group. For the third year students (advanced level) there were no more than two students per group. Each student-teacher and their group of UTA students would find a mutually agreeable time, determine content (based on a nine-week curriculum), and then each group would operate independently. Students were placed in appropriate levels based on their language ability. Classes were conducted in the morning in Taiwan, which corresponded to the evening in Texas. Tuesday to Thursday, Saturday and Sunday, classes were conducted in two sessions per day. Each session was an hour. Each student attended one session per week. At NTNU, besides classrooms for beginner, intermediate and advanced levels that were technically equipped for the online environment, there were also three spare classrooms that were technologically enabled and that could be used at any time.

2. Build course schedule and content

The content of this course was based on UTA's textbooks, Integrated Chinese 3rd Edition (Level 1, Part I) for beginner students, Integrated Chinese 3rd Edition (Level 1, Part II) for intermediate students, and Developing Chinese Fluency (Biao Da) for advanced students. In accordance with NTNU's Chinese Language Teaching Practicum, the curriculum contained nine topics. Student-teachers (graduate students) designed lesson plans to integrate with UTA's textbook, to be suitable for online classroom use, and appropriate for the students' level. For the NTNU student teachers, the objective of this class was for them to have an authentic experience with long-distance online teaching. The UTA students hoped to have the opportunity to communicate and practice Chinese with native Chinese speakers and improve their oral Chinese ability. The nine weeks of classes were based on a curriculum consisting of the following nine topic areas: the Chinese phonetic system (pronunciation and tones), Chinese character recognition, vocabulary, grammar, listening, reading, speaking, writing and culture. The participants were from three organizations: UTA , NTNU and program management (technical support). To help address technical issues there was a member of the NTNU technical support center and a member of Adobe Connect from Adobe's representative office in Taiwan. There were three main contacts for the planning: one professor at UTA responsible for Chinese teaching, Prof. Szu-yen Liang, one NTNU professor responsible for this practicum, Professor Chin-chin Tseng, and a program coordinator, Ms. Alice Lee.

## 3. Instructional planning

For online instructional materials, besides the teaching plans, there were also well-prepared Powerpoint presentations, class-related PDF files (such as activities designed as supplemental materials), and relevant teaching-related websites. For teacher training of the student-teachers, in addition to their practicum during which they observed teaching at well-known local Taiwan language centers, they could also observe recordings of teaching done by other student-teacher groups. Such continuous training was very valuable to improve their on-the-spot problem-solving abilities. During this nine-week course, without prior notice, UTA's Professor Liang, NTNU's Professor Tseng, and the program coordinator would participate in monitoring the interactive process. During class time, other student-teachers not engaged in teaching a class were also online as observers and helped out as needed.

### 3.3.2 Interactive online teaching

1. Adobe Connect configuration and practices

Online learning is more complex than traditional learning because before starting class, one must connect to Adobe Connect, set up a headset, set up classrooms, and upload relevant materials. During class, often there are issues such as a student without a headset or sound issues, issues with classroom sound such as no sound or lag, intermittent sound quality issues, overlapping sounds, echo, video camera issues, images freezing, background noise and interference, difficulty or inability to upload PPTs and PDFs, difficulties downloading files, offline recording problems, Internet disconnects, and online storage capacity issues.

2. Group teaching structure and leadership

The master teacher must observe each group's student-instructor interactions. Each group has an instructor leader responsible for the class operating smoothly, the overall level of interaction, quality interactions among the group members, ensuring the group does proper reflection, recording of such reflection, selecting a solid teaching structure that can create a positive learning atmosphere, and inter and intra-group interaction.

3. Group teaching ability

　　We referenced Brown's (2007) Teaching by Principles: An Interactive Approach to Language Pedagogy. In order to nurture the teaching ability of future teachers, one should establish the guidelines of linguistic competence, communicative competence, technological competence, and pedagogical competence of a teacher-to-be. Four teaching capabilities are defined as follows. For linguistic competence, one needs to have solid training in Chinese linguistics, and have the ability to transform linguistic knowledge into systematic comprehensible input for the learners. Furthermore, the teacher should be able to draw the learner's attention to what he/she can comprehend through language activities, which can help the learner to produce comprehensible output. For communicative competence, one needs to understand the learner's language and culture, and to facilitate positive transfer, in order to communicate effectively with the learner. For technological competence, one needs to become thoroughly familiar with the technology used as a teaching tool.  In this study it was the videoconferencing software (Adobe Connect) used for online teaching. The teacher must be able to utilize the various functions provided by Adobe Connect to display learning materials, and interact on audio or visual channels accordingly. For pedagogical competence, one needs to be trained in curriculum design, lesson planning, teaching principles, methodology and techniques for constructive error correction.

### 3.3.3. Online teaching reflection and communication

1. Recording teaching observations: Each week each student teacher observes the video file of their own group and other groups. There

were a total of 150 recordings made during the course of the study. Reflection on teaching and observing recordings is broken down into four types of content:

(1)The ratio of Chinese to English used by the teachers as well as the ratio of speaking in Chinese for the students compared to the teachers.

(2)Teaching and online operations issues

(3)Student difficulties

(4)Teaching strategies

2. Teaching self-assessment. After deducting scheduled classes that were not attended, there were ten groups which produced a total of 86 reflections.

3. Observations of other groups' teaching experiences. This peer assessment component resulted in a total of 168 data units. On average, each group gave each of the other groups 1.8 pieces of feedback, a ratio of about 1:2, which is considered an excellent level of communication in this context.

## 3.4 Data Collection Methods

### 3.4.1 Preparation for collaboration on teaching examples

The researchers of this online class created a class schedule, curriculum, and lesson plans using Moodle's platform to complete preparation activities. "Moodle is a learning platform or Learning Management System" (http://en.wikipedia.org/wiki/Moodle), which "promotes social constructionist pedagogy (collaboration, activities, critical reflection, etc.). It is a simple, lightweight, efficient, compatible, and low-tech browser interface" (http://www.cerait. com/learning-management-solution.htm). In a computer browser,

Moodle's course listing shows descriptions for every course on the server, including accessibility to guests (those who may be visiting the site, but are not enrolled in the course). Courses on Moodle can be categorized and searched; with one Moodle site capable of supporting thousands of courses. Each group's student-teachers uploaded their teaching plans and assignments to the Moodle interface by the required deadline.

### 3.4.2 Interactive teaching examples

This research used Adobe Connect for online virtual classrooms to conduct online classes. Because the Moodle system is asynchronous, and cannot directly do synchronous classes remotely, all online classes were conducted via Adobe Connect's online classroom feature. "Adobe Connect for eLearning provides a complete solution for rapid training and mobile learning, enabling rapid deployment of training accessible from anywhere, anytime, on virtually any device. An instructor may teach and collaborate from any distance and at any time as long as there is stable Internet access. All interactive, hands-on components — such as quizzes, simulations, and links — remain interactive even in recorded classroom sessions and meetings. Accounting for space and time restrictions and automatic conference recording functions, Adobe Connect online classroom is a very useful teaching platform for remote long-distance teaching, though students and teachers must be familiar with the equipment and functions in order for things to go smoothly." (Adobe Acrobat Connect Professional Demo, 2007)

### 3.4.3 Teaching feedback and communication examples

The study utilized Google Drive's ability to record four vital pieces of information simultaneously: learner attendance, student feedback, self-assessment (SA) and peer-assessment (PA). Teachers, students, and managers could all collaborate together in the process. Since Moodle is used for the NTNU's rating mechanism and ratings may only be done individually, self-assessment and peer-assessments were discussed with the student-teachers individually. Student-teachers could not see suggestions made by other groups. Thus, only after assignments are handed in were such assessments placed on Google Drive. Google Drive is a file storage and synchronization service provided by Google, which enables user cloud storage, file sharing and collaborative editing. People can work together on a site to add file attachments, information from other Google applications (like Google Docs, Google Calendar, YouTube and Picasa), as well as new free-form content. Creating a site with others is relatively easy, and the user always controls who has access, whether it's just the individual, a team, or the entire organization. The user can also publish a website to the world (http://en.wikipedia.org/wiki/Google_Drive). The Google Sites web application is accessible from any internet connected computer. However none of the information collected during the study was made available to the public. Only NTNU internal operations members were able to see this information.

Chart 2: Information on Google Drive

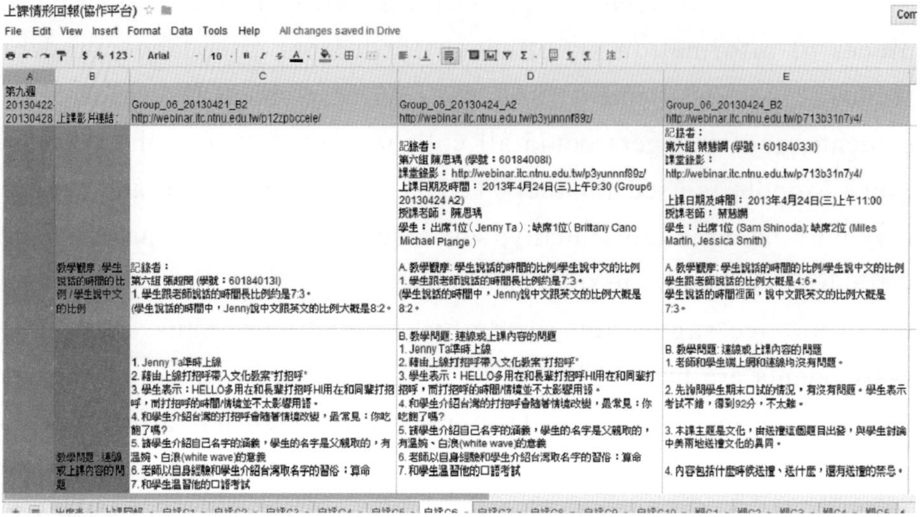


| A | B | C | D | E |
|---|---|---|---|---|
| 第九週<br>20130422-<br>20130428 | 上課影片連結： | Group_06_20130421_B2<br>http://webinar.itc.ntnu.edu.tw/p12zpbccele/ | Group_06_20130424_A2<br>http://webinar.itc.ntnu.edu.tw/p3yunnnf89z/ | Group_06_20130424_B2<br>http://webinar.itc.ntnu.edu.tw/p713b31n7y4/ |
| | 教學觀摩：學生說話的時間的比例 / 學生說中文的比例 | 記錄者：<br>第六組 張超閔 (學號：60184013I)<br>1. 學生跟老師說話的時間長比例約是7:3。<br>(學生說話的時間中，Jenny說中文跟英文的比例大概是8:2。 | 記錄者：<br>第六組 陳思瑀 (學號：60184008I)<br>課堂錄影：http://webinar.itc.ntnu.edu.tw/p3yunnnf89z/<br>上課日期及時間：2013年4月24日(三)上午9:30 (Group6 20130424 A2)<br>授課老師：陳思瑀<br>學生：出席1位（Jenny Ta）；缺席1位（Brittany Cano Michael Plange）<br><br>A. 教學觀摩: 學生說話的時間的比例/學生說中文的比例<br>1. 學生跟老師說話的時間長比例約是7:3。<br>(學生說話的時間中，Jenny說中文跟英文的比例大概是8:2。 | 記錄者：<br>第六組 蔡慧嫺 (學號：60184033I)<br>課堂錄影：<br>http://webinar.itc.ntnu.edu.tw/p713b31n7y4/<br><br>上課日期及時間：2013年4月24日(三)上午11:00<br>授課老師：蔡慧嫺<br>學生：出席1位 (Sam Shinoda); 缺席2位 (Miles Martin, Jessica Smith)<br><br>A. 教學觀摩: 學生說話的時間的比例/學生說中文的比例<br>學生跟老師說話的比例大概是4:6。<br>學生說話的時間裡面，說中文跟英文的比例大概是7:3。 |
| | 教學問題：連線或上課內容的問題 | 1. Jenny Ta準時上線<br>2. 藉由上線打招呼帶入文化教案"打招呼"<br>3. 學生表示：HELLO多用在和長輩打招呼HI用在和同輩打招呼，而打招呼的時間/情境並不太影響用語。<br>4. 和學生介紹台灣的打招呼會隨著情境改變，最常見：你吃飽了嗎?<br>5. 請學生介紹自己名字的涵義，學生的名字是父親取的，有溫婉、白浪(white wave)的意義<br>6. 老師以自身經驗和學生介紹台灣取名字的習俗：算命<br>7. 和學生溫習他的口語考試 | B. 教學問題: 連線或上課內容的問題<br>1. Jenny Ta準時上線<br>2. 藉由上線打招呼帶入文化教案"打招呼"<br>3. 學生表示：HELLO多用在和長輩打招呼HI用在和同輩打招呼，而打招呼的時間/情境並不太影響用語。<br>4. 和學生介紹台灣的打招呼會隨著情境改變，最常見：你吃飽了嗎?<br>5. 請學生介紹自己名字的涵義，學生的名字是父親取的，有溫婉、白浪(white wave)的意義<br>6. 老師以自身經驗和學生介紹台灣取名字的習俗：算命<br>7. 和學生溫習他的口語考試 | B. 教學問題: 連線或上課內容的問題<br>1. 老師和學生端上網和連線均沒有問題。<br><br>2. 先詢問學生期末口試的情況，有沒有問題。學生表示考試不錯，得到92分，不太難。<br><br>3. 本課主題是文化，由送禮這個題目出發，與學生討論中美兩地送禮文化的異同。<br><br>4. 內容包括什麼時候送禮、送什麼，還有送禮的禁忌。 |

# 4. Data Analysis

## 4.1 Online Collaborative Teaching

### 4.1.1 Establish a schedule for classes and online classrooms

Because of the large number of teachers and students in this online course and in order to meet the time limitations and different requirements, each week there were ten classes for beginner level students, seven classes for intermediate level students, and five classes for advanced students. There were 38 beginners, 19 intermediate, and 11 advanced students – 68 students in total. Each group's members collaborated on teaching methods, regardless of whether there were multiple teachers (collaborating online) for one student, one teacher for each student, or multiple teachers for each student (one teacher doing the teaching, while other teachers helped as needed with any issues that came up). It is believed that variation in the arrangement for dividing the work load and collaboration among the teachers can more effectively satisfy the needs of all participants.

Online attendance for the UTA students was 50% on average over the course of the program. This was primarily due to missed classes towards the last two weeks of April close to the time of UTA's final exams. Other reasons for missing class included problems getting online, lack of a headset, using the wrong classroom, simply forgetting, taking time off, or for no given reason.

### 4.1.2 Developing the curriculum and teacher planning

The curriculum consisted of nine topics. Including: the Chinese phonetic system (pronunciation and tones), Chinese character recognition, vocabulary, grammar, listening, reading, speaking, writing and culture. For each topic, a design and teaching plan were created that included the following: the stated goal of the topic, a selection of classroom activities, teaching methodology (for the student-teachers), the teaching schedule for the topic, supplementary materials, homework assignments, testing methods and an explanation of the proposed learning process. The week before classes began, each group of teachers met to design and plan nine to ten weeks of classes with appropriate content to accommodate the levels of the UTA language students.

## 4.2 Interactive online teaching

### 4.2.1 The Operation of Adobe Connect Platform

The most important component for success of the online teaching program was familiarizing teachers with operation of the Adobe

Connect platform. At minimum, the teachers needed to know the following: how to create and access meetings, how to install the Adobe Connect Add-in, the sharing screen function, the sharing PowerPoint content function, how to use voice-over-IP (VoIP) for audio communications, how to share webcam video, how to invite attendees to participate, and managing attendees during a session. The main problems the student-teachers experienced included: (1) inability to get into a meeting, (2) unable to hear any audio, (3) a user with the right to speak not being heard by the other participants, and (4) the screen shared by the host is fuzzy.

These operational issues were outlined in the manual which was designed for the online class for both teachers and students. It was recommended that before classes began, all participants should try out the platform. Also, during the first class both teachers and students were advised to go online 20 minutes early to practice using the interface functions and to upload class materials.

The following is a self-critique comment taken from the very first class meeting. The teacher in Taiwan was unable to hear the sound from one of the US based student's computer. The teacher typed a question, asking the student whether or not the headphone settings had been properly set. However, the student had just bought the earphones and didn't know how to use them, with the result that this particular student could hear no sound for the entire first class.

*SA01_G3: At the start, one of the students did not have any sound. The teacher asked repeatedly if their equipment was set up correctly. The student had just purchased a new headset and camera, and did not know how to use them yet. Fifteen minutes of time was spent trying to get the sound to work. In the end the headset still didn't work properly, and as a result there was an echo in the sound.*

The following issues occurred during implementation of the program (listed along with the number of times they occurred): Could not connect (4), Student did not have headset (3), Error with microphone settings (1), Could not hear any sound (9), Noise (2), Serious lag (2), Overlapping sounds (2), Intermittent sound (2), Sound feedback (8), Camera setup problems, whiteboard privileges problem (1), Issue with webcam setup (4), Image froze (3), Background noise (3), Lacked operational skills (3), Could not upload PPT & PDF files (6), Could not share screen (3), Offline recording problem (2), Lost connection (2), Storage space and retention limits (1), Audio and video not synchronized (9), and Network problems (2).

Above are some of the more serious issues that occurred which were resolved via help from technical support and support from the product's technical staff. Some of the smaller issues were resolved during class by the groups via the reporting system which was designed for the online class for teachers. Its purpose was to record any problems which occurred during the class.

Computers, the internet, a webcam and a headset with microphone were the basic equipment items that were needed. Some students attended class without a headset, which caused issues. In addition, when the headsets and/or microphone were not set up correctly, it negatively impacted class. Since many students have limited vocabulary and often couldn't hear the teacher clearly, this resulted in decreased student motivation. Also, the sound quality issues exacerbated student pronunciation and tone problems, making it difficult for teachers to give feedback and corrections.

Chart 3: Adobe Connect Operation Issues - number of occurrences

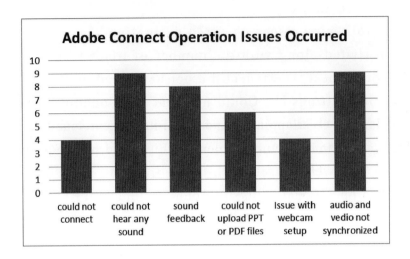

After downloading video files, sometimes the audio and video were not synchronized. Perhaps this was due to insufficient bandwidth or the screen sharing video quality was not adjusted well. Usually bad sound quality and/or echo could be resolved by using a headset that included a microphone. In addition, logging on more than once could cause this issue (which would be apparent by the student's name appearing twice in the participant's window). In such a situation, it was discovered that the problem could be resolved if the host simply removed one of them. To minimize background noise and alleviate this issue, we suggested adjusting settings appropriately as there is such normalization functionality built into the platform. Regarding the situation where files could not be uploaded, this issue had to be resolved by the platform company. For screen sharing, a required add-in must first be installed.

There were two issues related to disconnection during class. One was when the platform vendor would perform system maintenance during class. This could be resolved by communication with the vendor. The other was when there was a power outage. If such a loss affects a wide area and such notification occurs early enough, then contingency measures could be taken.

## 4.2.2 Online classroom structure and leadership

Because this was an online classroom experience, for the program to go smoothly, software and equipment issues were best taken care of in advance, before discussing effectiveness of the learning method. Resolution of on-the-spot operational issues had to be done by proper preparation and live third party support that could deal with the situation in a timely fashion.

The following represent examples of instructor involvement in the program. These records show the chronology of teacher efforts to help students resolve technical issues. During one class, a member of SA07 commented that one of the students had a technical problem. The instructor took the student into a 'chatroom' and worked with the student individually to resolve the problem. Once the problem was resolved, the student was asked to return to the digital classroom and rejoin the class. This remedial action was seen to be very helpful for the learning process. A member of PA08 commented that in addition to observing the learning process, the teacher was able to immediately and effectively handle issues that arose.

*SA07_G6: Sam's headset had an issue and he could not hear any sound, nor could he be heard. The teacher tried to reset his microphone but it did not help. She also asked the student to logout and then login again, but this didn't help either. Then the Coordinator happened to come into the classroom. She had me conduct class with another student, Jessica, and then went to assist Sam., Finally, after 15 minutes, Sam could successfully join the class.*

*PA08_G1: When many teachers were jointly working with only one student during the online classroom learning, one teacher could be assigned to monitor the situation and help facilitate if needed. By helping to correct any errors it was hoped that there would be better results. In point of fact, the monitoring teacher generally just served as an auditor.*

The following are examples illustrating overall interaction for the teams of SA11 and SA13~17. When unexpected situations occur in online class, teachers should be able to deal effectively with the emergency.

*SA11_G4: Because there was only one student in class and that student missed the previous week's class, the class content had to be changed at the last minute.*

*SA13_G9: One student's network connection had an issue, and the student twice was dropped from the classroom environment. After changing location, [Note: Does 'location' refer to a different computer? Or a wireless connection location? Or a different classroom? This isn't clear.]the student was OK. This issue took about ten minutes to resolve.*

*PA14_G1: The PPT stroke order activities illustrating for students how to write characters, was very helpful pedagogically. Teachers could very quickly tell if the student was writing characters correctly.*

*PA16_G1: After completing the first PPT with class materials, the teacher had an issue uploading the next PPT. In order to make the best use of time, the teacher used the chat frame to type in new vocabulary.*

*SA17_G6: For the first half of class, students were directed to write on the whiteboard, but students did not see this option due to the lack of proper 'permissions' for use of the software. After the permissions were granted, so that students were set as 'presenters', then they could use this functionality to draw on the screen.*

The following are examples of student-teachers reporting on their self-reflection assignments. The SA18 group suggested the online teaching materials should be simplified, and based more closely on the background of each student's knowledge. The SA19 group evaluated another group and found the guidance helpful.

After each group's lessons, the student teachers did self-reflection and gave suggestions based on observations of other groups, citing the first group's SA and PA for reference.

*SA18_G1: Simplifying lesson content. It's best to discuss topics with which the students are familiar. Remind students to use Chinese to express themselves and take advantage of practice opportunities. Use simple Chinese and do repetitive practice, or have students that understand the task explain to other students how to do it. If neither of these methods works, you can try explaining in English, but try to leverage the use of the whiteboard. You can also send the study material to students in advance. The teacher should go online twenty minutes early to minimize the possibility of unexpected issues.*

*PA19_G1: Advantage: Teachers were good at using classroom frequently used sentences, and the set of class materials was very logical. I could see the students learned a lot in the class. The teachers were methodical, asked good questions, and used previously studied material to lead into new material. It was also important that the content was of interest to the students (color, fruit), which helped the class go more smoothly. We recommend that when students have questions or cannot answer the teacher's questions, another teacher can use the chat room (text chat) feature to help answer the question, and allow the class to continue without interrupting other students; for example, by providing the student who needs help with sample sentences and combination characters. Sometimes the teacher would try using Chinese characters or pinyin to help the student guess the meaning, or have the student listen first so that students could practice their listening skills. When students pronounced words correctly, the teacher praised the student at the appropriate time, helping the student remember the correct pronunciation. When students did not know some grammar point very well, the teacher would provide a fixed sentence structure and sample phrases so that the student would have less pressure and could provide an answer with greater success. The teacher could teach slower, and not cover more than one sentence structure at a time. The teacher could help students speak in multiple related sentences rather than single sentences. If one can do these things it would be ideal.*

### 4.2.3 Teaching ability

In accordance with the stated goal to work on four skills: linguistic competence, communicative competence, technological competence, and pedagogical competence; the student-teachers were judged regarding online classroom competence for the following three approaches: a superficial approach, a detailed approach, or an achievement based approach. The achievement based approach is an ideal teaching method, and it is designed for students to be in a natural and relaxed environment. This approach requires pedagogical competence on the part of the teacher. For the teacher to the goal was to gradually adopt Krashen's "i+1" theory, wherein the teacher has strong communicative competence, and the questions asked of the students are relevant to the students' experiences, so that students can naturally be more confident. The following is an example of successful use of the achievement based approach.

*PA20: The teacher is good at encouraging the students to speak, and asking them relevant questions about their experiences. Students seem to feel no pressure. They appear relaxed and very satisfied with this chat experience. The teacher did not rigidly stick to her teaching materials, but rather naturally led students between topics based on their input. The teacher used Chinese exclusively, and only when necessary provided hints. The class was well paced, and students did not feel pressure. In addition, corrections were made at the appropriate time, as was positive feedback on pronunciation. Before class, students were told the agenda, and during class, varying usage in Taiwan versus Mainland China was pointed out. I found the whole experience very comfortable.*

The detailed approach refers to going through a lesson in a well prepared step-by-step manner, where interaction is limited to the scope prepared by the student-teacher, and the language student's learning tends to be passive. The following is an example of this type of classroom experience.

*PA21: Before class the teacher asked the students to count from one to twenty, helping students practice saying numbers, and then teaching students the difference between odd and even numbers. Then, the teacher taught students "add" and "subtract" and then they practiced simple calculations. The teacher introduced the Taiwan dollar (bills and coin currency), and explained the difference in units between Taiwan and Mainland China. In addition, the teacher asked students to compare differences between America and Taiwan. Lastly, the teacher helped students review measure words used for foods and drinks, and related vocabulary.  She also gave examples to use for conversation practice before doing exercises. Sometimes student and teacher would trade places (shop keeper and customer), allowing students to use the lesson's vocabulary during conversation practice. The ratio of teacher/student speaking was about 50%/50%, with Chinese used 85% of the time.*

The superficial approach was frequently a result of either insufficient technological competence, weak pedagogical and communicative competence, insufficient time for the activity, a low level of motivation from the student, or a combination of these factors. The result was that the original lesson plan could not be completed effectively. The following is an example of this type of observation.

*PA22: The teacher had limited knowledge and experience with Adobe Connect, so the first half of class was spent on technical issues. Next time if Supha (one of the students) cannot use the camera and microphone, she could type with other teachers and students to interact. I think more activities would be useful, such as matching games.*

## 4.3 Online teaching reflection and communication

Observations of teaching were recorded to identify the types of problems that occur when using an online classroom environment, such as teaching difficulties and problem resolution. The reported observations were all placed on Google Drive. Every person could look at these each week to see their own group and other group's recordings, and could regularly write and upload their teaching reflections (SA) and observations of other groups (PA).

If Google Drive is set up as a mechanism for communicating information, then teachers and students have one web platform for managing the sharing of every person's input. This platform can facilitate effective collaboration and cooperation, and that helps to improve and perfect the mechanism for online language learning.

## 5. Conclusions

The following are some conclusions and suggestions. The authors welcome feedback and suggestions from colleagues in the field.

1. An optimal online teaching management structure and related executional processes will have great value in research and analysis of online teaching. The influences of collaboration, interaction, and communication in the teaching management framework, use of an online teaching platform, and peer assessment has made the online teaching management structure closer to complete.

2. For online classroom management design, this writer recommends Google Site functionality, giving all three parties (managers, educators, and students) full communication capability. In this plan, Google Drive was used to keep track of NTNU's internal

information, including recording student attendance, reports on classes, self-assessment and peer-assessment. UTA students had no access to this information. Google Site can allow managers, educators and students to have a deeper understanding of the online classroom program and allow them to bring up questions, make announcements, and give feedback, thus allowing all parties a full and more accurate view of the learning environment.

3. The first hurdle in online teaching is for the users to learn operation of the platform, and it is also a real challenge. Students and teachers alike need to become familiar with online classroom operations to have an effective learning experience. It is important that internet bandwidth is sufficient, that the online classroom sound is normal, that the picture students and teachers are looking at is in sync, and that the tools available in the online classroom are well understood by both students and teachers. In order for collaboration to be effective, each group should not only have someone competent in Adobe Connect, but also have significant experience and practice in various online operations.

4. The quality of instructional videos influences peer learning. Many reports from student-teachers indicated that the recording of their lessons did not accurately reflect the situation during their lessons. Sometimes the recording's video and sound were out of sync or had lag, which reduced their reference value and ability to be analyzed. When the school's bandwidth was sufficient it was very important to use Adobe Connect's feature that allows adjustment of screen sharing quality.

5. Online teaching communication's self-assessment and peer-assessment reciprocity mechanism greatly helped all parties involved. Recording of online classroom reflections and observations of

other groups was a great channel for collaborative teaching. If one takes the approach that one can always learn and does not know everything, in addition to getting to know each other better, with effective collaboration, one can improve and succeed. This type of reciprocity mechanism requires dedication from those who are involved. By building a solid collection of materials in Google Drive, participants can see the whole picture with regards to communications and interactions. SA and PA materials were not placed on Google Drive by the student-teachers. Doing so would have certainly been helpful.

## Acknowledgements

In writing this paper I want to thank all the organizations involved. Firstly, I'd like to thank the sponsorship of NTNU's Aim for the Top University Project and NTNU's funding to support Better Teaching and Creativity Program. Secondly, I wish to thank NTNU's Chinese Language Teaching Practicum's Prof. Tseng and her students, and UTA's Prof. Liang and his Chinese language students' participation. Finally, I wish to thank NTNU's Moodle services, NTNU Technical Support Center, and the Taiwan representative office of Adobe Connect for their all-important assistance with the project.

# References

Adobe Connect. (2013). Adobe Systems Software product promotion. Retrieved form http://www.adobe.com/tw/products/adobeconnect.html

Adobe Systems Incorporated Web Site. (2007). Adobe Acrobat Connect

Professional Demo. Retrieved from http://www.adobe.com/products/acrobatconnectpro/

Boud, D. and Falchikov, N. (1989). Quantitative studies of student self-assessment in higher education: A critical analysis of findings, *Higher Education*, 18 (5), 529-49.

Boud, D. (1995). Enhancing learning through self-assessment. *RoutledgeFalmer.*

Broderick, C. L. (2001). What is instructional design? Retrieved November 2, 2004, from http://www.geocities.com/ok_bcurt/whatisID.htm

Burnett, W. & Cavaye, G. (1980). Peer assessment by fifth year students of surgery. *Assessment in Higher Education*, 2, 273-278.

Defazio, J. (2009). Collaborative learning communities: Evidence of theory-into-practice in instructional design. *International Journal of Instructional Technology & Distance Learning.* 6 (12).

Dochy, F. (Eds) (1996). Alternatives in assessment of achievement, learning processes and prior knowledge. Boston, Massachusetts: Kluwer Academic Publishers, 3-31.

Dochy, F. & Moerkerke, G. (1997). The present, the past and the future of achievement testing and performance assessment, *International Journal of Educational Research*, 27, 415-432.

Dochy, F., Segers, & Sluijsmans, D. (1999). The use of self-, peer and co-assessment in higher education: A review. *Studies in Higher Education*, 24 (3), 331-350.

Egbert, J. & Thomas, M. (2001). The new frontier: A case study in applying instructional design for distance teacher education. *Journal of Technology and Teacher Education.* 9 (3), 391-405.

Falchikov, N. (1986). Product comparison and process benefits of collaborative peer group and self-assessment, *Assessment and*

*Evaluation in Higher Education*, 11(2), 146-166.

Falchikov, N. and Boud, D. (1989). Student self-assessment in higher education: A meta-analysis, *Review of Educational Research*, 59 (4), 395-430.

Falchikov, N. (1991). Group process analysis: Self and peer assessment of working together in a group. *Standing Conference on Educational Development, SCED Paper,* 63.

Flachikov, N. (1995). Peer feedback marking: Developing peer assessment. *Innovations in Education & Training International*, 32 (2), 175-187.

Freeman, M. (1995). Peer assessment by groups of group work. *Assessment and Evaluation in Higher Education,* 20 (3), 289-299.

Gagne, R. M., Briggs, L. J., & Wager, W. W. (1992). *Principles of Instructional Design* (4th ed.). Fort Worth: Harcourt, Brace, Jovanovich College Publishers.

Garrison, D. R. (2005). Facilitating cognitive presence in online learning: Interaction is not enough (This study assessed the depth of online learning), *The American Journal of Distance Education,* 19 (3), 133–148.

Gates, B. (2013). Teachers need real feedback. [Video file]. Retrieved May 15, 2013 from http://www.ted.com/talks/bill_gates_teachers_ need_real_feedback.html/

Google Drive. Retrieved May 19, 2013 from http://en.wikipedia.org/wiki/ Google_Drive

Google Site. Retrieved May 19, 2013 from http://www.google.com/sites/ overview.html/

Harman, K. & Koohang, A. (2005). Discussion board: A learning object. *Interdisciplinary Journal of Knowledge and Learning Objects.* 1, 67-76.

Honebein, P. C. (1996). Seven goals for the design of constructivist learning environments. In B. G. Wilson (Ed.), *Constructivist*

*Learning Environments: Case Studies in Instructional Design.* Englewood Cliffs NJ: Educational Technology Publications.

Hung, D. (2001). Design principles for web-based learning: Implications for Vygotskian thought. *Educational Technology*, 41 (3), 33-41.

Hung. D. & Nichani, M. (2001). Constructivism and e-learning: Balancing between the individual and social levels of cognition. *Educational Technology*, 41 (2), 40-44.

Kanuka, H. (2006). Instructional design and e-learning: A discussion of pedagogical content knowledge as a missing construct. *Kanuka*. 9 (2), 1-47.

Koohang, A. & Durante A. (2003). Learners' perceptions toward the web-based distance learning activities/assignments portion of an undergraduate hybrid instructional model. *Journal of Information Technology Education*. 2, 105-113.

Koohang, A. (2009). E-learning and constructivism: From theory to application. *E-Learning and E-Learning Design* (Interdisciplinary journal of e-learning and learning objects. 5.)

Kwan, K. & Leung, R. (1996). Tutor versus peer group assessment of student performance in a simulation training exercise, *Assessment and Evaluation in Higher Education,* 21, 205-214.

Liu, Y. & Yao, T. (2008). *Integrated Chinese: Simplified Characters Textbook*, Level 1, Part 1 (3rd ed.) Boston: Cheng & Tsui Company, Inc.

Liu, Y. & Yao, T. (2009). *Integrated Chinese: Simplified Characters Textbook*, Level 1, Part 2 (3rd ed.) Boston: Cheng & Tsui Company, Inc

Meredith, S. and B. Newton (2003). Models of e-learning: Technology promise vs learner needs literature review. *The International Journal of Management Education*. 3 (3).

Moodle. Retrieved May 19, 2013 from http://en.wikipedia.org/wiki/ Moodle

Moodle's overall design. Retrieved May 19, 2013 from http://www.cerait. com/learning-management-solution.htm

Moore, M. G.(1989). Three types of interaction. *The American Journal of Distance Education*, 3 (2), 1-6.

Pimentel, J. R. (1999). Design of net-learning systems based on experiential learning. *Journal of Asynchronous Learning Networks (JALN)*. 3 (2).

Randall, B. (2001). Effective web design and core communication issues: The missing components in web-based distance education. *Journal of Educational Multimedia and Hypermedia*. 10 (4), 357-67.

Salmon, G. (2011). E-moderating: The key to teaching and learning online (3rd ed.). New York: Routledge.

Sambell, K. & McDowell, L. (1997). The value of self- and peer assessment to the developing lifelong learner, *Improving Student Learning--Improving Students as Learners [Note: Check This Journal for Proper Capitalization]*. Oxford, Oxford Centre for Staff and Learning Development. 56-66.

Schon, D. A. (1987). *Educating the Reflective Practitioner: Towards a new Design for Teaching and Learning in the Professions*. San Francisco, CA: Jossey-Bass.

Segers, M. (1996) Assessment in a problem-based economics curriculum. *Alternatives in Assessment of Achievement, Learning Process and Prior Knowledge,* Boston: Kluwer Academic, 201-226.

Somervell, H. (1993*).* Issues in assessment, enterprise and higher education: The case for self-peer and collaborative assessment. *Assessment and Evaluation in Higher Education*, 18 (3), 221-233.

Stefani, L. A. J. (1994). Peer, self and tutor assessment: Relative reliabilities. *Studies in Higher Education*, 19 (1), 69-75.

Topping & S. Ehly (1998). *Peer-assisted Learning*. Mahwah, N.J.: Erlbaum. 27- 42.

Topping, K., & Whitely, M. (1993*)*. Sex differences in the effectiveness of peer tutoring. *School Psychology International*, 14, 57-67.

Topping, K. J. (2001a*). Peer assisted Learning: A Practical Guide for Teachers*. Cambridge, MA: Brookline Books.

Topping, K. J. (2005). Trends in Peer Learning. *Educational Psychology*. 25 (6), 631–645.

Weaver II, & Cotrell, H. W. (1986). Peer evaluation: A case study, *Innovative Higher Education,* 11, 25-39.

Zhang, P. (2009). *Developing Chinese Fluency* (Biao Da). Singapore: Cengage Learning.

# 虛實相輔的數位華語文教學
## ——全球華文網Moodle之設計與應用

陳克曼（**Kerman Kwan**）

美國爾灣中文學校

kermankwan@gmail.com

## 摘要

　　僑校多為週末班，囿於場地與經費，每週上課時間非常有限。自僑委會於2008年開放「全球華文網」，許多僑校老師即開始使用Moodle創造一個有效的線上學習環境，希望能延伸學生使用中文的時間。

　　本文根據筆者過去五年自身行動研究與教學經驗，對美國爾灣中文學校的課後班幼齡學童、中級組及進階Advanced Placement（AP）高級組進行不同試驗，分析如何針對不同的教學對象，設計不同版面與內容的Moodle課程，並說明如何將虛擬教室內的教學資料配合實體課程，應用於華語文教學課程中，以期打造出一個虛實相輔相成的混合式教學環境（blended learning environment）。

　　以幼、中、高三個不同年齡為例：

1. 幼兒組的教學必須符合幼兒認知發展的特性。由於孩童受限於電腦素養，可能無法自行操作電腦。因此，虛擬教室的設計成Mommy and me的親子教學方式，在父母或是祖父母的協助下，一同完成任務。此外，由於兒童注意力時間較短，數位教室版面的設計，可求色彩鮮明，並將圖片、兒歌和影片直接放到首頁，除了能吸引孩子們的注意力以外，亦可以減少稚齡學童使用電腦的障礙。

2. 中級組的學生已有一些中文基礎，虛擬教室的內容應涵蓋中文聽、說、讀、寫，包括每週教學活動、教學講義、課文朗讀、生字筆順、動畫故事。此外，更可加入「遊戲學華語」引起學生興趣，並利用quizlet flash cards生字卡，Learn學習、Scatter遊戲和Quizlet test，設計不同的練習與任務。

3. 高級組AP班級中，有許多美國高中學生希望上了一年以後，能夠在AP中文考試中拿到滿分五分。因此，Moodle教室的設計必須配合AP教科書，並提供中國文化及歷史方面的補充教材，才能使學生更加熟悉與了解中華文化。線上作業尤其重要，須依照AP中文測試與ACTFL 5Cs標準，來加強學生的中文理解詮釋能力、人際溝通能力、口頭和書面表達的能力。

　　「工欲善其事，必先利其器」，老師們如能根據自身中文教學經驗，並善用Moodle虛擬教室，必能將資訊融入華語文教學之中，創造一個虛實相輔的數位華語文學習環境。

關鍵字：華語文教學、Moodle、線上學習、數位學習

　　海外僑校多為週末班，囿於場地與經費，一週只上課一次，課時也僅只有兩三小時，不但上課時數不夠，而且每次課程區隔較長，效果也不佳。根據德國的心理學家艾賓浩斯（H. Ebbinghaus）（reference 1）研究發現，遺忘在學習之後立即開始，在課後第一天，如果沒有再一次的複習，學生記得的比率只有33.7%，兩天後，剩27.8%，此後逐日遞減。若沒有良好的複習，到下一次上課時，學生對上一次課程的記憶大約只剩下20%了。因此對海外僑校的教師而言，虛擬教室是一個幫助學生課後學習中文的好平台，而Moodle又是虛擬教室中最佳的平台。

　　本文根據筆者過去五年自身行動研究與教學經驗，對美國爾灣中文學校的課後幼齡學童班、中級組及進階Advanced Placement（AP）高級組進行不同試驗，每班均在全球華文網開設一間專屬的

Moodle教室，將虛擬教室內的教學資料配合實體課程，應用於華語文教學課程中。

## 一、全球華文網Moodle簡介

　　全球華文網的Moodle和Blackboard、iCAN一樣，都是數位教學平台，不同的是：Blackboard的功能雖然比Moodle更強，但是，它是一個商業化教學平台，收費過高，不是一般僑校能夠負擔的，而全球華文網的Moodle平台，則是完全免費的。

### ㈠ Moodle簡介

　　Moodle是一個架設在網際網路基礎的課程和網站的軟體。簡單地說，Moodle是可以在網路上使用的課程管理系統（course management system）。Moodle的主要目標為幫助教學者建立有效的線上社群，透過學生的群眾參與過程創造一個有效的學習環境（林金錫等，2008）。

### ㈡ 全球華文網Moodle平台簡介

　　2007年僑委會執行「數位學習國家型科技計畫」，建置完成具備部落格（blog）、Moodle教學平台及華語文入口黃頁等功能之「全球華文網」網站，於2008年4月中旬開放，成為全球最大華語文師資社群暨優良線上教學平台網站之一。全球華文網有下列四個結合Moodle線上教學平台的學苑：語文學苑、文化學苑、師資培訓學苑和綜合學苑。絕大多數僑校的Moodle教室都建置在「語文學苑」裡，本文所提到的所有Moodle教室也均建置於該學苑。2013年，僑委會更將Moodle教室架設於雲端，與雲端學校相輔相成。

## 二、實驗課程的版面設計

　　教師可依照學生的年齡與程度，設計出不同版面的Moodle教室，以下為筆者實驗三個不同年齡層的範例：

(一) 幼兒組

由於兒童注意力時間較短，數位教室版面的設計，可求色彩鮮明，並將圖片直接放到首頁，下圖右邊紅框框內的兩張圖片是動畫檔，只是為了吸引兒童的注意，沒有什麼特殊的教學意義。

兒歌和影片也可直接放到首頁，除了能吸引孩子們的注意力以外，亦可以減少稚齡學童使用電腦的障礙。

幼稚組的教室，請參考筆者在全球華文網開設的「爾灣課後班陳克曼老師」。

http://cloudschool.huayuworld.org/moodle/course/view.php?id=335

(二) 中級組

雖然中級組的學生已有一些中文基礎，也比較成熟了，可是Moodle平台本身的版面太過樸實，老師在行有餘力時，亦可稍做裝飾。例如，把每課主題的名稱用不同顏色的字體，或加上圖檔，較為生動活潑。每一課的課程往往分兩三週來教，須加入每週日期標籤，讓學生一目了然。標籤可以用不同的顏色，凸顯出來。

中級組的教室，請參考筆者在全球華文網開設的「全新版華語第六冊陳克曼老師」。

http://cloudschool.huayuworld.org/moodle/course/view.php?id=356

(三) 高級組AP班

高級組AP班的學生都是高中生了，學生的年齡和中文程度都已經相當成熟，Moodle教室的版面應以配合實際教學為主。可依照每課課文標題來編排，也可依照主題或單元來編排，甚至交叉使用。

高級組的教室，請參考筆者在全球華文網開設的「2010爾灣Chinese 5陳克曼老師」。

http://cloudschool.huayuworld.org/moodle/course/view.php?id=983

## 三、實驗課程的內容設計

筆者仍以幼兒組、中級組和高級組三個不同年齡層來說明Moodle教室的內容設計。每組課程規劃思考是依照舒兆民老師的《使用全球華文網路教育中心素材開設Moodle課程》論文中所提到的「前置思考」、「教學目標」、「教學內容選定與分析」、「學習評量」及「線上作業」。

### (一) 幼兒組

幼兒組的教學必須符合幼兒認知發展的特性。由於孩童受限於電腦素養,可能無法自行操作電腦。因此,虛擬教室的設計成Mommy and me的親子教學方式,在父母或是祖父母的協助下,一同完成任務。

### 前置思考

1. 教學對象:幼兒組學生, 居住地語言為英語,有華裔子弟但是其中有好幾位父母是第二、第三代移民,不會說國語,也有一位母親是越南人,完全不會國語,學生年齡六歲左右。
2. 上課時數:每週上課四次,每次一小時。
3. 學習模式:除了每週實體上課之外,Moodle教室僅提供家長在家輔助兒童,沒有任何線上作業。

### 教學目標

幼兒組使用的教材以暨南大學「漢語拼音」教課書為主,以「學華語開步走」作為輔助教材。學生的程度是零起點,一年內要學會所有的漢語拼音。以「b、p」為例,具體教學目標如下(參考《學華語開步走》教師手冊):

1. 所有學生都能聽懂漢語拼音:b、p。
2. 所有學生都能學會漢語拼音:b、p的唸法和寫法。
3. 所有學生都能學會聲符:b、p的發音方法。
4. 所有學生都能學會如何將聲符b、p與之前學過的韻母合併,練習

唸讀漢字字音。

5. 所有學生都能學會認讀漢字:「爸爸」、「外婆」。

## 教學內容

每週教兩到四個拼音,以「b、p」為例:

## 1. 引起動機

**「實體教學」**(參考《學華語開步走》教師手冊)

(1)老師以問答方式,以實物為輔助,引導學生回答。

(2)老師拿著杯子提問:這是什麼?小朋友答:這是杯子。(母語)

(3)老師:杯子。(以手勢指示學生並發音)。

(4)老師把[b]的字卡貼在黑板上,帶領學生跟著老師一起讀。

(5)老師透過有趣的吹泡泡遊戲,引導學生學習[p]。

筆者所任教的班級男孩居多,非常頑皮,注意力又短暫,老師講課只要超過五分鐘,孩子們一定打打鬧鬧,到處亂跑,完全無法上課。這時候,虛擬教室裡的網路資源就派上用場了。

**「虛擬教室」**:點選Moodle教室內的「拼音一日通」,再選擇第二課韻母b、p、m、f、d、t、n、l,點選旁邊的「進入」,就可以播放b到l的卡通教學影片,學生喜歡五顏六色的動畫,每個人都目不轉睛地盯著螢幕看。老師可以要求學生跟著唸,不但輕鬆愉快,而且達到教學效果。

## 2. 主要活動

**「實體教學」**(參考《學華語開步走》教師手冊)

(1)說明[b]的發音方法。聲符的拼音練習,老師必須告訴學生:大部分聲符不可單獨發音,一定要和韻符或介音合拼。練習聲符拼音時要強調:從聲符開始唸,然後帶上韻符,由上往下,聲符連結單韻符或結合韻符一起拼出來。拼音時要快,不可以是一個符號一個符號地唸出來,要由上向下滑出聲音來。

⑵配合PPT，帶領學生由日常生活中的詞語開始練習發音，如：杯子、爸爸、白色，由常接觸的熟悉詞語帶入拼音與聲調。

⑶練習唸讀基本的語詞之後，開始講解[b]的拼音規則。

⑷書寫練習：老師要學生按照筆順，進行書空練習，之後在學習單上練習書寫。

⑸說明聲符[p]的發音方法，爲了使學生了解送氣的情形，學習[p]時，可以讓學生用手拿著薄面紙放在嘴邊，然後再唸，發音時紙就會因爲氣而飄動起來。

⑹練習唸讀語詞之後，開始講解[p]的拼音規則。

⑺配合PPT，帶領學生由日常生活中熟悉的詞語帶入聲調，並配合實物學習，以加深印象，如：外婆、朋友、跑步。

⑻老師要學生按照筆順，進行書空練習，之後在學習單上練習書寫。

3. 綜合活動

「**虛擬教室**」：聲調對非華裔的學童而言，有些困難，尤其是二聲和三聲，經常混淆不清。點選Moodle教室內的《說說唱唱漢語拼音——平揚拐彎降》影片，請學生跟著大聲朗誦。

4. 歌謠教學

「**虛擬教室**」：每天都點選Moodle教室內的「聲母韻母歌」，讓學生跟著唱。日積月累、孩子們對於聲母和韻母自然耳熟能詳了。

5. 學習評量

運用課程學習單進行評量，可於幾個主題單元完成後進行紙筆測驗。

6. 數位融入華語文教學

「**虛擬教室**」：香港中文大學出版的《漢語拼音練習版》http://resources.edb.gov.hk/~chi/frontpage.html可以點選聲母、韻母和聲

調，點選聲母和韻母時會發聲，方便學生認識該聲母、韻母，點選調號後所產生的字，也能發出讀音，是教漢語拼音的好工具。

線上作業

　　由於幼兒組學童年齡太小，加上部分父母在家不說國語，所以無法也不需要使用Moodle線上作業的功能。

㈡ 中級組

　　中級組的學生已有一些中文基礎，虛擬教室的內容應涵蓋中文聽、說、讀、寫，包括每週教學活動、教學講義、課文朗讀、生字筆順和動畫故事。

前置思考

1. 教學對象：中級組學生，居住地語言為英語，華裔子弟，年齡八歲以上。
2. 上課時數：每週一次，每次二小時。
3. 學習模式：混合式，除了每週實體上課之外，參考資料與作業均有線上學習。

教學目標

　　中級組使用的教材是全新版華語第六冊，學生能力為2，根據Krashen's 6 Hypotheses（Steve Krashen）的教學假設，教學內容應該為3 (i + 1)。各單元都需要涵蓋聽、說、讀、寫。第一課的教學重點是能讓學生對於好習慣和壞習慣有所知，好的習慣要繼續保持，壞的習慣要改正過來。

教學內容選定與分析（Note：沒有註明的是實體教學部分）

　　兩週教一課，第一週以教新知識為主，以第一課〈灰灰的改變〉為例子：

1. 引起動機：灰灰是一隻小灰兔，可以先讓學生們說出他們喜歡的動物。

2. 講述大意：老師先把本課大意說給學生聽。

3. 詞語教學：教導本課語詞，老師可用課本和紙本講義。

4. 生字教學：「**虛擬教室**」：用Moodle教室裡的生詞教導本課生字、部首，和字義。可以利用Moodle辭典功能或「教育部常用國字標準字體筆順學習連結快速產生器」製作本課生詞。老師在課堂上點選筆順書寫時，請學生書空或注意看筆順動畫。此時老師是面對著學生，比寫板書時背對著學生效果好多了。

5. 課文朗讀：在課堂上可以用範讀、領讀、團體讀、分組讀、個別讀的方式練習課文內容。「**虛擬教室**」：如若不希望學生過分依賴注音符號，老師可用「網頁瀏覽」或「連結到檔案」的方式，把沒有注音符號的課文放到Moodle教室，請學生在課堂上或課後朗讀，訓練學生認讀國字。

6. 第二週著重在複習及加入補充教材。

7. 內容深究：設計幾個理解文章的問題（可參考教師手冊），在課堂上提出問題，師生共同討論，指定學生在課後以書寫的方式將情意擴展的答案寫在作業紙上或在部落格迴響裡。

8. 學習評量：紙筆測驗、活動式評量、部落格迴響及Moodle錄音報告。

9. 遊戲融入華語文教學：利用「字中找趣」等簡報所製作的遊戲，以分組比賽的方式進行，表面上是在玩語文遊戲，實則複習生字及生詞。「**虛擬教室**」：也可用陳亮光、顏國雄、章薇菲、陳榮坤老師所設計的遊戲，將題庫更改為以該課為主的遊戲，讓學生開開心心地玩遊戲、學華文。Quizlet是一套免費又好用的中文軟體，老師們可以快速地把每課生詞輸入，再把系統自動輸出的Quizlet flash cards生字卡、Learn學習、Scatter遊戲用連結到Moodle教室，學生在課堂上或課後複習生詞。也可以利用Quizlet test讓學生練習做選擇題、填充題、是非題。

10. 文化及其他課外補充：「**虛擬教室**」：將動畫故事利用連結到檔案或網站的方式事先放在Moodle教室，如果有充裕的時間，在課

堂上播放給學生看，並簡單解釋，如果沒有足夠的時間，則可指定為課後作業。

### 線上作業

「**虛擬教室**」：Moodle最佳的功能就是線上作業了。中級組的學生還不太會打中文，所以作業可以出口語作業，任務式作業最好，例如：「我到超級市場去買水果」。但是，僑校的學生不比美國學校選修中文課那麼在乎成績，筆者試過出主題錄音線上作業，效果不是十分理想。退而求其次，可以讓學生做朗讀課文的錄音報告。請學生用Audacity將課文朗讀一遍，儲存成mp3檔案，然後上傳到Moodle教室。老師可以利用Moodle線上作業、線上評語及評分的方式直接將成績與評語輸入虛擬教室。

### (三) 高級組AP班

高級組AP班級中，有許多美國高中學生希望上了一年以後，能夠在AP中文考試中拿到滿分五分。因此，Moodle教室的設計必須配合AP教科書，並提供中華文化及歷史方面的補充教材，才能使學生更加熟悉與了解中華文化。

### 前置思考

1. 教學對象：高級組學生，居住地語言為英語，華裔子弟，年齡十八歲左右。
2. 上課時數：每週一次，每次二小時。
3. 學習模式：混合式，除了每週實體上課之外，參考資料與作業均有線上部分。

### 教學目標

高級組使用的教材是「超越」AP中文教材、「漫談中國」（文化輔助教材），教學內容還是i＋1（比學生現在的程度高出一點）。各單元都需要涵蓋聽、說、讀、寫。以第十七課〈我們只有一個地球〉為例子，具體教學目標為：

1. 學生將能夠討論環境污染和破壞的問題
2. 學生將能夠討論環保和社區規劃

**教學內容選定與分析**（Note：沒有註明的是實體教學部分）

　　三週教一課，第一週和第二週教新知識的part 1和part 2，以第十七課〈我們只有一個地球〉為例子：

1. 引起動機：「**虛擬教室**」先看《我們只有一個地球》（*Our Only One Earth*）影片，觸動孩子的心靈，美麗的山河大地、文化古蹟，如果不好好地愛惜，後果是何等地不堪，灌輸環保的概念。

2. 講述大意：老師把本課大意說給學生聽，由於學生已有中文根基，可以先用問答的方式，老師可了解學生對環保有沒有概念，學生亦可透過老師的問題與答案，知道本課大意。

3. 詞語教學：教導本課語詞，課文後面的語詞，有的國字學生已經學過了，可是，不見得了解該語詞的真正涵義。例如：「土石流」這三個字，每個單字應該都學過，可是他們並不知道放在一起，就是mudflows or landslides的意思。

4. 生字教學：高級組的學生，不需要再教生字筆順了，可是，生活環境中，除了中文學校以外，沒有使用中文的機會，學過的字詞，很容易忘記。

   筆者第一年教此組的學生時，體諒他們美國學校功課繁忙，並沒有要求學生書寫生字詞。後來聽從學生們的建議，仍然用紙本作業讓學生書寫該課生字詞。

5. 課文朗讀：在課堂上不太需要用範讀、領讀、團體讀或分組讀的方式，個別讀的方式可以讓老師清楚地知道學生無法讀出哪些字。不要總是叫一兩個程度最好的學生朗讀，而應該照顧到全班的學生。

6. 學習評量：紙筆測驗加上小組活動評量。

7. 內容深究：AP教材的設計非常適合以小組討論和報告的方式來進行內容深究。例如：將班上的學生分成兩人或三人一組，請他

們討論下面有關垃圾回收的問題：(1)你住的社區做了哪些回收工作？你認為還有什麼東西是應該回收的？(2)綠色商品是什麼？請舉幾個例子。(3)美國的綠色商品有標章嗎？(4)下面哪些垃圾可回收？哪些不可回收？錄影帶、手機、塑膠袋等等。(5)根據台灣的規定，把上列的垃圾分類。

學生討論完了以後，請小組到前面報告。如果時間不夠，可以指定每一組負責一到兩題，不需要全部討論。

第三週著重在文化部分。第十七課文化走廊的主題是「慈濟」。大意是：「慈濟」兩字的意思是「以慈悲心救濟需要的人」。簡介慈濟的創辦人證嚴法師的生平以及慈濟做功德、投入資源回收的善舉。

1. 資訊融入華語文教學：「**虛擬教室**」：在Moodle教室內，放入下列與「慈濟」有關的影片：

(1)匯集善意度眾生 —— 證嚴：短短三分鐘的影片，說明慈濟可以在台灣動員四百萬人，而證嚴法師認為「佛」不是泥雕像而是人心。

(2)慈濟音樂手語劇 —— 無量義經：受到證嚴法師的感召，許多醫生、護士及各行各業的大老闆都加入了慈濟的行列。

課文中提到了原住民，下面的影片可以做課文點的延伸：

(1)九族文化村 —— 山地歌舞表演：九族文化村位於台灣南投縣魚池鄉，是一座以台灣原住民九大族群為主題的樂園。九族文化村是結合台灣九大原住民族族群的各項文化特色展示，聽唱歌看跳舞和服飾，可以認識包括泰雅族、賽夏族、鄒族、布農族、卑南族、魯凱族、達悟族、阿美族、排灣族及邵族在內的九族。

(2)台灣的原住民的舞蹈：三個YouTube影片：①泰雅舞蹈表演 —— 出草祭。「出草祭」是到敵人的部落砍取敵人的人頭，目的是報仇，也可以提高自己在部落的地位。②阿美族的豐年祭。③

穿丁字褲的悟族舞蹈。

2. 文化及其他課外補充：中國歷史、文字、哲學、發明、節慶（新年、中秋節、端午節）、家族觀念、中國菜、中國俗語文化等等都是高級組非常好的補充教材，無論是影片、圖片或文章，都可以放到Moodle教室做補充教材。

線上作業

　　AP班級的線上作業尤其重要，須依照AP中文測試與ACTFL 5Cs標準，來加強學生的中文理解詮釋能力、人際溝通能力、口頭和書面表達的能力。AP中文測試的及格水平相當美國一般大學第四個學期中文課程的難度，分聽力、閱讀、寫作和說話四大部分。

1. 聽力（25%）
　　⑴10%聽中文對話後選擇正確回話
　　⑵15%聽情境對話後選正確答案

2. 閱讀（25%）──約三十五至四十題
　　⑴題目來源包括廣告、文章、電子郵件、書信等，有一小時可作答

3. 寫作（25%）──共有四題、不限字數
　　⑴看圖寫故事
　　⑵回覆電子郵件
　　⑶聽寫電話留言──可聽兩次

4. 說話（25%）
　　⑴有六小題，每題只有二十秒鐘的時間回答
　　⑵Presentation－四分鐘的時間準備，兩分鐘的時間record

　　高級組的學生聽力與閱讀能力都已經相當不錯了，上述聽力與閱讀部分可以規定學生依照AP教材的workbook自行練習。可是開放性問題（Free-Response Questions）（又分寫作技巧和說話技巧），非得長期苦練不可。由於學生已經會中文打字，每週作業都出口語作業

或書寫（打字）作業，反覆練習，才能熟悉AP考試方式，充分發揮實力。在出書寫作業前，需要提醒學生下列注意事項：

　(1)要非常仔細地看清楚題目，應考關鍵在於「問什麼、答什麼」，文要對題，語法、詞彙和文化知識是否正確都會影響成績。

　(2)選錯字會扣分。

　(3)千萬不要打英文，因為這表示中文詞彙不夠，想辦法用不同的字或詞。

　(4)考試中間不可以轉換正體字和簡體字，注音和拼音。

　(5)不強調標點符號，但是不要因為標點符號而影響內容。

　(6)寫回信時，結尾要加祝福語、名字、和日期。


　　學生可用Microsoft Word做書寫報告，用Audacity免費錄音軟體做二十秒鐘的口語練習或二分鐘的口語報告，再將報告上傳到Moodle教室，老師做線上評語、線上評分。下面是學生上傳到Moodle教室的看圖寫故事範例：


　　「小新和他的朋友正在計畫應該要如何去享受他們的環島旅行，可是他們最大的問題就是交通。他們要開車去呢，要租一台小車還是大車呢，他們想來想去，總於小新想到了又便宜又環保的方法，那就是騎腳踏車。小新和他的朋友都贊成這個主意，於是他們就跑去租三台腳踏車，開始他們的環島旅行。剛起程的時候，天氣都很好還陽光普照，可是到了下午，一片黑雲往小新的方向飄過來，突然下起了傾盆大雨。這一下就下了好久，都把小新和他的朋友淋成落湯雞。經過這場濕答答的狂風大雨，小新後悔地想早知道就應該還是開車出來玩。」

# 結論

　　至聖先師孔老夫子說得好──要因材施教。老師們一定要依照學生的背景、程度來規劃、建置Moodle課程，在使用時，如果發覺不夠理想，也需要隨時調整。

## 參考文獻

### ㈠ 期刊論文

Ebbinghaus, H. (1885). *Über das Gedchtnis. Untersuchungen zur experimentellen Psychologie*. Leipzig: Duncker & Humblot; the English edition is Ebbinghaus, H. (1913). *Memory. A Contribution to Experimental Psychology*. New York: Teachers College, Columbia University (Reprinted Bristol: Thoemmes Press, 1999).

林金錫、舒兆民、周中天、陳浩然、連育仁（2008）。Moodle在華語文教學上之運用，第五屆全球華文網路研討會論文，取自http://media.huayuworld.org/discuss/academy/netedu05/html/paper/sw57.pdf。

舒兆民──Moodle平台課程設計http://blog.huayuworld.org/gallery/10275/SHU4_Moodle.pdf。

舒兆民──使用「全球華文網路教育中心」素材開設Moodle課程http://edu.ocac.gov.tw/biweekly/543/g1.htm。

### ㈡ 網路資源

Moodle和Blackboard, 360doc, http://www.360doc.com/content/11/1227/02/8192435_175234718.shtml。

Steve Karshen, Krashen's 6 Hypotheses, http://www2.education.ualberta.ca/staff/olenka.Bilash/best%20of%20bilash/krashen.html。

# 雲端科技應用於美國高中之中文教學
## ——數位檔案夾計畫

姜滿

美國俄亥俄州森特菲高中

mjbroadstock@gmail.com

## 摘要

　　隨著雲端科技的進步和網際網路的發達，資料的存取和分享也隨之便利快捷。語文及文化之教學也就不再局限於只是教室或學校裡的活動。透過雲端科技，學生們可以在網路上建立一個溝通平台，分享他們的學習心得，展示他們的學習成果。美國俄亥俄州森特菲高中中文四及AP學生透過Google site，建立個人數位E-Portfolio。將他們的中文學習成果記錄下來與教師及同學們分享。本文主旨在分享應用雲端科技於美國高中中文教學之實務經驗。

　　爲了使學生能分享，蒐集及檢視自己的中文學習，美國俄亥俄州森特菲高中的高年級中文課學生皆須參與數位檔案夾計畫：E-Portfolio project。E-Portfolio計畫的主要目的在提供學生一個數位環境讓學上能分享交流他們的中文學習成果。在學期初學生透過Google site建立一個個人的中文學習網站，以此網站作爲其中文學習的數位文件的檔案夾。在這個網站上，學生在學習每一個單元時，必須建立以下不同的網頁：一）學習目標I can statement，二）課前預習Preview，三）學習成果How well I learn，四）學習反省Reflection，五）說故事story telling，及六）成語篇Idioms。也就是在學習每個單元時，學生可以依據學習目標，驗證學習成果，可以預習生詞並延伸詞彙及練習寫作，可以轉載或張貼該單元的學習成

果，如任務型評量活動報告，自製電子漫畫書，口語練習影片檔案，影音檔案連結等各單元的活動設計。透過雲端技術，學生不會受到地域、瀏覽器、電腦系統，及檔案格式等限制，可以簡便地連接與使用數位資料。只要能連接上網便可以隨時隨地進入自己的網站，張貼作業和存取檔案。教師可以透過網路給予即時的建議和修正，同學們也可以瀏覽彼此的網站，互相交流分享，同儕學習。此一計畫同時提升學生的科技應用能力，設計個人化的學習網站，讓中文的學習更生動有趣。

　　參與E-Portfolio的學生並於學期結束前填寫問卷調查，針對E-Portfolio計畫的學習效果及使用難易提出意見。本研究將依據學生的反應及教師的反省日記做檢討，並提出E-Portfolio計畫之優缺點及未來改進之方向。

關鍵字：雲端科技、網路教學、華語教育、美國高中華語教學

　　隨著雲端科技的進步和網際網路的發達，資料的存取和分享也隨之便利快捷。語文及文化之教學也就不再局限於只是教室或學校裡的活動。透過雲端科技，學生們可以在網路上建立一個溝通平台，分享他們的學習心得，展示他們的學習成果。美國俄亥俄州森特菲高中中文四及AP學生都架設個人Google網站，以建立數位檔案夾E-Portfolio。將他們的中文學習成果記錄下來與教師及同學們分享。本文主旨在分享應用雲端科技於美國高中中文教學之實務經驗。

## 一、緣起

　　森特菲高中是一所典型的美國中西部公立高中。學生人數約二千八百人，少數民族學生佔總人數的10%，亞洲裔學生佔總人數約6%。森特菲學區於2006年正式在高中部開設中文課程。2012年中文課程包括中文一、二、三、四，及AP中文。然而為了讓初中外國語文學分得以認可，大部分學生上高中後都延續選修初中所學的外

國語言。因為學區初中部沒有開設中文，因此選修中文的學生中文課的學生中高中一年級人數不多，而學習總人數大多維持在四十到五十人次。中文一人數約二十人，中文二約十五人次。由於學生陸續畢業，高年級中文班人數減少，因此學校採取合班上課制。於2009年起中文三和四合班上課。2012年中文課課高級班更包括中文三、四，及AP三個不同的程度。因此如何有效地針對不同的程度學生給予適當的教學活動，對任教老師而言相當具挑戰性。

　　為了有效地幫助學生學習，高級班的教學採翻轉教室教學方式（flipping classroom）。傳統的教學是老師主導的講演式教學，上課的時間以老師主導講述課程內容為主。但是在不同層次合班上課的教學環境下，語文課老師主講的方式在時間上及實用性皆不適用，而且教師主導的教學方式效果也不彰。因此筆者改變傳統的教學方式，採用翻轉教室教學法。每週上課方式為隔日替換方式，也就是週一和週三老師給中文三學生上課，中文四及AP中文的學生則透過活動單自行學習相關課程內容。週二及週四老師給中文四及AP課程上課，中文三學生則給予活動，讓學生自行學習課程內容。

　　翻轉教室設計是把學習的主導權移交給學生，讓學生自己負責學習的過程。學生能透過視訊或教學活動，自行學習基本的內容。教師上課的時間則主要用在教學活動及討論課程的內容及學生的問題。對中文課程而言，高年級的學生已有相當中文詞彙及文法概念，因此自行閱讀單元內容並學習生詞及語法點是可行的。教師在上課的時間則多用在口語的對話練習、文化內容的分享，並針對語法結構及生詞的應用和比較，及其他學生無法自行理解的內容做講解。

　　但如何能讓學生透過活動自行學習課程內容是一個挑戰。為了能讓學生有效學習單元生詞，並展現所學的成效，筆者決定讓學生建立個人網站，透過編輯網站內容，學生能練習所學生詞及語法，並可蒐集及檢視自己的中文學習。因此森特菲高中的高級中文班，中文三、四，及AP中文學生皆須參與數位檔案夾計畫：E-Portfolio Project。

## 二、數位檔案夾計畫

　　數位檔案夾計畫，E-Portfolio，主要目的在提供學生一個數位環境讓學生能利用雲端科技，以蒐集、分享和交流他們的中文學習成果，並透過編輯過程反省自己的學習，進而改進將來學習的方式。在學期初學生申請建立Google帳號，然後在Google site上架設一個個人的中文學習網站，以此網站做為該年度中文學習的數位文件檔案夾，儲存所有學習資料及成果。學生在開學第一週即學習如何架設個人的Google網站（見附件一）。在這個網站上，學生在學習每一個單元時，必須預習生詞及練習寫作，再依據學習目標，驗證自己的學習，並張貼各單元的學習成果。因此學生必須建立以下的五至六個不同的網頁：

㈠ 學習目標I can statement

　　在教育實踐理論裡提到，當學生對自己學習的過程及目標能有所認知及了解時，將有助於其學習效果。此學習目標網頁即在幫助學生在課前預習的過程中，思考並寫下各單元的學習目標，了解學習的過程，並在單元結束時，寫下句子以驗證自己的學習成果。因此在此網頁裡，每位學生須用英文以「I can...」的句型列出四到六個具體的學習行為目標，單元結束後，再以中文輸入句子以檢驗自己是否達到此一學習目標。以下是芮同學在其E-Portfolio上學習目標的實例。

1. *I can ask for and give direction*…你知道圖書館怎麼走嗎
2. *I can identify locations by using landmarks as references*…圖書館在活動中心旁邊。
3. *I can describe whether two places are close to or far away from one another*…圖書館離活動中心很近。
4. *State where you are heading and the purpose of going there*…我到圖書館去看書。

（二）課前預習Preview

　　爲了幫助學生能自行預習課文、學習每單元的生詞，及了解生詞的用法，學生必須在E-Portfolio上建立「課前預習」網頁。學生將輸入每一課的所有新生詞、生詞的拼音及英文解釋，並用此生詞造一個句子。此作業須在老師開始上課前完成，利用自行學習的頭兩天來製作此項網頁，學生們先和同學一起討論課文內容再做生詞預習輸入。除了新生詞練習外，還需要選擇五個生詞，針對這五個生詞，拆開後延伸出新生詞以學習更多生詞。由於E-Portfolio需要用電腦輸入，教室內的小電腦速度太慢，鍵盤打字極不方便，因此在第二單元後生詞預習的電腦輸入部分，改成以作業單手寫輸入形式，在學生的E-Portfolio上只保留新生詞延伸學習部分。以下爲葉同學的生詞延伸實例。

1. 豆腐：*dou4 fu3*：*tofu*：來一盤家常豆腐。

　　豆漿：*dou4 jiang1*：*soymilk*：我喜歡喝豆漿。

　　反腐：*fan3fu3*：*against corruption*：我是反腐的。

2. 放：*fang4*：*put*：請不要放味精。

　　放棄：*fang4qi4*：*give up*：我不會放棄。

　　放開：*fang4kai1*：*let go*：放開我。

3. 肉：*rou4*：*meat*：我愛吃肉。

　　豬肉：*zhu1 rou4*：*pork*：我常常吃豬肉。

　　雞肉：*ji3 rou4*：*chicken*：我不喜歡吃<u>雞肉</u>。

4. 碗：*wan3*：*bowl*：來一碗酸辣湯。

　　洗碗：*xi3 wan3*：*wash dishes*：我不喜歡洗碗。

　　碗櫃：*wan3gui4*：*cupboard*：我碗櫃有放碗。

5. 酸辣湯：*suan1 la4 tang3*：*Hot and sour soup*：蛋花湯比酸辣湯好吃多了。

　　辣椒：*la4jiao1*：*hot pepper*：我爸爸每天吃辣椒。

　　酸梅：*suan1mei3*：*preserved plum*：我小時候常常吃酸梅。

㈢ 學習成果How well I learn

　　每一個單元，教師根據單元目標及學生必須學會的項目，設計IPA（Integrated Performance Assessment）整合式評量活動，來檢視學生的學習成果。學生透過此一整合式評量來表現自己的中文的認知及表達能力。該活動以任務為導向，並讓學生在理解、溝通、表達三個不同的模式中表現學習成果（interpersonal, interpretive, and presentational modes）。每個整合式評量以真材實料（authentic materials）讓學生以三種不同模式來完成任務，並藉由學生在任務完成的過程中評量其學習成果。例如，在在生日派對單元裡，活動的任務是給自己開一個生日派對，學生需要完成的三個模式是：

1. Presentational mode：設計一張生日邀請卡，說明生日派對的日期、時間、地點、活動內容、路線說明，及注意事項。
2. Interpretive mode：用￥500到中國最大網購網站——淘寶網上購買生日派對所需的水果、飲料、點心等食品。選購後將物品以分類、項目、數量、單價、照片，及價錢詳細列出清單。
3. Interpersonal mode：以電話方式或發短信方式邀請同學來參加生日派對。電話通話以Voki或Video錄製在E-Portfolio上。
學生將完成的整合性評量活動每個模式的成果都張貼在E-Portfolio的學習成果（How well I learn）網頁。教師再依據學生所展現的成果依據評量表給予成績。（見附件二）

　　每個單元的任務型整合式評量活動方式不同，有的需要自製電子漫畫書，有的是建立口語影片檔案，檔案如果太大，則將檔案上傳到Google雲端硬碟，Google drive，再在E-Portfolio上加入連結。有的需要用網路上的影音軟體，學生在其他網站，如Viki、Toodoo網製作成品後，複製程式碼再把程式碼貼在HTML程式碼裡，使其他網站的成品可以呈現在E-Portfolio上，以完成繳交各單元的活動設計。

## (四) 學習反省Reflection：

在每個單元學習結束時，學生以英文完成學習反省網頁，在此學生反省自己在這一個單元裡學習的過程，及所遇到的困難及問題，並藉此與老師溝通。以下是斐同學的學習反省實例。

Reflection:

*Although the vocabulary was easy to learn and remember because I felt it applied to my life (more relevant = easier to remember) the grammatical structure using* 了 *was a bit confusing. The book said that* 了 *indicates that an action has occurred, but it was hard for me to understand that it can also be used to talk about the future, as in* 我明天吃了早飯去機場 *I will go to the airport tomorrow after I have eaten breakfast.*

## (五) 說故事Story telling：

說故事網頁是以四幅連環圖畫讓學生就圖畫串聯起一個故事。學生可以練習描述故事的邏輯性，學習連結詞的運用，以及寫作打字技巧。圖片來源是中文聽說讀寫作業本的圖片。中文三使用中文聽說讀寫Integrated Chinese Level 1 Part 2，中文四／AP使用中文聽說讀寫Integrated Chinese Level 2 Part 1。以下是聞同學的說故事實例。

家偉在路上走常看到<u>男才女貌</u>。他想如果他也有一個好女朋友，他會很高興。他不<u>知道</u>很多女人所以他<u>出</u>網上找一個女人。家偉要的女人要喜歡跑步、吃素、不喜歡買東西。可是最<u>嚴重的判據</u>，是她要愛他。可是，哪知網上給他一匹女馬！

## ㈥ 成語篇Idioms：

　　中文四及AP中文的學生也需要依據單元裡的生詞找一個相關的成語，把它的拼音及定義寫在成語篇網頁裡，並造一個句子。成語學習是學生較難自行學習的部分，學生不知道有哪些成語或該怎麼找成語。網上的成語網通常是全中文，學生不容易理解，因此這個部分老師需要上課時補充相關的成語教材。以下是杜同學的成語篇實例。

　　火上澆油：*huo3 shang4 jiao1 you2: to aggravate a situation:* 不要火上澆油，他們現在比剛才更生氣。

　　高班的中文學生在課堂上或下課後在電腦上編輯個人的E-Portfolio檔案夾。將每一單元的學習目標、學習反省、生詞學習，和學習成果都展現在個人的網站上。教師在每單元結束後一定檢視每位學生的網站，透過網路給予即時的建議和修正。然在網路上修改學生作業並不容易。爲了讓學生發現自己在寫作上的錯誤，教師修正的方式必須事先和學生統一說明，如：多餘的字轉成紅色、文法錯誤則以藍色括弧修正說明、畫底線的字是用詞錯誤的字，之後讓學生自行改正。教師也透過閱覽學生的網站，了解學生的學習困難及常犯的錯誤，之後可以在上課時與學生討論分析。

　　透過製作E-Portfolio個人的數位檔案夾，學生能在剪輯的過程中學習中文，並在檔案夾裡保留完整的中文學習成果，也可以在其他同學們的網站上交流觀摩，互相學習。此一計畫同時提升學生的科技應用的能力，學習如何設計個人化的網站，也讓中文的學習更生動有趣。

## 三、雲端科技的應用

　　拜網路科技之賜，此數位檔案夾計畫能夠利用Google免費協作平台及雲端技術，使學生能將所有資料檔案都上傳到Google。讓

學生在使用時不會受到地域、瀏覽器、電腦系統，及檔案格式等限制，能很簡便地儲存、連接，及使用數位資料；只要能連接上網便可以隨時隨地進入自己的網站。由於學生的數位檔案夾個人網站是設置在Google站上，因此可以自由選擇其網站的隱私權限，可以選擇與特定人分享，或和全世界人共用。本校過去一直使用Moodle教學平台，Moodle 為教師設計的教學平台，教師為主要設計者，學生處被動的單向學習角色。本計畫的各項網頁活動雖然都可以以Moodle活動單方式進行，但為讓學生能有主動權去設計編輯和學習，也考慮學生學習的效果及自主權，筆者決定採用建立Google協作平台。以下表格比較Google協作平台和Moodle教學平台的不同。

|  | Moodle教學平台 | Google協作平台 |
| --- | --- | --- |
| 主要使用人及權限 | 教師設計編輯 | 學生即網站站主，可以自行設計、編輯、張貼、上傳，及在平台上交流 |
| 其他使用人 | 註冊學生可以單向閱讀，下載及上傳檔案，或使用教師已設計好之活動單 | 受邀人士可以閱覽、發表意見，或張貼修改 |
| 交流互動 | 只有在form活動中可以交流 | 任何網頁凡受邀請的人皆可交流討論 |
| 上傳檔案大小 | 由學校設定上限，一般5MB | 每個平台100MB，上傳附加檔案20MB |
| 限制 | 不受到地域，瀏覽器，電腦系統的限制<br>部分視頻格式不被接受<br>部分功能受限於瀏覽器<br>部分功能校方不提供 | 不受到地域、瀏覽器、電腦系統的限制，功能由Google提供，站主可以選擇使用與否 |
| 保存期限 | 一年 | 只要Google站存在，檔案存在，不受限制 |

## 四、學生意見

　　參與E-Portfolio的中文三、四、及中文AP學生共計十五人。除了一位同學缺席外，其餘同學皆完成E-portfolio問卷調查。學生於學期結束前兩週填寫問卷調查，針對E-Portfolio計畫的學習效果及使用難易提出意見。以下就問卷調查結果進行討論。學生針對E-Portfolio個別網頁及整體提出同意／不同意下列的敘述。表1爲學生對E-Portfolio網頁的問卷調查百分比結果。

表1　學生對E-Portfolio各網頁的意見調查結果

| | 問題 | 不同意／非常不同意 | 同意／非常同意 |
|---|---|---|---|
| 1 | 「I can...」教學目標幫助我了解學習目標和自我檢視我的學習成果 | 21.4% | 78.6% |
| 2 | 課前預習部分輸入生詞及造句幫助我學習生詞 | 35.7% | 64.3% |
| 3 | 課前預習生詞中，延伸新生詞對我認識新的生詞很有幫助 | 57.2% | 42.8% |
| 4 | 學習反省網頁對我審視自我學習和自我評量學習成果很有益處 | 38.5% | 61.5% |
| 5 | 說故事部分讓我能夠應用所學練習寫作 | 21.4% | 78.6% |
| 6 | 學習成果部分透過任務型活動幫助我學習中文 | 42.9% | 57.1% |
| 7 | 成語篇讓我能夠學習成語並能運用在日常對話中 | 83.3% | 16.7% |
| 8 | 編輯數位檔案夾讓我學會如何使用網路工具，使我對建立網站網頁更有信心 | 21.4% | 78.6% |
| 9 | 總體而言，我覺得E-Portfolio數位檔案夾是學習中文及自我學習檢討的有效方法 | 28.6% | 71.4% |

　　第二部分調查學生在各網頁編輯輸入時所花費的時間。表2為使用時間的調查結果。

表2　學生各網頁編輯所需時間

| # | 使用時間 | 小於十分鐘 | 小於三十分鐘 | 小於一小時 | 小於兩小時 | 超過兩小時 |
|---|---|---|---|---|---|---|
| 10 | I can ... statement | 69.2% | 30.8% | | | |
| 11 | Preview-New vocabulary | | 23.1% | 53.8% | 23.1% | |
| 12 | Reflection | 92.3% | 7.7% | | | |
| 13 | Story Narrative | 38.5% | 53.8% | 7.7% | | |
| 14 | How well I learn/ project | | | 46.2% | 30.8% | 23.1% |
| 15 | Idiom | 80% | 20% | | | |

　　表1顯示除了對生詞延伸認識新詞和成語篇（僅中文四及AP中文學生）的的學習效用功能不贊同外，超過半數的學生同意其他網頁對其中文學習有正面的作用。總體而言，78%同學贊成E-Portfolio幫助他們學習如何使用網路工具、架設網站，及編輯網頁，讓他們更有信心地建構網站。71.4%的學生同意數位檔案夾是中文學習及個人學習檢討的有效方法。

　　學生對學習成果網頁針對任務型活動有助於中文學習的看法呈現正反面相似比例，在開放式問題的回答中，學生提及主要原因是在於部分學生覺得任務型活動花費時間太長。一般紙筆測驗只需要花五十分鐘時間，但整合式評量大部分學生需要花一到兩小時時間。學生表示他們認同任務型活動的必要性，但要把活動設計做好，要用上太多課外時間。

　　表2顯示除了課前預習及學習成果兩個網頁需要花費較長的時間編輯輸入外，大部分的網頁學生可以在三十分鐘內完成。課前預習學

生需要花約一小時時間製作，而學習成果－任務型整合評量活動則需
要兩小時左右完成。

　　在開放式問題中學生提出他們認為數位檔案夾E-Portfolio計畫對
他們而言的最大收穫、對困難的地方，及最喜歡和不喜歡的部分，並
提出建議。雖然課前預習和完成任務型活動需要花很多時間，絕大部
分的學生們提出E-Portfolio最大的收穫是在編輯課前預習及在呈現學
習成果當中檢視自己的中文學習。AP學生也提到說故事部分對他們
的AP中文考試非常有幫助，讓他們能實際演練AP考試的項目。也有
學生提到喜歡學習反省網頁，讓他們的回顧自己的學習過程。

　　學生在建立E-Portfolio最大的困難是網頁編輯的問題。部分學生
對Google site的編輯方式不太了解，在側欄編輯、版面設置、數位檔
案連結時常出現問題，造成作業困難，也花費時間。針對E-Portfolio
內容本身除了少數中文三學生對生詞延伸部分有困難外，其他內容學
生都能掌握。許多學生提到他們喜歡E-Portfolio的地方是E-Portfolio
除了能學習生詞練習中文外，也提供他們機會去反思自己的學習，此
外所有的文件檔案都在同一網站上，很容易查閱整理，也可以作為他
們未來大學選修中文時中文程度表現的證明。

## 五、教師的省思

　　這是一個網路網際的時代，培養學生能善用現有的網路資源，有
效地使用學習的工具是當初設計E-Portfolio的首要目的。經過兩年的
嘗試，在此依據學生的反應及教師的反省日記做檢討，就兩年來學生
使用E-Portfolio學習的成效及教學的實用性，提出本計畫之優缺點及
未來改進之方向。

1. 網頁設計問題：去年首次介紹E-Portfolio時，學生在網頁的編輯和
　 版面配置遇到許多的困難，讓部分學生卻步。這些學生第二年這
　 方面的問題顯著地減少。當學生了解Google site的操作模式後，第
　 二年就相當得心應手。中文三的學生雖然是第一次學習，但也很
　 容易上手，在網頁設計上的困難相對去年而言較少，其原因之一

在於學期初對Google site的使用方法有較詳細的說明和操練。這些網際時代的學生，在網路活動的操作上非常順手，因此教師實在可以多善加利用現有的網路資源，讓學生藉由網路所提供的免費平台，作爲學習的工具。

2. 綠色教學環境：在E-Portfolio裡的網頁，其實許多活動，例如生詞預習、教學成果、說故事，都可以用紙筆作業單方式讓學生練習。當初考慮使用E-Portfolio的主要動機之一，就是作業電腦化，以減少紙張的使用及浪費。除了之後因電腦使用的困難，在生詞預習部分改爲手寫單之外，其他項目全部保留在網路上。其實就老師批改作業而言，批改紙質的作業單是比較容易，既方便又快速。在網路上修改作業所需花費的時間較作業單要多上三到四倍，修改方法也不是紅筆一圈便能完成，爲了要點出學生的錯誤，常需要變換顏色、字體、加註批等，相當耗時。可以不再需要列印活動單，讓教學綠色化是E-Portfolio的優點，但相對地教師得花上較多的時間在網上批改作業是E-Portfolio的缺點之一。

3. E-Portfolio內容要求：從學生的問卷調查中可以看出學生的困難所在，大部分學生都認同E-Portfolio對他們中文學習的幫助，但是程度不同學生對內容要求意見不同。中文四學生喜歡生詞延伸單元，讓他們能自行選擇學習不同新詞。然而對中文三學生而言，因爲所學有限，生詞延伸及造句相對困難些，因而變成負擔，這是設計之初所沒有料想到的。之後在內容設計上需要考慮學生的學習能力，針對不同程度的學生，給予適合的要求。

4. 學習成果的儲存與展現：E-Portfolio讓學生把學習成果儲存起來，可以和他人分享，可以隨時取用、編輯修改。有學生提到E-Portfolio讓他們有效地管理學習的檔案，不怕遺失或忘記帶上課，畢業以後還可以使用。相較其他科目學期結束後他們通常都把上課的資料丟進紙張回收箱，不再檢視。但是E-Portfolio讓他們能把整年的課程資料有效率地整理歸檔存儲，作爲以後學習的參考，需要時不會找不到個人的檔案夾。

5. 網站交流溝通功能：E-Portfolio和Moodle最大的功能差異，除了學生主導網頁設計外，還在於其功能可以讓學生閱覽彼此的網頁，相互留言進行交流。然今年學生們雖然將網頁開放給同班同學，但整個計畫裡並沒有特別設計活動，讓學生能主動地到別人的網站去瀏覽並上貼意見。教師雖然鼓勵學生們互相瀏覽其他同學的網頁，但是學生以事情太多、沒有時間做藉口，而錯失了E-Portfolio相互分享的功能。明年將設計不同的活動，讓學生能參考同儕的網站資料，或評量其他同學的作業，互相修改，讓學生們能從瀏覽別人的網站時也能同時學習中文。

## 六、總結

　　總體而言，學生對數位檔案夾E-Portfolio計畫是肯定的，他們認同數位檔案夾對其中文學習及網路設計的功能。雖然少數抱怨網頁編輯耗費時日，但都認為他們的付出對其中文學習是值得的。明年因財務問題，本校的中文三課程將改為線上課程，而E-Portfolio計畫正好可以配合線上課程，讓學生在網路上編輯學習，展現所學。筆者也將修改網頁要求，讓網頁活動適合學生的程度，同時給予學生更具挑戰性的活動設計，讓學生能相互學習，彼此交流。希望透過Google雲端科技，讓學生的中文學習更有趣，更有變化，也讓學生更能跟得上網路網際的腳步。

## 附件一

## Chinese upper class E-Portfolio project

**What is E-Portfolio:**

E-Portfolio is an electronic portfolio providing an environment where students can:

(1)collect their work in a digital archive;

(2)select specific piece of work (hyperlink to artifacts) to highlight specific achievements;

(3)reflect on the learning demonstrated in the portfolio, in either text or multimedia form;

(4)set goals to improve future learning; and

(5)celebrate achievement through sharing this work with an audience, whether real or virtual.

When used in formative, classroom-based assessment, teachers and peers can review the portfolio document and provide formative feedback to students on where they can improve.

**How to create**

Before you start, you need to go to http://google.com to create a Google account. Once you have a Google account, you go to http://sites.google.com and log in with your Gmail account. Then follow these steps to create your own site.

1. Select "Create new site"

(1)You can leave "Blank template" selected or choose your own theme.

(2)For your site name, use "your name's E-Portfolio-Chinese 3"

(3)For your site URL, use "yourfirstnameeportfolio"

(4)Click on "+" next to "Choose a theme" and select the theme that you like for your E-Portfolio

(5)Click on "+" next to " More options" and click on "Only people I specify" can view this site.

(6)Type the code and click on "Create site"

2. Create your home page:

(1)You can insert text, pictures, links, table, and other html objects. Play around and see what you can do with Google site.

3. Your E-Portfolio will be an ongoing project throughout the year. Therefore, you will be adding new content and pages daily.

⑴Under the home page, you will start to add pages for each lesson

⑵Create a new page for each lesson by clicking "Create page" and this time select "Announcements" This template will allow you to create posts for your assignments. Name this page 《Lesson XX》 with page title 《Lesson XX》

⑶Within each lesson page, click "New post" to add four required sub pages

⑷**I can statement**學習目標：List the lesson goal using I can... statements. The "I can" statements are listed on the first page of each lesson. You can also make your own I can statements.

⑸**Preview**課前預習：Here you type all the new vocabulary you will learn in this lesson, pinyin, English definition, and an example sentence. To expand your vocabulary learning, pick five new words and use each character in these words to find four more new phrases. Write their pinyin, English definition, and make a sentence for each phrase. For example: a new word, 討論，you can expand the new phrases from討to討飯，檢討and 論can expand to論文and無論。Use online dictionary to expand your vocabulary.

⑹**How well I learn**學習成果：Here you post your lesson project or assessment to show how well you have learned this lesson. Post every parts of the project. If you create an object on another website, copy the HTML codes, then go to edit, then click HTML, then paste the HTML code in your site.

⑺**Reflection**學習反省：Write a paragraph to reflect how you have mastered the content of this lesson and what difficulties you have faced when you learned this lesson

(8)**Story telling說故事**：You need to include the story telling from the workbook in each lesson. Type one or two sentences for each picture in the workbook and make a story out of these four pictures.

(9)**Idioms成語**：Write down the idioms you learn in each lesson. If there is no idiom learned in the lesson, search online to find any idiom with the characters in the lesson. You need to write at least one idiom per lesson with pinyin, English definition, and a sentence or pictures to show what this idiom mean.

4. Go to "More actions", and select "Site permissions"

(1)Invite your teacher and classmates by typing their email addresses. For teacher, select "can edit", for students, select "can view".

# 附件二

學生E-Portfolio數位檔案夾實例——同學製作
1.生日派對單元任務型整合評量實例——葉同學製作

## 2. 電話約會單元任務型整合評量實例──成田同學製作

## 3. 出租房子單元任務型整合評量實例──區同學製作

# 二、漢字及詞彙之數位輔助學習

# The distribution and grouping effect in character learning: Using data-driving E-learning materials in language teaching

**Yi Xu National Taiwan Normal University Charles, A. Perfetti**

University of Pittsburgh

xuyi@pitt.edu    liyunchang@ntnu.edu.tw    perfetti@pitt.edu

## Abstract

The logographic nature of the Chinese writing system creates a huge hurdle for Chinese as a foreign/second language learners. Existing literature suggests that radical knowledge can facilitate character learning. In this project, we used the Chinese Orthography Database Explorer and selected 48 compound characters in eight radical groups, and examined the role of presentation sequence in digital learning. We found learning radical-sharing characters in groups imposed challenges during the learning stage but consistently led to better recall in all measures. Learners were able to generalize radical knowledge based on autonomous learning, and the learning characters in groups was especially facilitating. We concluded that the appropriate material sequencing can facilitate orthographic knowledge development, and self-learning enabled by digital resources in learners' own time and space can complement traditional classroom learning.

Keywords: Chinese characters; radicals; orthographic knowledge; digital learning; self-learning

# Introduction

Due to the logographic nature of the Chinese writing system, learning how to read and write is frequently identified as one of the biggest challenges for Chinese as Foreign Language (CFL) learners (Everson, 1998, etc.). Characters are constructed with three layers of orthographic structure, including character, radical, and stroke (Shen & Ke, 2007), and it is well-acknowledged that radical knowledge can greatly facilitate one's learning (Shen, 2010; Shu & Anderson, 1999, etc.). In this project, we examine if the acquisition of radical knowledge can be achieved through CFL learners' autonomous learning. Further, we evaluate if grouping radical-sharing characters together in presentation can result in a difference in the form, sound, and meaning representations in lexical memory, and in developing radical knowledge.

More than 95% commonly used characters in modern Chinese are standard compound characters consisting of a semantic radical and a phonetic component (Dictionary of Chinese character information, 1988). The semantic radical generally gives useful cues to the meaning of the whole character. According to Feldman and Siok's (1999) summary based on approximately 4500 commonly used characters, there are about 200 semantic radicals, and on average, 20 standard compounds are formed on each. It stands to reason that learners who possess and who can apply radical knowledge would be greatly facilitated in character learning. Taft and Chung (1999) found that explicit radical instruction immediately before the first exposure of character facilitates memory retention. Wang, Liu, and Perfetti (2004) compared the implicit and explicit learning of the orthographic structure of Chinese characters and found that explicit instruction helped learners to make meaning inferences of characters based on radicals. Learners frequently rely on familiar radicals to learn new characters (Shen, 2005), and can make meaning inferences in unfamiliar characters based on their radical knowledge (Jackson, Everson, & Ke, 2003). Recently, Chen et al. (2013) used groups of radical-sharing characters as materials, and compared the learning effectiveness under two situations, one through explicit orthography learning enabled by an E-learning platform, and the other the traditional word-based instruction focusing on comprehension and grammar. Chen et al's study verified the possibility of using online learning to facilitate radical-based character instruction. In the current project, we followed the direction and conducted a project in which orthographic knowledge development is achieved primarily through learners' self-learning enabled by digital presentation. Previous studies suggest that radical frequencies in compound character in one's print exposure affects character recognition for L1 adults (Taft & Zhu, 1997), L1 children (Peng, Li, & Yang, 1997), and L2 adults (Wang, Liu, & Perfetti, 2004). In this project, we hypothesize that learning radical-sharing compound characters in radical-focused groups, would lead to different learning outcome than learning those characters in distribution. If sequencing characters by their shared radicals results in better lexical memory, then digital learning materials online or in language learning software can be arranged in such a way to facilitate orthographic knowledge acquisition.

## Methodology

A between-subjects experimental design was adopted with character sequencing (grouping vs. distribution) as an independent variable. 88 CFL learners enrolled in 1st and 2nd-year Chinese language classes in an American university participated in the project. Half of the participants in each proficiency level were assigned to the "grouped" condition, whereas the rest were assigned to the "distributed" condition.

## Materials

We used an online database, namely the Chinese Orthography Database Explorer (CODE) 中文部件組字與形構資料庫 (Chen, Chang, Chou, Sung, & Chang, 2011), to determine experiment materials. This database systemizes subcharacter components (i.e., orthographic units internal to a character) and the compound characters that they compose, and was established especially to facilitate learning character through their sub-components including radicals and chunks. (CODE emphasizes on subcharacter components in general: aside from radicals (*bùshǒu*), which are the smallest orthographic units with meaning associations, orthographic units internal to a character can be chunks (*bùjiàn*), which are simply the smallest visually integrated units and which, by definition, do not need to have semantic or phonetic functions. This paper focuses on learning through radicals, the particular type of subcharacter component that contributes to characters' meanings.)

We selected eight radicals that were explicitly taught to the participants in their regular curriculum before the experiment. We then selected six compound characters formed by each radical. These characters were selected based on the following criteria: First, they were beyond 1st or 2nd year participants' course curriculum; second, the characters' number of strokes, the characters' number of chunks, and their English translation frequencies (Brysbaert & New, 2009) are matched across the eight radical groups. The radicals and characters include 女（婚、嫁、媳、娃、嬌、姑），食（饞、饅、餡、飽、蝕、饒），心（忽、患、急、忌、忍、愁），貝（販、賑、敗、賠、賊、財），金（銀、鈔、鑽、鎖、鑰、釣），日（晌、曠、曬、晾、暄、暗），火（爐、烘、焰、炮、煙、燭），木（棚、柱、梯、板、材、概）。Two sets of texts, with eight texts each, were created to allow instruction under each condition. For texts used in the grouped condition, each text contains all the six characters in one radical group, such as 婚、嫁、媳、娃、嬌、姑 for the 女 radical group. In the distributed condition, characters in one radical group are distributed in different texts and each text never contains two target radical-sharing characters.

## Procedure

Prior to the learning sessions, pretests including written sound/meaning production and a radical semantic awareness test were conducted. (See examples in the Measures section.) In each learning session, participants learned two texts, i.e., 12 target characters. Immediately after each learning session, participants completed an immediate form production task and three computerized tasks: a lexical decision task, a sound matching task, and a meaning matching task. On the fifth day, participants had a chance to rehearse all the 48 target characters learned, and then completed posttests, including sound/meaning and form production tests and a semantic awareness test. A delayed test with all the components in the posttest were conducted two weeks later. All sessions took place in a language lab classroom. The same instructor taught all 1st-year classes (under both conditions), and a second instructor taught all 2nd-year classes.

In each learning session, the instructors spent 20 minutes teaching the two texts, by leading participants to read based on flashcards, asking comprehension questions, and practicing grammar. The instructor did not give instruction regarding the orthographic structures of any characters. Participants then continued to learn the target characters in that learning session on individual computers, with approximately 30 seconds on each character. During the 30 seconds, they were exposed to the character's form, sound, and meaning presented on computers.

## Measures

In the written sound/meaning task (conducted in pretest, posttest, and delayed test), participants were asked to write the *pinyin* and meaning for the 48 target characters. For sound production, we used two measures: a *pinyin* measure, in which a response was considered correct only if both the tone and the syllable were correct, and a syllable measure, in which tone marking does not matter. Table 1 shows two items in these written sound/meaning production tasks. In form production (conducted as immediate test, posttest, and delayed test), participants were asked to write a character based on its meaning in English. We also adopted two measures: a character measure in which the response is considered correct only when the complete character form was correctly produced, and a radical measure, in which partial credits were given based on the number of correct chunks appearing in their correct positions produced divided by the total number of chunks in that character. Table 2 shows two items in the form production task.

**Table 1. Examples in written sound/meaning production tasks**

|   |   | *Pinyin* & Tone | Translation |   |   | *Pinyin* & Tone | Translation |
|---|---|---|---|---|---|---|---|
| 1 | 婚 |   |   | 2 | 晾 |   |   |

**Table 2. Examples in the character form production task**

|   | Meaning | Character |   | Meaning | Character |
|---|---|---|---|---|---|
| 1 | diamond |   | 2 | candle |   |

Among the computerized tasks, the lexical decision task assesses participants' visual-orthographic representation of the characters. They were asked to judge whether the stimuli was a real character or not by pressing one of the two keys on keyboard, and to respond as quickly and as accurately as possible. Non-characters were created by deleting or adding a stroke. Each stimulus was presented for 1000 milliseconds (m.s.) followed by a blank of 3000 m.s. before the screen moved on to the next trial. In the meaning matching and sound matching tasks, a character was presented for 1000 m.s., followed by an English translation, or a *pinyin* display, accompanied by a female native speaker's voice pronouncing the sound. Participants had 3000 m.s. to make a judgment in both tasks. Participants' accuracy rate and reaction time (RT) on target characters were analyzed.

The radical semantic awareness test was modeled after Chen et al. (2013). (1) gives an example. This task assesses the participants' ability to generalize the meanings and the legal positions of the radicals and to apply this knowledge to unfamiliar characters. Different items were used in the pretest, the posttest, and the delayed test.

(1) (        ) Which word is related with "wood" or "timber" ?
　　①稔　②杻　③欣　④嶸
　　　　　　　　　　　　　　　　　(The correct answer is ②.)

## Results and Discussions

In the following, the mean accuracies and standard deviations were calculated using proportion of correct responses, and numbers in RT results are in milliseconds. For computerized tasks, a one-way ANOVA with character sequencing (grouped vs. distributed) as an independent variable was conducted on each measure. In the lexical decision task, there were no differences between the distributed and the grouped condition in mean accuracy (distributed: $M = 0.77$, $S.D.$ = 0.07; grouped: $M = 0.74$, $S.D.$ = 0.13), $F$ (1, 86) = 1.63, $p$ = .205. Nor is there a significant difference in RT (distributed: $M = 1206$, $S.D.$ = 219; grouped: $M = 1191$, $S.D.$ = 174), $F$ (1, 86) < 1, $p$ = .724. At the same time, participants' accuracy in both conditions and in both levels was significantly higher than 0.5 chance level (Distributed: $t$ (43) = 24.668, $p$ < .001; Grouped: $t$ (43) = 12.141, $p$ < .001), suggesting that participants developed robust orthographic representation of the target characters and were able to differentiate them from non-character visual stimuli. For the sound matching task, the distributed condition ($M$ = 0.66, $S.D.$= 0.15) had significant higher accuracy than the grouped condition ($M = 0.59$, $S.D.$ = 0.13), $F$ (1, 86) = 5.57, $p$ = .021, while there was no difference between the two in RT (distributed: $M = 1188$, $S.D.$ = 269; grouped: $M = 1167$, $S.D.$ =233), $F$ (1, 86) < 1, $p$ = .703. For the meaning matching task, there was no significant difference between the two conditions in accuracy ($M$ = 0.73, $S.D.$ = 0.14 for both conditions), $F$ (1, 86) < 1, $p$ = .837, or in RT (distributed: $M$ = 1108, $S.D.$ = 230; grouped: $M$ = 1069, $S.D.$ = 178), $F$ (1, 86) < 1, $p$ = .368. The inhibition observed in the sound matching task in the grouped condition was likely to be caused by the similar visual attributes among target characters in one radical group, which made it difficult for participants to differentiate target characters from one another. Previous L1 reading studies reported that orthographically similar characters, including radical-sharing characters, can inhibit each other on certain experimental tasks (Feldman & Siok, 1999; Zhou & Marslen-Wilson, 1999).

For the production and the generalization tasks, a repeated-measures ANOVA with sequencing as a between-subjects factor and testing time as a within-subjects factor was conducted on each measure. In all measures, the sequencing $\times$ testing time was significant or near significant (*pinyin*: $F$ (2, 172) = 4.41, $p$ = .030; syllable: $F$ (2, 172) = 4.57, $p$ = .026; Meaning: $F$ (2, 172) = 6.29, $p$ = .007; Semantic awareness: $F$ (2, 172) = 2.90, $p$ = .064; form production with character measure: $F$ (2, 172) = 4.57, $p$ = .012; Form production with radical measure: $F$ (2, 172) = 8.43, $p$ < .001). A simple main effect analysis of testing time using one-way ANOVA revealed that differences under both conditions in in all measures were significant, and pairwise comparisons with Bonferroni adjustment were conducted. The detailed statistical results are summarized in Table 3. For sound production (including the *pinyin* and the syllable measures) and the meaning production, accuracy in the posttest was higher than that in the delayed test, which in turn was higher than that in the pretest, suggesting positive learning outcome in both conditions and retention loss after two weeks' interval. For form production (including both the character measure and the radical measure), under the distributed condition, performance in both the immediate test and the posttest were higher than that in the delayed test, suggesting retention loss. Under the grouped condition, performance in the posttest was better than that in the immediate test, which was in turn better than the delayed test. This indicates that under the grouped condition, the rehearsal on the fifth day strengthened the participants' orthographic representation, but without repeated practice, memory was subject to retention loss regardless of the learning conditions. For the semantic awareness task, there was significant improvement in participants' performance in the posttest, and that knowledge gain from learning retained as a long-term application knowledge.

**Table 3. Analysis of the simple main effect of testing time (n = 88)**

| | | Simple main effect analysis of testing time | Accuracy differences in testing time | Detailed pairwise comparisons |
|---|---|---|---|---|
| Sound (pinyin) | D | $F(2, 86) = 75.64$, $p < .001$ | post > delayed > pre | $p < .001$ in all pairwise comparisons |
| | G | $F(2, 86) = 117.36$, $p < .001$ | post > delayed > pre | $p < .001$ in all pairwise comparisons |
| Sound (syllable) | D | $F(2, 86) = 111.35$, $p < .001$ | post > delayed > pre | $p < .001$ in all pairwise comparisons |
| | G | $F(2, 86) = 163.32$, $p < .001$ | post > delayed > pre | $p < .001$ in all pairwise comparisons |
| Meaning | D | $F(2, 86) = 109.30$, $p < .001$ | post > delayed > pre | $p < .001$ in all pairwise comparisons |
| | G | $F(2, 86) = 236.96$, $p < .001$ | post > delayed > pre | $p < .001$ in all pairwise comparisons |

| | | Simple main effect analysis of testing time | Accuracy differences in testing time | Detailed pairwise comparisons |
|---|---|---|---|---|
| Form (character) | D | $F(2, 86) = 46.75$, $p < 0.001$ | immediate/ post > delayed | Immediate vs. post: $p = .335$; Immediate > delayed: $p < .001$; Post > delayed: $p < .001$ |
| | G | $F(2, 86) = 57.24$, $p < .001$ | post > immediate > delayed | Post > immediate: $p = .021$; Immediate > delayed: $p < .001$; Post > delayed: $p < .001$ |
| Form (radical) | D | $F(2, 86) = 53.49$, $p < .001$ | immediate/ post > delayed | Immediate vs. post: $p = 1.00$; Immediate > delayed: $p < .001$; post > delayed: $p < .001$ |
| | G | $F(2, 86) = 67.52$, $p < .001$ | post > immediate > delayed | $p < .001$ in all pairwise comparisons |
| Semantic awareness | D | $F(2, 86) = 13.49$, $p < .001$ | post/delayed > pre | Post > pre: $p = .009$; Delayed > pre: $p < .001$; Delayed vs. post: $p = .218$ |
| | G | $F(2, 86) = 33.55$, $p < .001$ | post/delayed > pre | Post > pre: $p < .001$; Delayed > pre: $p < .001$; Delayed vs. post: $p = .364$ |

*Note.* Rows marked by D report results under the distributed condition, and rows marked by G report results under the grouped condition. Pre, post, and delayed stand for pretests, posttests, and delayed tests. For form production tasks, the three testing points were the immediate test, the posttest, and the delayed test. > indicates that the former testing point has higher accuracy than the latter, and / means no significant difference.

We then examine the simple main effect analysis of sequencing under each testing point. The mean accuracies in each measure were reported in Table 4. There were no differences between the participants' knowledge regarding those target characters in the pretest, except that with the syllable measure, participants under the distributed condition performed better than those under the grouped condition. (But note that those participants under the distributed condition had only 1% proportional knowledge of the target characters.) After learning, the grouped condition yielded better results than the distributed condition in all measures. In the delayed test, the grouped condition continued to have an advantage in form production with the radical measure, and the semantic awareness test.

Table 4. Means and standard deviation (S.D.) in production task and generalization task (n = 88)

| | Distributed | Grouped | Comparisons | Significance |
|---|---|---|---|---|
| | Mean *(S.D.)* | Mean *(S.D.)* | | |
| **Pretest** | | | | |
| Syllable | 0.01 (0.03) | 0.00 (0.01) | $F (1, 86) = 4.40, p = .039$ | * |
| Pinyin | 0.00 (0.01) | 0.00 (0.01) | $F (1, 86) = .39, p = .532$ | |
| Meaning | 0.01 (0.03) | 0.00 (0.01) | $F (1, 86) =.49, p = .487$ | |
| Semantic awareness | 0.69 (0.19) | 0.68 (0.23) | $F (1, 86) = .04, p = .85$ | |
| **Immediate test** | | | | |
| Form (radical) | 0.36 (0.20) | 0.36 (0.15) | $F (1, 86) = .01, p = .906$ | |
| Form (character) | 0.29 (0.18) | 0.29 (0.19) | $F (1, 86) = .01, p = .943$ | |

|  | Distributed | Grouped | Comparisons | Significance |
|---|---|---|---|---|
| **Posttest** | | | | |
| Form (radical) | 0.36 (0.20) | 0.44 (0.19) | *F (1, 86) = 4.10, p = .046* | * |
| Form (character) | 0.26 (0.19) | 0.33 (0.20) | *F (1, 86) = 2.84, p = .095* | † |
| Syllable | 0.36 (0.22) | 0.44 (0.22) | *F (1, 86) = 3.47, p = .066* | † |
| Pinyin | 0.28 (0.21) | 0.38 (0.22) | *F (1, 86) = 4.2, p = .044* | * |
| Meaning | 0.35 (0.21) | 0.46 (0.17) | *F (1, 86) = 6.6, p = .012* | * |
| Semantic awareness | 0.79 (0.23) | 0.88 (0.16) | *F (1, 86) = 4.43, p = .038* | * |
| **Delayed test** | | | | |
| Form (radical) | 0.20 (0.15) | 0.27 (0.16) | *F (1, 86) = 4.75, p = .032* | * |
| Form (character) | 0.13 (0.13) | 0.18 (0.14) | *F (1, 86) = 2.28, p = .135* | |
| Syllable | 0.17 (0.14) | 0.18 (0.15) | *F (1, 86) = .11, p = .742* | |
| Pinyin | 0.10 (0.11) | 0.12 (0.13) | *F (1, 86) = .54, p = .463* | |
| Meaning | 0.16 (0.14) | 0.19 (0.12) | *F (1, 86) = .97, p = .328* | |
| Semantic awareness | 0.84 (0.20) | 0.92 (0.12) | *F (1, 86) = 4.43, p = .038* | * |

*Note.* The means and the standard deviations for accuracy were calculated using proportion of correct responses. * signals significance at the $p < .05$ level and † stands for significance at the $.05 < p < .10$ level.

In other words, though the grouped condition imposed more challenges in the learning stage, as seen by the lower accuracy rate in sound matching, and there was no indication of its advantage in form representation in the immediate test, it consistently led to better form, sound, and meaning recalls than the distributed condition later. We suggest that grouping radical-sharing characters together had such a beneficial effect because it encourages "deeper processing" and the application of orthographic knowledge in learning. The idea of deep (i.e., more elaborate) vs. shallow (i.e. sheer rote) processing originated from Craik and Lockhart (1972). Taft and Chung (1999, p.248) and Shen (2004) suggested that deeper processing is involved when one analyzes characters in terms of its radicals, and that would result in better lexical memory retention. In the grouped condition, the recurrence of the radicals drew participants' attention to the radicals' shape and position. The semantic relatedness of target characters also enhanced their awareness of the radical's semantic cueing functions. Further, in order to differentiate those orthographically similar characters, participants were made to realize that those characters can be differentiated from one another by their distinctive phonetic components. The grouped condition therefore encouraged the semantic and structural analysis of the characters and prompted learners to make associations between the radical and the characters, as well as between the characters themselves.

Grouping characters also encouraged learners to apply orthographically-based strategies in learning. Once the radicals are perceived as a character-forming unit, learners in the grouped condition can more easily decompose the whole character's structure. They are then not dealing with a pile of random strokes, but a few larger subcharacter components with fixed spatial layouts. Thus, memory burden can be substantially reduced. Radicals are thought to be orthographic representational unit associated with meaning by themselves (Perfetti & Tan, 1998; Taft & Zhu, 1997, etc.), and the activation of radical-level processing would facilitate character encoding and decoding, and support form, sound, and meaning representations.

While the advantages of the grouped condition disappeared in most measures after the two-weeks' interval, grouping still produced better results in form production with the radical measure in the delayed test. In other words, learners under the grouped condition established better orthographic representation of the radical, including their meaning associations, and that memory lasted long-term. Results in the semantic awareness tests showed that learners made rapid improvement in radical application knowledge, and such knowledge retained long-term. Compared to Chen et al. (2013), who showed the benefit of explicit orthographic instruction, we suggest that automatous learning enabled by presenting learners with compound characters over a short period of time is also highly effective. Further, learning radical-sharing characters in groups, in comparison with learning them in distribution, helped learners to better generalize the position specificity and the semantic cueing functions of radicals.

## Implications

This project is the first study that examines the effect of material sequencing in CFL learners' character learning. Results bear direct implications to autonomous learning through digital materials such as online resources or software. Online learning affords much benefit such as the flexibility in time and space, but it differs from traditional language classrooms in the lack of instructor-student interactions in reality. Our results suggest that learners can develop implicit radical application knowledge when online or digital materials are presented to them in a sequence that promotes generalization. That is, when a list of characters sharing the same radical and the same semantic associations are presented close together in digital materials, learners develop radical awareness, which in turn helps with their character acquisition. This study also shows a successful example of combining traditional classroom teaching with students' self-learning without explicit instruction from the teachers. Learning to read and write can be labor-intensive and time-consuming. Our study suggests that a potential scenario to optimize learning with limited class time is to have teachers focus on comprehension and communication in the classroom, while digital materials can be created to develop CFL students' orthographic knowledge through self-learning outside the classroom. We also hope to have shown an example of using online tools such as large databases in doing pedagogically-oriented research. To explore the application of CODE, readers are directed to the Chinese Radical-Based Character-Family E-Learning Platform: http://coolch.sce.ntnu.edu.tw/chinese2/fonts.php. Instructors and researchers alike can choose appropriate learning materials based on rich information made available through such online resources.

This research is not without limitations. First, the current discussion does not extend to variations of characters' meanings in different compound words or the acquisition of those variations. Second, the advantage of the grouped condition in delayed tests did not consistently reach significance in some measures; thus, how to achieve better memory retention needs to be further explored. Nevertheless, this study is significant in using digital resources to bring out the beneficial outcome of using radical-based grouping in character learning and radical knowledge development.

# References

Brysbaert, M., & New, B. (2009). Moving beyond Kucera and Francis: A critical evaluation of current word frequency norms and the introduction of a new and improved word frequency measure for American English, *Behavior Research Methods,* 41, 488-496.

Chen, H. C., Chang, L. Y., Chou, Y. S., Sung, Y. T., & Chang, K. E. (2011). Construction of Chinese Orthographic Database for Chinese Character Instruction [中文部件組字與形構資料庫之建立及其在識字教學的應用]. *Bulletin of Educational Psychology,* 43, 269–290.

Chen, H.-C., Hsu, C.-C., Chang, L.-Y., Lin, Y.-C., Chang, K.-E., & Sun, Y.-T. (2013). Using a radical-derived character E-learning platform to increase learner knowledge of Chinese characters. *Language Learning and Technology,* 17(1), 89-106. Retrieved from http://llt.msu.edu/issues/february2013/chenetal.pdf

Craik, F. I. M., & Lockhart, R. S. (1972). Levels of processing: A framework for memory research. *Journal of Verbal Learning and Verbal Behavior,* 11, 671– 684.

*Dictionary of Chinese Character Information* [漢字資訊字典] (1988). Shanghai, China: Science Press [科學出版社].

Everson, M. E. (1998). Word Recognition among Learners of Chinese as a Foreign Language: Investigating the Relationship between Naming and Knowing. *Modern Language Journal,* 82(2), 194-204.

Feldman, L. B., & Siok, W. W. T. (1999). Semantic radicals in phonetic compounds: implications for visual character recognition in Chinese. In J. Wang, A. W. Inhoff, & H. C. Chen (Eds.), *Reading Chinese script: A Cognitive Analysis* (pp. 19-35). Mahwah, NJ: Lawrence Erlbaum.

Jackson, N. E., Everson, M. E., & Ke, C. (2003). Beginning readers' awareness of the orthographic structure of semantic-phonetic compounds: Lessons from a study of learners of Chinese as a foreign language. In C. McBride-Chang and H.-C. Chen (Eds.), *Reading Development in Chinese Children* (pp. 142–153). Westport, CT: Praeger.

Peng, D.-L., Li, Y.-P.,& Yang, H. (1997). Orthographic processing in the identification of Chinese characters. In Chen, H-C. (Ed.), *Cognitive Processing of Chinese and Related Asian Languages* (pp. 85-108). Hong Kong: The Chinese University Press.

Perfetti, C. A., & Tan, L. H. (1998). The time course of graphic, phonological, and semantic activation in Chinese character identification. *Journal of Experimental Psychology: Learning, Memory, and Cognition,* 24, 101-118.

Shen, H. H. (2004). Level of Cognitive Processing: Effects on Character Learning Among Non-Native Learners of Chinese as a Foreign Language, *Language and Education,* 18, 167-182.

Shen, H. H. (2005). An investigation of Chinese-character learning strategies among non-native speakers of Chinese. *System,* 33, 49–68.

Shen, H. H. (2010). Analysis of radical knowledge development among beginning CFL learners. In M. E. Everson, & H. H. Shen (Eds.), *Research Among Learners of Chinese As a Foreign Language* (Chinese Language Teachers Association Monograph Series, Vo. 4). (pp. 45-65). Honolulu: University of Hawaii, National Foreign Language Resource Center.

Shen, H. H., & Ke, C. (2007). Radical awareness and word acquisition among nonnative learners of Chinese. *The Modern Language Journal,* 91, 97–111.

Shu, H., & Anderson, R. C. (1999). Learning to read Chinese: The development of metalinguistic awareness. In J. Wang, A. W. Inhoff,

& H. C. Chen (Eds.), *Reading Chinese Script: A Cognitive Analysis* (pp. 1–18). Mahwah, NJ: Lawrence Erlbaum.

Taft, M., & Chung, K. (1999). Using radicals in teaching Chinese characters to second language learners. *Psychologia,* 42, 234–251.

Taft, M., & Zhu, X. (1997). Submorphemic processing in reading Chinese. *Journal of Experimental Psychology: Learning, Memory, and Cognition,* 23, 761–775.

Wang, M., Liu, Y., & Perfetti, C. A. (2004). The implicit and explicit learning of orthographic structure and function of a new writing system, *Scientific Studies of Reading,* 8(4), 357-379.

Zhou, X. & Marslen-Wilson, W. (1999). Sublexical processing in reading Chinese. In J. Wang, A. W. Inhoff, & H. C. Chen (Eds.), *Reading Chinese Script: A Cognitive Analysis* (pp. 37-63). Mahwah, NJ: Lawrence Erlbaum.

# 概念圖與數位學習結合應用探究[1]

蕭惠貞　周俞姍

國立台灣師範大學華語文教學系暨研究所

huichen.hsiao@ntnu.edu.tw　sparkle-tte@hotmail.com

## 摘要

　　本文主要介紹並演示華語詞彙學習網站之特色，融合認知概念圖於華語詞彙教學中，希冀探究本網站於學生自學與教師導學應用之可行性與優勢。近年來詞彙教學逐漸受到重視（胡明揚，1997；孫德金，2006）。詞彙的多義性一直是對外漢語學習者的難點之一（邢志群，2011；陳建生等人，2011），而如何有效地運用教學材料幫助二語學習者學習和擴充相關詞彙量是本研究主要關心的議題。本網站的教材主要以文化意涵豐富（顏色詞與溫度詞）的詞彙學習內容爲主，設計上則從認知語義學理論導入。一方面，學習內容結合了Lakoff（1987）提出的理想化認知模式（ICM）、隱喻映射原則（metaphorical mappings）和轉喻（metonymic），以及Taylor（1995：2003）語義鏈（meaning chains）機制所描寫之語義聯想途徑，建立詞彙群之間的相關性：即「概念圖」（Novak & Gowin, 1984）；另一方面，前人的研究亦指出配合多媒體視聽教學工具的二語學習，能有效提升二語學習者詞彙學習的效益（Chun and Plass, 1996; Duquette et al., 1998）。因此，本學習網站除以「隱喻」與「轉喻」映射來串聯詞彙間的延伸關係外，並融入視覺與聽覺刺激之情

---

[1]　本研究計畫特此感謝教育部與國立台灣師範大學邁向頂尖大學計畫之研究補助（Project No. 101J1A0703, and Project No. 102J1A0505）。感謝助理周俞姍、李佳霖、林倩如、廖思涵等人協助計畫相關事項及王政凱、林瑋如助理等人協助架設本網頁。

境對話數位動畫與練習題，希冀幫助華語學習者詞彙的學習：即從高頻「基本義」詞彙擴充延伸至「抽象義」詞彙，期盼能有益於鞏固學習者多義詞的相關詞彙文化知識，展現華語詞彙教學數位化之優勢。

關鍵字：多義詞、概念圖、詞彙學習、華語教學、數位教材

## 一、前言

　　近年來，由於科技發展的日新月異，網路資訊與科技媒體已成為人們生活中不可或缺的要素之一。除了在通訊方面的應用，網路與科技的發展在教育上也有相當程度的影響。全球資訊網路（World Wide Web, WWW）因適合儲存和發送教學材料，加上多媒體的特色，許多學者均已投入網路輔助語言教學（Web-assisted Language Learning）（周健慈，2000）。近年來電腦科技為學生學習或娛樂的主要方法之一（舒兆民，2002），因此網路課程教學（數位學習）勢在必行。在這樣的潮流和趨勢下，數位科技顯然帶給傳統板書教育不小的震撼。傳統教育不再全然適用於教學，數位科技輔助之教學則為後起之秀，越來越多人使用數位學習且需要此類型的教學模式。

　　以華語文教學的情況而言，其二語／外語（CSL/CFL）學習者廣泛分布於世界各地，要在當地取得相關學習資訊或材料實屬不易，網路資訊科技無空間限制的特色為其提供最好的解決辦法。然而，現有之華語教學的網路資源多以發音、漢字、文化、閱讀等為主，與詞彙學習相關的網站仍屬少數，例如，與詞彙相關之學習網站多為辭典解釋性質或是以「字」（character）筆畫（如：《蘭亭字典》[2]）為主軸，較少有與學習者互動之詞彙練習或動畫輔助。

---

2　《蘭亭字典》（http://orchid.shu.edu.tw/dic/）內容，包含以筆順與常用詞介紹為主。

　　為此，本研究旨在設計以認知概念圖爲架構之詞彙學習網站[3]，並加入相關的詞彙動畫與即時回饋練習，探討其在自學與導學上之可行性與趨勢。第二節透過文獻回顧，我們討論了認知理論與詞彙教學、概念圖應用和數位教學的優勢；第三節依照ADDIE模式，我們針對本研究架設之網站提出更進一步的介紹；最後，我們結合理論與實務進行總結並建議未來相關規劃。

## 二、理論背景

　　以下內容分爲兩大部分：分別是認知理論與詞彙教學，及數位教學於二語學習優勢之探討。

### (一) 認知理論與詞彙教學的相關性

　　詞彙是構成語言的重要要素之一。在語言學習中，詞彙則是學習者建構更大語言單位的基礎之一（胡明揚，1997；孫德金，2006；Milton, 2009）。然而，詞彙的多義性卻常是學習者的學習難點（Boers, 2000；Verspoor and Lowie, 2003；陳建生等人，2011）。根據 Richards（1976）對於已知詞彙的定義，學習者必須知道該詞彙的語義特性和延伸或隱喻用法，或是其他功能語境的變化，才是所謂的知其然。

　　此外，詞彙的複雜多義性已受到多方面的探究，例如從早期Fillmore（1976）的框架語義（Frame Semantic）到Lakoff & Johnson（1987）提出概念隱喻（conceptual metaphor）、Fauconnier & Turner（2002）提出概念整合理論（Conceptual Blending Theory），都建立了認知方法和語言結合的可能性，特別是詞彙的語意延伸或從認知原則的途徑，皆爲詞彙教學開闢新徑。在英語教學應用方面，黃晶偉和董志友（2012）的研究指出學習者若

---

[3]　網址chinese-elearning.tcsl.ntnu.edu.tw版權所有師大蕭惠貞etal，研究團隊。

能釐清目標語某個範疇的隱喻機制，則可提高學習速度與語言使用的正確性。Boers（2000）針對EFL（English as a Foreign Language）學習者的實驗結果也證實運用隱喻原則習得詞彙的效果優於傳統提供單純詞義對應、或以功能分類的詞彙表，並有良好的長期記憶表現。MacLennan（1994）也指出，如果讓EFL學習者了解語言擴展和認知發展的隱喻作用，學生便能用以辨識現行語法和詞彙中的隱喻性模式。Lazar（1996）則認為在英語中，能夠理解詞彙的隱喻擴展，會是學生詞彙建構很重要的工具。

在漢語研究方面，潘玉華和李順琴（2011）針對漢語詞彙的研究也提出人類的記憶是有限的，但詞義的擴展是無限的，但大多數的詞義擴展是經由隱喻延伸的，因此學習者如果可以透過隱喻概念掌握相關詞彙，應有益於詞義擴展的提升。如果能深入詞彙的隱喻義，還能避免學生受到母語負遷移的影響。此外，曾貽（2012）也指出學生母語若與目標語的隱喻概念一致，其就能較輕鬆掌握目標語的詞彙。

除了隱喻概念理論，概念圖（concept map）亦是認知教學中的重要工具。概念圖的概念起源自J. D.Novak（1984），他根據Ausubel（1962）的概念同化理論[4]（assimilation theory）在科學教育上設計了以概念圖理解知識的方法。概念圖是一種用來理解和展現知識的圖解工具，其應包含概念與概念之間的連結；概念通常以封閉的圓或圖形展示，每個連結上都會有一些字或片語以顯示兩個概念之間的關係，概念圖的特色為：⑴可將複雜的觀念階級化，階層越高的概念越普遍，階層越低的則更具體；⑵概念圖包含交叉結合（cross-link），人們可藉由這些交叉結合知道概念圖中某概念與某概念的關

---

4　概念同化理論：Ausubel（1962）提倡有意義地學習，他認為當學生遇到的新知識和已有概念（個人認知結構）交互作用，便能達到有意義地學習，其中新知識和已有概念都可能受到對方影響而有新的不同的意義，此為同化理論。

係、連結；(3)具體事物的範例可融入於概念圖中（Novak & Cañas, 2006）。

概念圖現今已被廣泛運用於各個科學領域。在外語教學領域中，概念圖的引導一開始用於幫助學生理解文章脈絡，提高學生閱讀速度（Cicognani, 2000）。近年來，概念圖的引導輔助也逐漸用於外語詞彙教學中，詞彙教學中若引入概念圖則可幫助學生克服抽象語言教學模式的障礙。王君（2010）的實驗結果也發現大學生以詞彙概念圖學習英語詞彙之策略是具有優勢的，意即概念圖不但可以使詞彙之間的語義關係清晰化，也能將詞彙關係化隱爲顯，幫助學生記憶。

## (二) 數位教學於二語學習之優勢探討

資訊科技與教學的關係可分爲三類：(1)計算機[5]學習（computer as tutee），即學習如何操作電腦；(2)計算機教學（computer as tutor），計算機如教導者，引導學生學習特定知識；(3)計算機工具（computer as tools），計算機處理、通訊等功能提供學生學習非特定知識。上述三類又以計算機教學、計算機工具爲重要分類（壽大衛，2001）。壽大衛（2001）進一步指出由於批評者認爲電腦難以取代師生之間角色，故計算機輔助教學（computer aids instruction）與計算機協助教學（computer-assisted instruction）或電腦輔助語言學習（computer-assisted Language Learning, CALL）更爲常見，兩者區別在於電腦輔助教學更強調自我學習的效果（李世忠，1999；林奇賢，1998；邱貴發，1998）。

運用網路科技和多媒體的優勢，能幫助二語學習者在時間與空間的限制之外提升學習的效能。例如，以網路進行語言教學的模式有日益增多的趨向，並且有(1)超連結（hypermedia），利用網路超連結，學生可迅速查詢資料；(2)教學策略改變，網路教學以學生爲主，學生

---

[5]　現今稱之爲「電腦」。

可不斷反覆練習；(3)使用生活實際教材，網路上的資源豐富且多與生活相關；(4)整合學習環境，網路允許同時查找多筆資料，且具備記錄功能；(5)會議系統，可與母語者進行會話溝通，加強口語能力等優點（周健慈，2002）。結合多媒體的詞彙教學能有效提升學習者的詞彙辨識及輸出能力（Chun and Plass, 1996; Duquette et al., 1998）。此外，在華語教學應用方面，實證研究也支持網路電腦教學與多媒體輔助效果佳、其可幫助在非目標語國家學習者發展聽力、網路和數位科技可提供學習者更多元、活潑、可應用於日常生活的中文學習環境等優點（林金賢，2004；涂鈺亭，2010；邱美智、黃玲玲，2011）。

因此，本研究冀望結合認知語言學理論與概念圖的輔助，針對華語相關文化詞彙，設計一套數位學習網站。結合理論與前人研究的成果，奠定本研究以隱喻和轉喻概念設計概念圖的理論基礎，並在此基礎之上藉由數位教學之優勢，設計本網站，期許能為華語二語詞彙學習數位化方面，提供學習與教學相關資源。

## 三、網站介紹

本研究依照ADDIE[6]模式設計網站，包含「分析」、「設計」、「發展」、「執行」、和「評估」等五大部分。前三部分，主要突顯本網站之特色和設計理念，介紹自學與導學應用之可行性與優勢；後兩個階段屬於「應用」層面，現階段已於台北歐洲學校做了初步的問卷回饋，探究實際運作之可行性。

### (一) 分析階段

在人類的共同感知範疇（如：空間、時間、溫度、顏色等）中，

---

[6]　ADDIE是一種教學設計模式，包括了Analysis分析、Design設計、Development發展（開發）、Implement建置（執行）、Evaluation評估等階段。

溫度詞和顏色詞除有跨文化的共性外，亦有其個性之差異。引申概念中特殊的文化性，如：「白包」、「紅包」，和抽象延伸義如：「熱鬧」、「黑心」、「黑箱作業」等皆為教學中的難點之一。詞語中文化意涵的差異是造成跨語言溝通交際衝突的主因，是教學中必然會遇到的問題，詞彙學習中更是不容忽視（孫德金，2006）。因此，本研究以溫度與顏色此二感知範疇的高頻單字詞（冷溫熱[7]、黑白紅綠）為基礎，透過隱喻和轉喻概念原則的輔助，分析這些華語教材中單字與延伸詞彙之關係。運用概念圖展示，以英文敘述和語義延伸關係，協助二語學習者建立個人的語義詞彙庫（mental lexicon），加強建構、組織化其詞彙記憶，因而習得相關延伸詞彙。

　　本研究材料主要以網路辭典（《教育部國語辭典》、《蘭亭字典》）與各大華語教材（《新實用視聽華語》、《遠東生活華語》、《中文聽說讀寫》等）中與「冷、溫、熱、黑、白、紅、綠」相關之詞彙為主，並參照語料庫之頻率，分為初階與進階詞彙，如下表所示：

| 目標詞 | 初階詞彙 | 進階詞彙 |
|---|---|---|
| 冷 | 冷飲、冷氣（機）、冷凍、冷靜、冷冰冰 | 場子／氣氛很冷、冷場、冷笑話、冷門、冷知識、冷戰、冷淡、冷血、心灰意冷 |
| 溫 | 溫水、溫暖、溫柔、溫和、溫度、高溫、體溫、溫習 | 恆溫、降溫、保溫、溫室、溫泉、溫馨、溫故知新 |

---

[7] 本研究網站尚也列入高頻常用單音節多義詞「貴」，然因本文涵蓋內容僅以溫度域及顏色域相關文化詞彙為主，故主要介紹時暫不論述「貴」一詞。

| 目標詞 | 初階詞彙 | 進階詞彙 |
|---|---|---|
| 熱 | 熱飲、熱鬧、大熱天、熱呼呼、熱情、熱心 | 熱帶、悶熱、場子熱、熱烈、熱門、蘋果熱、熱潮、熱點、熱線、熱愛、熱戀、冷熱（相似詞：暖——溫暖、人情冷暖） |
| 黑 | 深黑、黑板、黑暗、黑夜 | 黑名單、黑箱作業、黑市、黑社會、白髮人送黑髮人、扮黑臉、是非黑白、黑心商品 |
| 白 | 白天、白包、白開水、白飯 | 白費、明白、清白、白吃白喝 |
| 紅 | 紅燒、紅茶、臉紅、紅包、走紅 | 大紅人、眼紅、亮紅燈、牽紅線、紅利 |
| 綠 | 紅綠燈、綠地、綠化、臉都綠了 | 綠意、綠洲、綠建築、戴綠帽（相似詞：青——鐵青著臉、青澀、青春、踏青） |

　　在網站的呈現上，我們將詞彙分為初階與進階詞彙概念圖，從詞彙本義出發，以隱喻或轉喻概念，導入具有相同概念之詞彙，學習者可直接在此入口一覽詞彙延伸的途徑。詞彙本義延伸至抽象義途徑如下例1所示：

1.

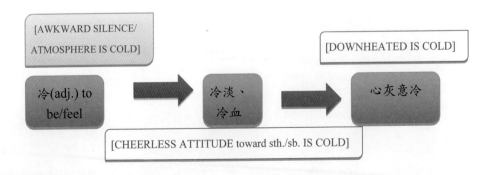

例如，在「冷」進階概念圖本義中，其中一項延伸的意項包含下列目標詞彙：「冷淡」、「冷血」，及「心灰意冷」。在意義關聯的呈現上，希望藉由概念原則導出的介紹，學習者可以加深對該詞彙的記憶。因此，在代表詞彙本義的圖形中，與此概念圖相關之重要概念皆以中括號及英語大寫呈現，也就是，出現[UNPOPULARITY/TRIVIA IS COLD]、[CHEERLESS ATTITUDE IS COLD]兩個重要概念原則，展示其與本義中的[AWKWARD SILENCE/ATMOSPHERE IS COLD]概念原則之串聯。

華語的詞彙教學除詞義教學外，應包括詞義的聚合和組合關係（Lyons, 1968）、具體語境等詞彙知識，使學習者具備相關詞彙知識而能有效運用。此外，視覺刺激和多媒體展示於教學上的重要性也逐漸提高（Reiser, 1987；何淑貞等，2008；Mayer, 2005），而且，結合數種輸入方式的學習模式亦能使學習者學到更多。

綜上所述，本研究在網頁上的設計呈現以下重點：(1)學習網站須以動畫展示情境對話，同時提供學生語境與視覺多媒體的輔助學習，加強學生記憶；(2)網站須有「句式搭配」提供學習者點選，內含目標詞彙之常見的語義組合關係（常用搭配詞）或句法組合關係（常用句式），讓學生以詞組的方式學習目標詞彙；(3)網站須設計「解釋較難的目標詞彙之文化意涵」之內容，以降低學生學習難點；(4)網站須有練習題與即時對錯回饋，幫助學生自我評估是否已經學會目標詞彙。

(二) 設計階段

本研究依照分析階段所歸納之結論，設計出以下主要目標詞彙學習內容：(1)詞彙概念圖（初階、進階）、(2)句式搭配、(3)主要學習目標詞彙之對話動畫，以對話方式引入目標詞彙、(4)文化講解小博士（Dr. Ideas）、及(5)練習題。經數名經驗豐富之國內外華語教師審查

修改校訂，並聘請台灣師範大學國語中心資深華語配音教師[8]進行情
境對話與詞彙練習語境錄音，最後由數位設計團隊結合語言材料，進
行動畫分鏡圖繪製和網站架設等相關工作。主要的動畫人物以四位主
角（兩位母語者、兩位來台學中文的外籍學生），設計真實情境對
話。

㈢ 發展／開發階段

　　本網站入口頁面如下圖一所示。詞彙學習頁面分爲(a)教師版和
(b)學生版，學習者可根據需求選擇登入的頁面。教師版的頁面主要
是增設了含有該詞彙概念圖及其「教學目標」的相關建議。此外，
本網站亦根據所選之目標詞彙，設置了測驗試題與詞彙練習加強頁
面，學習者可在詞彙學習之後，進入測驗試題頁面，檢測自我的學習
情況、或是至詞彙練習頁面，加強複習單一詞彙。

圖1　本研究網站入口頁面

8　特別感謝國語中心劉崇仁老師和張黛琪老師的協助。

　　圖2為網站首頁，使用者可在此選擇欲學習之詞彙，亦可依照自己的華語程度及需求，選擇「進階」或「初階」詞彙概念圖。

圖2　本網站首頁（教師版）

　　點擊詞彙「初階」或「進階」後，頁面即顯示該目標詞彙之初階或進階概念圖。此概念圖從詞彙本義延伸至抽象詞義，途徑輔以英語註解方式呈現隱喻或轉喻概念原則，以供學生學習、記憶參考。當滑鼠移至詞彙上，便會出現拼音（考量到對二語學習者而言，該詞可能為全新詞彙），學生可以任意在概念圖中選擇欲學習之詞彙。此外，網頁右上方還增設了「句式搭配」按鈕供學習者點選，學習者可在正式進入動畫網頁前，先學習目標詞彙之常用搭配慣用句式，網站之概念圖與句式搭配設計詳如圖3與圖4所示。

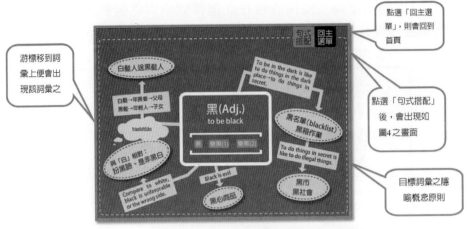

圖3　本網站詞彙認知概念圖範例之一（黑）

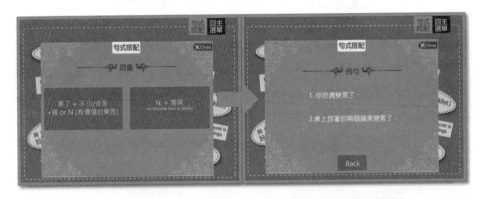

圖4　網站點擊「句式搭配」後出現之後續畫面範例

　　點擊「句式搭配」後，首先會出現如圖4左邊之畫面，先展示了詞彙常用之搭配句式，學習者於句式方框再點擊後，則會出現如圖4右邊之帶有例句的畫面。概念圖中的每個詞彙都可以點選連結至該詞彙動畫與其他相關資訊，點選後，學習者將會看到以對話組成之動畫來學習目標詞彙意義，動畫首次播放爲中文，可反覆播放。此外，亦有拼音、英語等版本供學生點選，但無論字幕呈現方式爲何種方式（中、英、拼），背景聲音皆以「中文」播放。若學生仍有不懂之

處，可點選下方之小博士人偶圖形（Dr. Idea），便會出現與目標詞彙相關之更深入的解釋。最後，學生也可點選並完成目標詞彙練習題方能回到該詞彙之概念圖，再另選其他詞彙繼續學習。

　　以「黑」進階詞彙「白髮人送黑髮人」為例，圖5為動畫起始畫面，點選「PLAY」按鈕後，動畫便會開始；點選「BACK」按鈕則會回到詞彙概念圖畫面。圖6則為動畫之分鏡圖示。

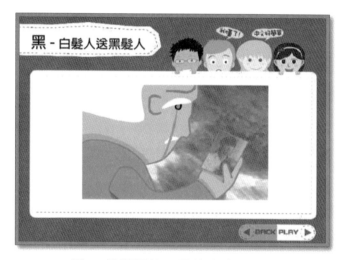

圖5　點選目標詞彙後之畫面範例

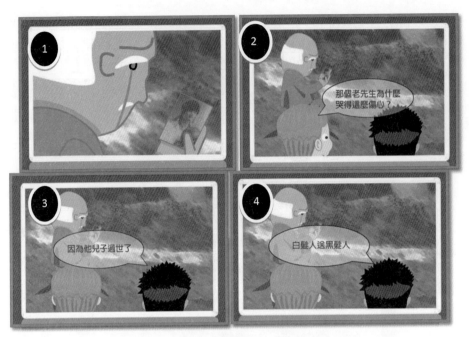

圖6 「白髮人送黑髮人」動畫分鏡圖示

　　圖7是該動畫的對話結束後的最終畫面，使用者可以點選最左側的箭頭圖案回到詞彙概念圖頁面，或可選擇重複播放的箭頭按鈕重複動畫。此外，為進一步加強學習者的詞彙知識，在頁面中設有Dr. Idea小博士圖像的按鈕，頁面如圖7（小博士圖案）、及圖8所示；根據詞彙的不同，使用者可以看到詞彙常見的語義延伸途徑、英文翻譯或是相關延伸詞即搭配詞。使用者對於動畫中的詞句有所疑慮，亦有中文、英文和漢語拼音的按鈕可供學習者選擇，即在動畫中搭配不同的字幕出現，加強提升學生聽力與理解。

圖7　動畫最終畫面

圖8　小博士（Dr. Idea）頁面

　　最後，學習者可在完成詞彙學習後，點選進入練習題頁面，如圖9所示。在練習題的旁邊，使用者可點選「喇叭按鈕」聽取題目錄音。練習題作答方式為直接點選該選項，並設有立即回饋。作答錯誤時，學習者可點選「RETRY」按鈕再次作答，如圖10所示；若作答正確，如圖11所示，學習者則可任意點擊該頁面回到原概念圖。

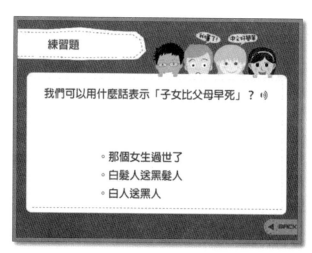
圖9　「白髮人送黑髮人」練習題畫面

圖10　作答錯誤畫面　　　　　圖11　作答正確畫面

　　以上為本研究所設計之網站內容，網站以意義鏈、隱喻或轉喻認知概念圖為架構，設計出一連串結合視覺刺激、互動特性的學習材料（如：動畫、練習、搭配、文化解釋等），供華語二語學習者學習中文溫度詞與顏色詞的另一輔助學習途徑。

㈣ 結合運用本網頁於教學應用上

　　總之，本研究所設計內容，主要定位是為華語二語學習者提供輔助學習的網頁內容。就學習者而言，在概念圖中，學習者可就個人欲學習的目標詞彙（例如：黑箱作業），了解其與基本義的關係。點選後，學習者進入動畫，可以再次決定點選「中文」、「拼音」或「英文」之選項，來輔助情境對話的理解（如圖12所示）。

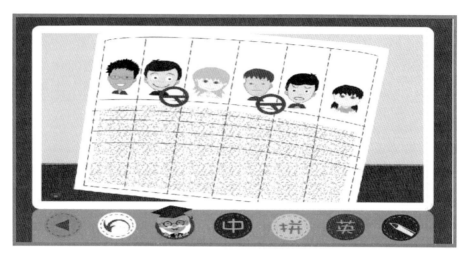

圖12　中文、拼音、英文之選項畫面範例

此外，針對詞彙練習部分，如圖13所示，學習者在此頁面可複習，統整自身已學過的相關詞彙，包括漢字與詞彙之正確發音（點入漢字後，再點擊喇叭按鈕即可）。

圖13　詞彙複習界面：「綠」相關詞彙範例

　　同樣地，在教師方面，除了文章先前所提及每一單元的「教學目標」、「概念圖」和「句式搭配」使用之外，教師亦可參酌「綜合比較」這部分，如圖14，適切引導學習者了解相近的其他詞彙比較。簡言之，每個學習區塊的應用，若能搭配教師的說明引導，則更能使數位教材輔助應用更為靈活、實用。

圖14　詞彙綜合比較之界面範例

## ㈤ 初步評估階段

　　根據李英哲（1997）針對網路課程與教材設計所提出之五項原則：⑴適合課程目標和方法、⑵便於沒有電腦專業訓練的教師與學生使用、⑶充分利用電腦的各種優點與功能、⑷充分體現人機互動的特點、⑸充分提供一系列完整的學習程序和內容，本研究之詞彙學習網站皆達到上述之原則。另一方面，我們也初步完成台北歐洲學校學生的試用問卷調查，分別針對本網頁「整體印象」、「頁面使用」、「詞彙學習內容」、「詞彙練習內容」、「試題測驗內容」及「開放式建議」，以五分量表，給予回饋。以下為些許問題範例：

1. 詞彙練習的例句對我很有幫助。（非常同意、同意、無意見、不同意、非常不同意）

2. 搭配漢語拼音，能幫助我了解對話。（非常同意、同意、無意見、不同意、非常不同意）

3. 概念組織圖對我很有幫助。（非常同意、同意、無意見、不同意、非常不同意）

4. 進階的內容對我來說太簡單了。（非常同意、同意、無意見、不同意、非常不同意）

　　整體而言，受試者偏向「同意」詞彙學習整體內容對於學習上有實質幫助。在詞彙練習內容上，也同意其複習與統整的正面效益。然而，在試題測驗內容上，受試者普遍認為測試題目過少或是題目內容過難。另外，在開放式問題部分，部分受試者肯定本網站的建置，但也有些受試者建議「頁面的操作」仍有進一步待改善的空間，例如應該更加「簡易化」。上述這些寶貴意見，皆為本網頁未來待改善的主要要點之一[9]。

## (六) 小結

　　本研究主要以認知概念、輔以隱喻原則為架構，引導學習者自學華語新詞彙，並提供教師教學相關輔助。本網站主要特色在於(1)區分學習內容的層次性；(2)運用隱喻（或轉喻）的認知原則，融合於概念圖中現，引導幫助學習相關延伸詞彙；(3)動畫學習舉例清楚易懂，串連新舊知識，適用於華語二語學習者。

　　不同於一般詞彙學習網站，本網站化整為零的學習概念使學習者在一開始就能知道各個溫度詞或顏色詞之間的語義關係，加強學生對即將學習之詞彙的認識；而網站第二個特色是動畫學習，透過視覺刺激或動畫的模式，來加強學生記憶，同時增添詞彙學習的樂趣與多元

---

[9]　囿於篇幅，僅呈現主要結果綜述。

性；即本網站畫面以視覺導向b、及以學習者爲中心的直觀設計，則降低使用的障礙，學習者僅需點擊頁面，無需經過上傳、下載、註冊等繁複的手續，一般人皆能使用。此外，本網站也善用了網路多媒體的特性，結合了文字、圖像、聲音，給予學習者充分的感官刺激，提升學習者的學習動機與成效；最後，在人機互動方面，本網站針對詞彙所設計的互動練習題，也充分展現了人機互動的特點，學習者可藉由網站這些練習題檢視自己是否已學會目標詞彙（即時性回饋），此功能也補足學生在自學時無法落實自我檢視的缺點。

## 四、結語

　　本網站設計程序依照ADDIE模式進行，目前已完成「分析」、「設計」、「發展」、「執行」等階段。網站內容取材，主要篩選自各大常用華語教材與相關辭典，並以「貴、黑、白、紅、綠、冷、溫、熱」等常用多義詞詞彙爲主，學習內容包括(1)詞彙認知概念圖、(2)詞彙情境動畫、(3)互動練習題、(4)詞彙句式搭配、與(5)詞彙相關知識。

　　在網站內容部分，學習者可於網站內選擇欲學習之詞彙，經由概念圖頁面得知該詞彙字詞與本義字詞之意義延伸原則，其後有中文、英文、拼音等三種情境動畫供學習者鞏固學習內容。學習者可於動畫中學到該詞彙的情境對話，並推敲詞彙意義。此外，另有詞義解釋供學習者確認詞義。有些含有文化詞彙的詞義則經由跨語言的補充說明，輔助學習者延伸學習。最後，互動練習的回饋設計，能讓學習者確定自己是否已學會該詞。在「執行」（或建置、應用）階段，本研究未來的實施、評估階段，擬請華語學習者與華語老師實際使用本網站自學或導學，並進一步提出可行之課程教學設計；此外，囿於現實因素考量，網站僅先針對數個高頻、且能產性高的形容詞做初步的概念圖與數位學習之應用，此爲本研究待改善之處。本研究希望未來能同時增加目標詞彙範圍，進而研究設計更多相關的詞彙概念圖與學

習網站內容，希冀為華語數位教學界提供不同面向的輔助教材之選擇。

## 參考文獻

王君（2010）。基於概念圖的大學英語詞彙教學策略研究。**齊齊哈爾大學學報**（哲學社會科學版），第五期，頁124-127。

王明輝（譯）（2007）。**資訊科技與教學**（原作者：Myint Swe Khine）。台北市：台灣培生教育。

邢志群（2011）。對外漢語詞彙教學法初探。**中文教師學報**，第四十二卷第二期，頁71-97。

李世忠（1999）。**教學科技：評鑑與應用**，台北：五圖書出版有限公司。

李英哲（1997）。自學式華語電腦課程的內容設計與應用方法。**教學科技與媒體**，36：20-28。

何淑貞、張孝裕、陳立芬、舒兆民、蔡雅薰、賴明德等人合著（2008）。**華語文教學導論**，台北市：三民書局。

林奇賢（1998）。網路學習環境的設計與應用。**資訊與教育**，第六十七期，頁34-50。

林金賢（2004）。結合網路同步教學與多媒體網站輔助華文新聞教學的探討。台灣師範大學碩士論文。

邱美智、黃玲玲（2011）。南密西中文學校——個案討論學校背景、電腦輔助教學發展、困難挑戰及應用，台北：**第七屆全球華文網路教育研討會論文集**。

邱貴發（1998）。網路世界中的學習：理念與發展。**教育研究資訊**，第六期，頁20-27。

胡明揚（1997）。對外漢語教學中詞彙教學的若干問題。**語言文字應用**，第一期，頁12-17。

周健慈（2002）。中文網路教學面面觀。世界華語文教學研討會論文集，5(2)，頁257-262。

孫德金（2006）。對外漢語詞彙及詞彙教學研究。北京：商務印書館。

涂鈺亭（2010）。華語網播教學發展——以中級華語為對象。台灣師範大學碩士論文。

國立台灣師範大學編輯群（2011）。新實用視聽華語，新北市：正中書局。

舒兆民（2002）。網路華語語體及文化課程教學設計。台灣師範大學碩士論文。

陳建生、夏曉燕、姚堯等（2011）。認知詞彙學。北京：光明日報。

曾貽（2012）。英漢基本顏色詞的隱喻認知對比分析及對英語教學的啓示。海外英語，第十一期，頁106-107、109。

黃晶偉、董志友（2012）。英語熟語學習的認知語言學視角。教書育人，第三十期，頁90-91。

葉德明主編（2001）。遠東生活華語。台北市：遠東。

潘玉華、李順琴（2011）。隱喻理論對對外漢語詞彙教學的啓示。雲南師範大學學報，9(4)，頁28-30。

壽大衛（2001）。資訊網路教學。台北市：師大書苑。

Ausubel, D. P. and Fitzgerald, D. (1962). Organizer, General Background, and Antecedent Learning Variables in Sequential Verbal Learning. *Journal of Educational Psychology*, 53(6), pp.243-249.

Boers, Frank (2000). Metaphor Awareness and Vocabulary Retention. *Applied Linguistics*, 21(4), pp.553-571.

Chun, D. M. and Plass, J. L. (1996). Effect of Multimedia Annotations on Vocabulary Acquisition. *The Modern Language Journal*, 80, pp.183-198.

Cicognani, Anna (2000). Concept Mapping as a Collaborative Tool for Enhanced Online Learning. *Education Technology & Society*, 3(3), pp.150-158.

Duquette, L., Renié, D., and Laurier, M. (1998). The Evaluation of

Vocabulary Acquisition when Learning French as a Second Language in a Multimedia Environment. *Computer Assisted Language Learning*, 11(1), pp.3-34.

Fauconnier, G. & M. Turner. (2002). *The Way We Think: Conceptual Blending and the Mind's Hidden Complexities*. New York: Basic Books.

Fillmore, Charles J. (1976). Frame semantics and the nature of language. In Annals of the New York Academy of Sciences: Conference on the Origin and Development of Language and Speech, volume 280, pp. 20-32.

Lakoff, George (1987). *Women, Fire, and Dangerous Things: What Categories Reveal about the World*. Chicago, IL: University of Chicago Press.

Lazar, G. (1996). Using Figurative Language to Expand Students, Vocabulary. *ELT Journal*, 50 (1): 43-51.

Lyons, John (1968). *Introduction to Theoretical Linguistics*. Cambridge: Cambridge University Press.

Novak, J. D. & Gowin, D. B. (1984). *Learning How to Learn*, NY: Cambridge University Press.

Novak J. D. & Cañas A. J. (2006). *The Theory Underlying Concept Maps and How to Construct Them* (Technical Report No. IHMC CmapTools 2006-01). Pensacola, FL: Institute for Human and Machine Cognition.

MacLennan, Carol H. G. (1994). Metaphor and Prototypes in the Teaching and Learning of Grammar and Vocabulary. *International Review of Applied Linguistic*, 32(2), pp.97-110.

Mayer, Richard E. (2005). Principles for Managing Essential Processing in Multimedia Learning: Segmenting, Pretraining, and Modality Principles. In Richard E. Mayer (Ed.), *Cambridge Handbook of Multimedia Learning* (pp. 169-182). New York: Cambridge University Press.

Milton, J. (2009). *Measuring Second Language Vocabulary Acquisition,* Buffalo: Multilingual Matters.

Reiser, Robert A. (1987). Instructional Technology: A History. In R. M. Gagné (Ed.), *Instructional Technology: Foundations* (pp.11-40). Hillsdale, NJ: Lawrence Erlbaum.

Richards, J. (1976). The Role of Vocabulary Teaching. *TESOL Quarterly*, 10(1), pp.77-89.

Taylor, J. (1995). *Linguistic Categorization: Prototypes in Linguistic Theory*. Beijing: Beijing Foreign Language Teaching and Research Press.

Taylor, John R. (2003). *Linguistic Categorization* (3rd edition). Oxford: Oxford University Press.

Verspoor, M. and Lowie, W. (2003). Making Sense of Polysemous Words. *Language Learning,* 53(3), pp.547-586.

Yao, Tao-Chung and Yuehua Liu (1997). *Integrated Chinese*. Boston, MA: Cheng & Tsui Company.

# Concept Map and Digital Learning Materials Application

**Huichen S. HSIAO**　**Yushan Charlotte CHOU**

Department of Chinese as a Second Language,

National Taiwan Normal University

## Abstract

This paper aims to explore the feasibility of cognitive concept map application in Chinese vocabulary learning through online learning. In recent years, the importance of vocabulary learning has been increasing [Hu, 1997 (胡明揚)；Sun, 2006 (孫德金) ] and the issue about the difficulty in learning polysemous words has also been brought up [Xing, 2001 (邢志群)；Chen et al., 2011 (陳建生) ]. Therefore, this paper seeks to propose an efficient way to assist L2 Chinese learners with their vocabulary learning. On the one hand, we chose Chinese color-related words and temperature-related words with high frequency as learning materials and analyzed them on the basis of cognitive semantics. In order to provide an efficient way of vocabulary learning, we accomodated the work of Lakoff (1987) on ICM, metaphorical mappings, metonymic mappings, Taylor's (1995; 2003) proposed meaning chains by developing various concept maps (cf. Novak & Gowin, 1984) integrated with cognitive principles and explanations. On the other hand, we are aware of the advantages of vocabulary learning by means of multimedia from previous research (Chun and Plass, 1996; Duquette et al., 1998); thus, the website is presented with the concept maps and multimedia assistance in dialogues (for practice purpose) designed by our teams. All in all, our major aim is to explore the feasibility of Chinese vocabulary online learning through the assistance of cognitive principles by illustrating the route from core meanings to more abstract meanings, supplemented by concept maps and multimedia as well.

Key words: polysemy, concept map, vocabulary learning, TCSL, online learning materials

# 遠距同步漢字入門課之教學規劃與實驗
## ——以印尼亞齊大學學生為對象

官志皇　舒兆民

台北市立教育大學華語文教學碩士學位學程

國立聯合大學華語文學系

wjf1216@gmail.com　zhaomin@nuu.edu.tw

## 摘要

　　漢字教學是對外華語教學中的重要環節，對於外籍人士而言，除了少數國家（如：日本、韓國、越南）的學習者外，多不具有圖像平面式的文字概念。根據以往的文獻及研究成果，學者專家主要從漢字本體特色出發，開展針對漢字的教學與引導，這些教學的方式往往是運用在實體課程或是面對面個別指導的教學環境。在教學的方法中，對外籍人士的漢字教學也不可能一字一字地教導，而漢字的教學則多由部首、部件、字源、字根來拆解，從聲符義符來介紹，然而，學習的時間則不免過長，從精緻教學的角度來看，又缺乏在學習開始給予一個漢字系統的總體概念，以致策略學習方式無法在之後的漢字學習中主動應用。

　　目前，作為漢字的網路平台課程且透過遠距混成式教學的模式還不多。侷限在視訊螢幕大小與線上的對話方框，教師無法明確地掌握學生的學習狀況，師生間的互動也受平台功能而有限制，許多的教學策略或是教學活動並不適用在遠距教學上。因此，本研究即思考漢字教學與學習策略引導的「數位化」與「混成式課程化」，藉由融入漢字造字與識字之策略優勢於漢字入門課程，分別對海外實施教學。本實驗教學建置混成式課程，配合遠距同步教學與移地

式的教學，觀察教學過程、學生學習情形，以及成效評估。經與印尼亞齊大學的遠距教學實驗後，就平台之運用，探討功能與活動設計之良窳，利用多媒體的製作與運用、悅趣化的學習導入教學中。隨後分析並提出平台教材與教學之功能需求與教學技巧之建議。

關鍵詞：遠距教學、漢字教學、教學策略、漢字學習平台

## 一、前言

　　對外華語文教學中，在語言的指導上，漢字學習一直是非圖像文字為母語的學習者在學習漢語初入門時的難處。如何提高漢字教學的效率，解決這個學習「瓶頸」，在華語文教學界是許多教研學長期關注的部分。在本體研究方面，已有許多學者深入探討（王寧，2001；裘錫圭，2001；黃沛榮，2003；賴明德，2003），也有許多對外籍人士的漢字教學研究，然而，在研究過程中，未能發展出適合的漢字入門教學模式，以及對於漢字習得之過程與規律的整理與描述。

　　教學界了解學生的認知特點、有效的學習策略，以及所運用的工具學習，與漢字作為第二語言的文字教學特點，是我們設計漢字的教學具體計畫、步驟、方法與教學技巧的根據，但目前相關的學習策略研究，以及適合各不同母語人士自學或輔學的學習資源與工具，都僅局限在實體課程，還未有適合而有效的遠距教學課程。因此，本研究期從兩個角度來研發網路漢字入門課程教學系統：一為研究華語文教學中，對外籍人士學習漢字之教與學的策略，二為分析並提出平台教材與教學之功能需求與教學技巧之建議。

## 二、本計畫之平台系統簡述

　　因應全球不同國家學習華語者使用的母語語系眾多、學習者華語文能力也有所差異，以母語為媒介進行華語初學者開發教材課程是必要的步驟，據此提出適合不同母語者之漢字初學字卡製作與教學系

統，希望達成漢字教學協同製作平台，具有以下目標：

1. 提供以多語而適合各地之教材進行華語課堂或線上同步教學，構思如何以一套多語系統的教材，提供具不同華文程度者，符合其母語轉借學習的適性學習環境，提高學習效率。

2. 透過網路提供教材的協同編撰機制，結合華人在華語上的優勢，與在地各國教師對在地語言的了解進行分工，以利第二語言華語初學者的教材開發，讓教材可以因地制宜。

3. 系統提供便利的字卡[1]與文章教材製作機制，讓教材製作者可以編製多語系教材，供華語教學教師可以利用因地制宜之教材，進行華語課程之設計。

4. 在文章教學方面提供自動智慧斷詞功能，簡化建立詞卡教學的工作。學習者在閱讀時，配合斷詞功能搭配彈出母語小提示以顯示字詞的簡義，讓學習者自然適應華語文章閱讀時的切割斷句。

5. 結合Google™公司的字詞翻譯功能，翻譯尚無人工翻譯之多語字卡、詞卡的簡譯以供使用。

　　系統方面的說明如下：

## (一) 線上教學子系統

　　平台線上教學情境為教室混有不同國籍學生或在不同地區的學生同時在線上上課，老師授課的內容為全中文版本，學生在上課時，學習的是老師準備的中文課堂內容，而系統會另外提供資料庫內有的多語系教材作為輔助教材幫助學生學習，所有的教學流程都會依照老師的控制為主，學生的上課畫面上，可以利用本平台所提供的斷詞功能，在滑鼠指標所移動到的詞彙或字上，看到顯示出的多語系簡譯，且只要點選詞彙就另開一個視窗，呈現詞、字卡的多語內容，以更明確了解該詞彙內容，亦不會阻礙到老師上課的流程。

---

[1]　未來依教材所需，分別串聯各課文中的相關詞卡。

## (二) 補課與適性化的課後複習

上課過程中，老師可利用錄製的功能，錄製上課的完整流程，上課結束之後，將成為一份離線教材，學生想要複習或補課時，可以利用錄製下來的課程閱讀、學生閱讀時，多語輔助教材會依照學生當時的華語能力來顯示，上課時所看到的輔助教材，跟往後想要複習時的輔助教材，會依學生程度來呈現（圖1）。

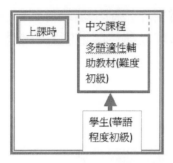

圖1　符應學習需求之課後複習示意圖

## (三) 平台系統

本研究平台包含五個系統：管理者子系統、素材管理子系統、教材管理子系統、教學平台、會員子系統。系統流程如下：

1. 以管理者子系統管理使用者登入權限。
2. 建置者利用素材管理子系統上傳動畫、圖片。可提供教材管理子系統製作教材的元素。
3. 利用教材管理子系統製作字卡、詞卡、文章、課本，以提供編撰教學之使用。
4. 教學平台管理教學活動，提供老師教學編輯機制，利用教材資料庫已有的教材進行教學活動。
5. 會員子系統可以讓成員修改本身的基本資料，查看自身創建或收藏的素材、教材、教學，以及瀏覽參加過的課程資料。

## ㈣ 教學平台

此平台主要進行線上教學、記錄學習歷程、課程管理。

### 1. 申請開課

老師向管理者提出申請開課。申請表內容有：課程名稱、教學目標、教學內容、預計學習時間、教學要點概述。

### 2. 審核課程

管理者審核課程，結果通知該課程申請的老師。

### 3. 加入課程

學生可向開課老師申請加入課程，在老師上課的時間進入該課程上課。

### 4. 開設課程

⑴設定課程大綱

設定課程大綱，如課程目標、教學內容、預計學習時間、教學要點概述。

⑵課程單元管理

①開設課程單元

建立課程中的單元，單元內容為老師所挑選的字卡、詞卡、文章的組合或老師可以直接使用課本內容上課。

②單元說明

編寫每一個單元的單元說明、單元上課預估時間。

③管理課程單元

可以修改或刪除課程單元。

⑶上課學生管理

①核可申請上課的學生

②除名上課學生

③上課人數限制

## 5.目前系統成果

### ⑴素材管理子系統

提供建置者上傳動畫與圖片，以供教材建置使用。提供上傳素材和瀏覽功能（圖2）。藉由專業的媒體創作者，上傳素材以供建置教材之使用。

圖2　此為本計畫漢字學習平台中的字卡，左為漢字筆順，右為漢字圖片，底下尚有拼音、詞性、部首、意思、常用詞等介紹

### ⑵教材管理子系統

進行教材建置與管理，利用素材管理子系統提供之圖片與動畫，增加教材多媒體的呈現。

### ⑶教學平台

①同步呈現

教學情境為老師用全中文教材教導，而學生畫面跟老師畫面一致。

②詞彙多語適性簡譯呈現

系統斷詞功能將該詞彙簡譯出來。學生華語能力會影響可顯示簡譯的詞彙數量，當學生程度高於該詞彙所設定的難度時，簡譯將不會顯示。

③適性化輔助教材

藉由斷詞功能，學生點選自己想看的詞彙，查詢該詞彙的內容，詞、字卡內容依照學生華語能力不同，有不同的顯示。此功能不會影響到老師上課流程。

④課後複習

學生可再次觀看老師的完整教學，並依自己需求，調整觀看課程的時間點。

## 三、本計畫之實驗研究

　　本計畫之實驗歷經主要三期次教學，第一次為2012年3至4月間，透過臺灣與印尼亞齊大學學生遠距之交流，進行漢字入門策略教學，並施測了解學生的學習成效，同時也測試平台使用情形，包含本計畫自製之平台、Skype運用情形（圖3）。第一次的實驗過程為測試平台情形，然因平台之使用受限亞齊大學的網路基礎設施之影響，同時也因系統字卡抓取圖片耗時，多數漢字之教學改採Skype結合網路上免費之動態筆順進行備案教學。雖說教學過程中受限於設備與系統之影響而成效有所折扣，但也因此獲得啟示，不管是平台或教學等，也能在未來提供修正方向。

　　在同步教學準備過程，硬體方面要準備電腦、耳機麥克風、Webcam、投影器材等設備，軟體方面須熟悉同步平台的介面操作，如使用Skype的「語音」、「影像」、「文字」的同步功能，也要事前模擬教學，適應實際教學環境外也可避免當天教學過程碰到突發狀況才能臨危不亂，還要先了解當地的禁忌，以免說錯話引起誤會；由於這是漢字學習平台之建置計畫，所以筆者在教案設計上著重漢字教學策略，除了透過平台上的動態筆順動畫及字源演變過程，也在白板上實際講解漢字筆順和部件結構，不只是單純使用漢字教學法，也將線上多媒體運用在教學中。

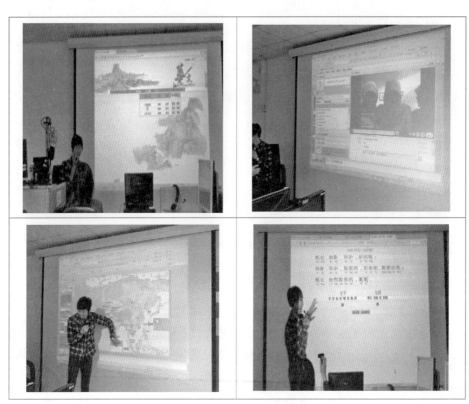

圖3　第一次試教過程紀錄

　　第二次為2012年6至8月間，採移地實驗教學方式，地點於印尼亞齊大學與伊斯蘭大學兩校的暑期中文學習短期班中進行。本期運用自製平台於課堂教學，以資訊融入方式來進行教學，同樣也因為當地設施等問題，操作也不易，以本計畫之初直接攜帶類主機赴當地操作，也因操作者不熟系統與主機之建置，且幾台筆電雖已裝入系統可供單機操作，但仍不敷六十餘人學習之用。為此，本計畫則以系統資料改製PPT後，供學生學習，並配合課堂教師之引導，對學習內容有所了解。本次亦同時了解當地數位教學之實況，並思考未來解決之道。

　　第三次為2012年11至12月間，採遠距實驗教學，同時以Skype並

配合後續自學之非同步網路課程學習，設計學習時程與練習功能，以結合本計畫之自製平台與Moodle平台練習。從本教師端記錄學生上線學習情形，由小老師提供12月至1月間之後續輔導，採遠距式的混成式教學。遠距同步教學內容依序為 1.漢字教學策略：筆順、筆畫；2.漢字教學㈠；3.漢字教學㈡；4.漢字教學㈢；5.總複習；最後還針對這五次教學內容整理出試題，請印尼亞齊大學當地老師代為測驗。在此次也加入了悅趣化的教學策略、設計數位化的教學活動，以PPT給予一個故事情節做一闖關遊戲（圖4），設計十題問題，答對之後可以得到獎勵，並完成關卡，反之答錯卻得重頭來過，也可藉此檢視學生是否真的了解問題或者僅是猜對的，此教學活動可當作最後的總複習，也可當作隔天上課前的暖身活動。

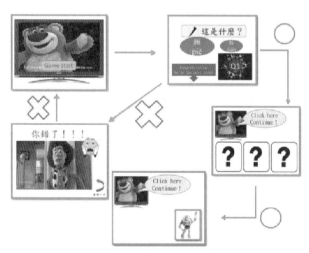

圖4　以PPT製作悅趣化的教學活動

　　另外，也以線上網站「教學魔法變變變」[2]所提供的自製題庫遊戲─配對卡遊戲，自行修改語法，將教學過的部首，以此款配對遊戲，在課堂間讓學生練習（圖5）。

---

2　教學魔法變變變http://blog.huayuworld.org/esthchangchua/19496/2010/06/24/68466。

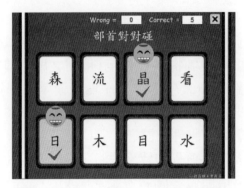

圖5　配對卡遊戲──部首對對碰

## 四、教學結果評估與修正

　　本計畫之實施,在教學與系統運用上,目前有以下幾個方面的啓示:

### (一) 對遠距同步教學的難點及建議

　　筆者認爲線上遠距同步教學的難點分爲兩大項,一爲軟硬體設備上的難點,另一個是教學內容的難點,在軟硬體上大致是網路、電腦與通訊平台的問題,雙方網路只要有一方不穩定,視訊或音訊極有可能延遲、斷斷續續甚至是斷訊的狀況;而電腦只要過於老舊就無法安裝新版本的通訊平台(如Skype),造成兩方的版本不相容無法共同通訊;至於通訊平台的多人視訊大都須付費,所以免費版本無法應付太多人同時視訊是其缺點。對於軟硬體設備的建議爲雙方在網路上以使用有線網路爲主,無線網路爲輔,前者的網速流量及穩定度皆高於後者;而電腦上也以最低限度的版本安裝通訊軟體即可解決;通訊平台可改採Google的Hangouts爲考量,不過多人即時視訊也只有十人爲最高上限,在免付費的情況下,如果要進行線上教學,還是只能以小班制進行。線上遠距同步教學不似實體課程授課,教學內容的難點在於教學活動與教學法等方面都會受到限制,如教學活動少,僅能透

過口頭方式請學生回答問題；教學法受限，無法以情境教學、團體語言教學等帶入遠距教學之中。對於教學內容的建議為教學活動可讓學生與學生互相進行角色扮演，不只是單方面回答問題；而在教學法可以精熟其他教學法，以彌補一部分教學法無法使用。

## ㈡ 當地網路資訊基礎與數位落差

　　以當地的網路傳輸，以及平均的數位落差來觀察教學的推動情形。目前的教學測試中，以遠距教學形式的效果較差，由於傳輸速度與電腦系統效能等的差異，在使用過程中常受到設備的左右，教學備案方式必須事先思考，如運用Connect8不能進行時，即改用Skype，再無法使用，則須當地督導教師以備份硬碟協助區域性播放，配合教學教師之進行。移地教學的做法也類似，唯獨此種教學備案則無法順利進行教學錄製，以及運用教師所編製的線上在地適性的字詞卡。

## ㈢ 學習活動的數位化有待再研發

　　以漢字學習過程來看，大量的活動練習，甚至是遊戲活動實施以階段性的複習，都是重要的教學設計，然而，在目前的數位化教學工具與遊戲模組中，尚無法大量或完整地將活動遊戲的成效達到如同在實體課堂一般，光靠平台原有的部件及連連看練習是不足的，因此在之後的遠距實驗教學中加入PPT自製闖關遊戲及配對卡遊戲以彌補這部分。

## ㈣ 學生偏誤情形

　　以現有印尼學生在漢字學習表現上可以看出與一般外籍人士學習的偏誤類同的部分，這些在印尼學生的學習狀況也相同，如：
1. 部件的置換，包含了形近替換、意近替換、類化改換及聲符改換等（打→扛、超→迢、陪→倍、源→沅）。
2. 部件的增減，像是多加意符或減少意符（桌→槕、故→古）。
3. 部件的變形或變位，源於母語干擾或鏡面變異〔可→（○

丁）〕。

4. 字形筆畫（田→由、甲）、空間結構、自創新字、同音錯字與形近誤用。

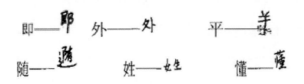

### ㈤ 學習檢測與成效

　　學習期初與期末為期八個月，移地實驗教學時間為兩個月，期末以策略學習為測驗例子（圖6），可以看出學習者對於拆解字形、猜測字義，以及在文字書寫上有了進展。唯受試人數不多，且入門教學為期四週，教學為分散隨文形式，尚未能判定是否單純為本教學的成效。然而，與之前未實施數位教學相較，教師意見表示確實比往年的教學具有效果。

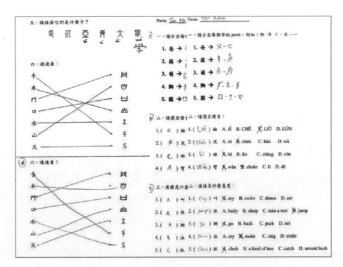

圖6　學生期末策略教學檢測試卷示例

#### ㈥ 教師意見反饋

　　教學教師與當地督導教師反應意見，在從事數位化的漢字教學，備課時間高於一般課堂教學，因為多了系統操作與網頁友善度的因素，教學順暢與否常影響了學習進度與教學心情。往往一個在課堂中簡單的帶領轉換成線上帶領時便會處處掣肘，這點在研究者反思部分亦常見，只有期待未來在技術上與相關的習得教學實驗能更多地研究。

　　在課後的練習與回答問題的正確率的確是提升了，尤其是漢字的形音義間關係的理解，其熟稔程度相較以往學生學習的效果高，足見在非同步的功能上，字卡搭配字源教學法的解說是有效的。學生在漢字部分可利用錄製的影片，以及介面、說明等的適性多語功能，對於學生確有成效，實可再進一步實驗設計，觀察教學的效果，以推廣此類的教學模組。

#### ㈦ 學生訪談

　　學生訪談部分蒐集資料，完整的計有十四名，學生表示學習趣味與新奇是其引發動機的重點。網站上單純漢字教學是相當枯燥的，但透過自製遊戲與動態筆形仿寫是有趣的部分，由此可見悅趣化的教學策略有其成效。至於漢字的構成與基礎知識，學生雖無法說出所以然，但已見造字原則與意義上模糊的掌握能力。

#### ㈧ 遠距同步教學的優點、好處

　　最主要為打破「時間」、「空間」的限制，因為不受地理環境的限制，所以教師教學範圍擴大、學生學習機會增加，即使身處不同兩地，也可做到即時雙向溝通；與非同步教學相比，師生互動頻繁，學習者必須積極參與課程，可增加學習者參與感，遠距同步教學特別強調溝通。

# 五、結語與建議

## (一) 結語

在執行計畫的過程中，從課程規劃、設計發展與實驗教學，本計畫常有變動，原因在於人事上的掌握、聯繫不易，教學對象程度、人數也不明，媒體設備與通訊差異，影響著太多因素。筆者認為只有這一年多的接觸交流還不足，尤其是未能長期與多次到當地接觸了解，這是需要時間與人力的配合。

透過兩次的遠距同步教學，不難發現印尼亞齊大學學生對於此種教學方式感到新奇有興趣並且不排斥未來繼續使用此方式學習漢字。我們也發現在漢字教學中，學生對於筆順、部件的拆分與結構及字源的演變都有一定程度的掌握，可以從圖6的測驗中看出。但是，在部首教學上，我們也注意到學生對於形聲字的部首與聲符的搭配不甚理解，原因在於當地較少教授部首，所以當我們進行此部分的教學，學生大都茫然，後來是透過當地老師以母語解釋學生才了解部首教學的重點。此外，相較於第一次遠距同步教學只使用兩個多媒體教學遊戲（原本平台內建的部件及連連看練習），就教學而言遊戲或複習活動的比例少，在教學時多為講課較為單調，無法引起學生太大的興趣，而在第二次教學中又多帶入新的多媒體教學遊戲（PPT闖關遊戲、部首對對碰），學生的反應比之前好，可見將悅趣化的教學策略帶入教學中，是有幫助的，除了提高學生的學習興趣，也可透過遊戲再幫學生複習一次，達到精熟原則。

本計畫雖然已經結束，但研究實施尚持續進行，系統與課程部分已建置完成，前測實驗教學也有一定的成效，在地化教材也逐步完成。然而，實施人數尚嫌不足與策略漢字入門教學課程的循環修正還在進行之中，不過因為與印尼亞齊大學簽訂合作備忘錄，所以計畫在未來的五年中，與亞齊大學合作下，繼續實驗教學，擴大教學的成效研究與學習者的學習效果與態度研究，期能對印尼亞齊大學的學生在學習漢字有所助益。

## ㈡ 建議

　　在遠距同步教學結束之後，實驗教學的教師有些教學心得，前面已經談述的教學難點不再贅述，試整理出幾點建議以供參考：1.對於教學上所使用的軟硬體皆須熟悉使用方式，適應實際教學環境才能臨危不亂；2.實際教學時間較少，教學內容的量要適中，才不會有教不完或延後教學的情況；3.考量網路連線品質，講話語速要放慢，下達指示語只要說關鍵字即可；4.可用較爲誇張的肢體動作表現，學生更容易理解，在視訊畫面上的效果也較爲鮮明；5.漢字教學的遊戲活動不可少，能夠適時引發學生學習興趣，提振學生精神，不至於感到枯燥乏味；6.遠距同步教學的狀況多，要有隨機應變能力，如動態筆順無法播放立刻改以白板書寫。以上六點是我們經過實驗之後所得出的教學建議。

　　後續除了繼續將漢字學習平台的功能與內容更完善的建置，如再加強數位化的教學活動，期待能將悅趣化的教學概念完整呈現，以用在遠距教學上，也希望透過這個平台能有其他的規劃，像是推展遠距的混成式教學以及發展行動式學習並推出相關App應用程式。

　　在遠距的混成式教學中，希望能建立一制度，在學期之中安排兩校的學生或爲該地的成人、青少年進行遠距同步教學，設計教材與教學課程，另外提供平台讓印尼當地的學生可非同步自主性學習，而當學期結束後，可利用寒暑假時間，由台灣派學生至當地進行實體課程的教學，一方面可讓兩方有長久性的遠距教學規劃，另一方面也可以確保華文系學生能有機會前往當地進行教學實習，平時爲遠距混成教學，寒暑期進行短期的銜接式實體課，可爲當地開展適當的外語教學。

　　（本論文爲何照清教授國科會專案「華語文網路漢字學習平台之建置㈡」研究成果之一，計畫編號：101-2631-S-239-001）

# 參考文獻

王建勤（2005）。漢語作為第二語言學習者語言系統研究，北京：商務書局。

王駿（2009）。字本位與對外漢語教學，上海：上海交通大學出版社。

周健（2009）。漢字教學理論與方法，北京：北京大學出版社。

計惠卿、張秀美、李麗霞（2005）。華語文數位教材之內涵與互動設計之研析，第四屆全球華文網路教育研討會。

姚麗瑩（2011）。印尼高等學校的零起點生漢字教學設計——突出聲符、意符與正字法的漢字教學，石家莊：河北師範大學碩士論文。

孫德金主編（2006）。對外漢字教學研究，北京：商務印書館。

陳秀如（2008）。多媒體教學策略對外籍生華語文學習成效、認知負荷與學習動機之影響——以漢字筆畫書寫及義類辨識為例，台北：台灣師大資教所碩士論文。

張笑怡（2011）。對印尼人的漢字教學研究，長沙：湖南師範大學碩士論文。

舒兆民（2007）。多媒體正體漢字之教學實驗，2007第五屆全球華文網路教育研討會，頁221-232，台北：僑委會。

舒兆民（2011a）。華語文網路混成式平台課程之教學實施與觀察——以線上平台與即時互動工具結合之課程為例，2011華語文科際整合學術研討會會後論文集，頁165–182，苗栗：國立聯合大學華語文學系。

舒兆民（2011a）。漢字策略教學結合自選漢字輔學卡融入華語網路初級課程之實驗，第二屆「華文作為第二語言之教與學」國際研討會暨第九屆「東南亞華文教學」研討會，新加坡：新加坡華文教研中心。

黃沛榮（2003）。漢字教學的理論與實踐，台北：樂學書局。

溫敏淦、何照清、舒兆民、楊宗珂（2011b）。華語文網路漢字學習平台分析，2011華語文科際整合學術研討會，頁126–142，苗栗：國

立聯合大學華語文學系。

裘錫圭（2001）。文字學概要，台北：萬卷樓圖書出版社。

萬業馨（2003）。從漢字識別談漢字與漢字認知的綜合研究，語言教學
　　與研究，頁73，北京。

賴明德（2003）。中國文字教學研究，台北：文史哲出版社。

本篇感謝科技部經費補助。

# 三、語言技能及文化之數位輔助資源

# 一個全新互動的數位學習方式
## ——中文多媒體簡報比賽

黃清郁（**Ching-yu Austin Huang**）[1]

新澤西州肯恩大學資訊系

chuang@kean.edu

劉景秋（**Jing-Chiou Liou**）[2]

新澤西州肯恩大學資訊系

jliou@kean.edu

## 摘要

　　在華人的傳統語文教育中，各種中文競賽大都是單方向的。這些比賽對學生只是一種單方向的學習成果展現或測驗，跟聽眾並沒有雙向的互動，也無法表達個人的學習觀點與心得。使得這樣的競賽缺乏一個整合語文多元表現、知識性與才藝性的可能性。隨著中文數位教學的日漸普及以及網路資訊的發達，學生們除了在課堂上學習之外，更應該要善用數位多媒體的方式來展現學習的效果。本論文將介紹一個全新的學藝競賽學習方式，利用現代多媒體工具來鼓勵學生用中文簡報中華文化常識、連接過去與現代中國、台灣、香港、澳門以及華人在世界的社會實況，並與老師，或裁判們互動，以促進練習用中文思考與表達創作能力，也同時讓學生、老師

---

[1] 新澤西州立醫學暨牙醫大學資深電腦科學家，新澤西中文學校協會義工會長，新澤西維德中文學校老師。

[2] 新澤西肯恩州立大學資訊系助理教授。

之間能相互觀摩學習不同有趣的中文知識，達到教學相長的境界。

關鍵字：多媒體教學、網路學習、中華文化知識、語言學習的規範、互動式學習、中文學校

# 一、前言Introduction

傳統中小學的各種中文競賽大都是單方向的，例如演講比賽、詩歌朗誦比賽、壁報比賽、歌唱比賽；或是記憶性的，例如認字比賽、中華文化常識比賽；或是文化才藝的，例如扯鈴比賽、書法比賽。這些比賽對學生只是一種單方向的學習成果展現或測驗，跟聽眾並沒有雙向的互動，也無法表達個人的學習觀點與心得，而文化才藝性的比賽也只是展現技巧，並沒有讓學生真的了解到該才藝的相關中華文化知識，在華人的教育中缺乏一個整合多元表現、知識性與才藝性的比賽。

隨著中文數位教學的普及以及網路資訊的發達，學生們除了在課堂上學習之外，更應該要善用數位多媒體的方式來展現學習的效果。本論文將介紹一個全新的學藝競賽學習方式，利用現代多媒體工具來鼓勵學生用中文簡報中華文化常識、連接過去與現代中國、台灣、香港、澳門以及華人在世界的社會實況，並與老師，或裁判們互動，以促進練習用中文思考與表達創作能力，也同時讓學生、老師之間能相互觀摩學習不同有趣的中文知識，達到教學相長的境界。

美國大學理事會這幾年在學習世界語言上特別訂出五大規範[1]，除了第一項溝通（Communications），包括上課教的聽、說、讀、寫之外，其他四項都在強調文化知識、溝通與互動的重要性，包括生活習俗跟文化（Cultures）、連接現實社會（Connections）、比較不同的語言跟文化（Comparisons）、實際體驗環境（Communities）。所以這種新的數位學藝競賽方式也正好配合了這些規範——學習語言除了基本的聽說讀寫之外，還必須有互動跟了解語言的文化內涵，而且學生透過準備跟參與這項活動，對於準備AP

中文考試也將會有莫大的助益。

## 二、中文多媒體簡報比賽Chinese Multimedia Contest

　　在美國許多知識性競賽的作品都是學生在家裡事先做好，比賽當天學生只需要做簡報並跟裁判互動回答問題，例如科學類的競賽有州內Jersey Shore Science Fairs[2]，跨州區域的Delaware Valley Science Fairs[3]，全國與世界的英特爾Intel International Science and Engineering Fair (ISEF)[4]，文科類的有美國歷史日National History Day (NHD)[5]，科技與設計類的有科技學生協會 Technology Student Association[6]，許多這些競賽學生必須從從地方、區域、跨州比賽中獲獎，才能進入到全國與世界比賽，這些競賽都是屬於課後或是社團活動，學生利非上課時間準備競賽，由家長、學校老師、大學教授指導，有些競賽每年都會有特定主題，例如美國歷史日（NHD）2013的主題是「Revolution, Reaction, Reform in History」，科技學生協會（TSA）2013主題是「A Tradition of Excellence」，學生可以針對主題自由選擇題目發揮，在作品上列出參考書籍、網路資料，最後利用文字、照片、影像、聲音來展現作品，因為學生必須大量閱讀與引用許多參考資料，甚至訪談相關領域專家。

　　隨著小孩在美國的中學念書，我們有機會深入比較華人傳統學校的競賽與美國中學的競賽，發現美國這些競賽整合式的學習效果非常好。在台灣與美國各地中文學校舉行的壁報比賽也是鼓勵學生了解成語與中華文化，但與美國的競賽比較之下，壁報比賽最大的缺點是無法滿足美國大學理事會對於互動與溝通的要求，以及學生花在準備材料的時間遠比研究與學習中文的時間多；例如，由於題目是當場抽籤，學生必須事先在家裡模擬製比賽的幾個主題，事先要把全部題目所需的材料與工具都準備好，在比賽有限的兩個多小時時間內，學生再把之前模擬做過的作品當場重做剪、寫、貼、畫一次，這些大都是屬於美勞而很少有中文知識的學習。由於時間限制，裁判在評分時學

生並不在旁邊介紹，裁判們無從知道學生在壁報上寫、貼、畫的東西代表什麼，裁判們只能用自己主觀的了解去詮釋，這可能完全背離學生的意思，裁判們也無從知道學生到底懂不懂主題內容跟整體作品的含意，所以壁報比賽幾乎就是以藝術為主要打分數的基礎，競賽過程中學生既沒有表達的機會也沒有與他人互動，不符合語言學習的五大規範。在現在資訊科技發達的時代，我們需要更好的競賽方式讓學生能真正有效率地學習中文。因此，我們從2009年起在美國新澤西州的維德中文學校把原有的壁報比賽改成中華文化多媒體的整合學習競賽。

　　新推出這項中文多媒體簡報比賽讓學生以中文簡報一個有興趣的主題，時間約三到四分鐘，學生簡報後將回答裁判的提問，問題以學生介紹內容為主。題目範圍必須針對中華文化，例如，人物：現代、過去中華歷史或故事人物，包括在美國或是世界其他地區的華人；歷史或是時事：正在發生或是歷史上的傳說、故事、事情與事件；地理與名勝：只能涵蓋台灣、中國大陸、香港、澳門等相關地方；生活習俗或是常識：任何中國人現代或是古代的習俗、節日、華人特有的生活；藝術、建築與科學：任何中國人現代或是古代的發明、建築、醫學、數學等等；成語、文學與故事：包括中文成語、古代與現代中文書籍（非翻譯）、《詩》、《辭》、《三字經》等等；電影與電視節目：必須是以華人為主角，在美國或是世界其他地區、台灣、中國大陸、香港或是澳門拍攝中文發音為主的影視節目，以非華人為主角的英文、日片與韓片等其他語言的中文版不包括在內。

　　學生可以使用電腦、iPad、DVD Player、電子多媒體、肢體表演或平面壁報展示學習成果，準備口語說明並與裁判就內容進行問答，學生必須當場以口頭做中文簡報給裁判與聽眾。簡報方式有靜態展出，例如：電腦、壁報、海報、書籍、論文等形態做簡報；或是透過動態語音與表演簡報，例如：學生作品一部分可以包括事先錄好或是找好的中文影音；有些主題必須以影片或是紀錄片方式介紹比較合適，因此，學生也可以透過現場表演來介紹，例如：扯鈴、舞蹈、國

劇的動作技巧。這比賽應該是著重在中文簡報內容與學生是否懂他們所介紹的內容，而不應該太注重在藝術、發音準確度、表演，或是技巧等方面。中文表達只要裁判或老師能聽得懂就可以。而裁判的問題不要過於刁難與艱深，例如，資料來源、分工情形、請學生把某部分再講一次、學生本身的經驗等等，而不要問不在學生介紹範圍內的問題。如果學生的介紹或資料有誤，裁判們可以在該組學生比賽結束後或是總結時間指正跟提供建議。

我們建議各僑校除了比賽方式之外，學校跟老師們可以從用專題、作業、討論的方式開始，讓學生透過自己製作的影片、影音、投影片、壁報、表演等不同創意的方式現場介紹自己的主題。在以中文做口頭簡報之後，學生應該還要當場回答老師或學生所提問的各種跟簡報主題有關的問題，確認學生是否了解主題，同時訓練以中文思考跟應對。這些投影片與簡報影片更可以保留讓學校與老師們當作教學教材。同時，因為海外僑校有些學生中文程度與知識無法完全獨立製作作品，而且網路上的資訊不一定是真實的，在準備過程中，我們鼓勵家長、中文學校任何老師、幹部，或其他成人參與並擔任指導老師，畢竟語言跟文化知識的正確性也很重要。而且我們也建議學生如果剛開始作品無法用中文寫出，可以先用英文尋找，再透過谷歌翻譯[7]或是其他翻譯網頁把英文翻成中文，這樣才能有效地學習中華文化。

新推出的多媒體簡報比賽受到許多家長與老師的推崇，而逐漸把這項中文多媒體競賽推廣到新澤西中文學校協會（2010年開始），以及美東中文學校協會（2012年開始），學生與家長們對於這項新型的學習方式反應非常熱烈。當然，這種比賽方式還是很新，也需要一些設備跟願意投入的老師與幹部的支持，有些僑校還在觀望。我們希望透過這次的全球華文網路研討會，討論與分析一些實際的學生作品與經驗分享，希望能把這種語言學習方式推廣到全美國的中文學校，以及全球所有的華人教育團體，包括台灣一般的中小學教育的國文與外語學習。除了背誦之外，語言跟文化的學習應該要多注重了解

與分析、培養資料查詢能力、比較不同文化、整合表達與應對，希望所有的學校能多加強在這方面的教育。

## 三、比賽形態與評分標準式Contest Style & Scoring Criteria

主題簡報跟作品形式，學生可以使用電子多媒體、肢體表演或平面壁報展示介紹主題，口語說明並與裁判就內容進行問答，可以參考以下形態：

| 靜態展出 | 當場以口頭做中文簡報給裁判與聽眾。學生可以拿稿照唸，但會酌量扣分。例如：壁報、海報、書籍、論文等任何展示形式。學生應該把這些作品主動提供給裁判們看，裁判應該要看過學生所有的作品。 |
|---|---|
| 動態語音與表演 | 作品一部分可以包括事先錄好或是找好的中文影音，但不能超過簡報時間的一半，簡報仍必須以學生當場報告詮釋為主。簡報可以利用下方式：<br>a.電腦與投影機：透過電腦檔案呈現的形式。<br>b.影音：電影、CD / DVD / 電視、錄影帶、錄音帶、任何電器用品形式。<br>c.道具：扯鈴、樂器、玩具、衣物、任何物品形式。<br>d.話劇：相聲、歌唱等任何演唱或是表演方式。 |
| 靜態與動態語音混合 | 學生可以混合以上形式或任何其他形式，穿插靜態展示、口頭介紹、結合任何動態語音與表演。 |

在比賽以前，所有的學生都應該測試自己的電腦或影音器材是否能正確地展現效果，學生作品必須在該組比賽以前完成與布置好，家長與老師可以協助與指導學生製作，但是比賽時只有學生才能簡報、控制電腦跟設備與回答問題，除了主辦單位與比賽學生之外，其他人不得在比賽時提供學生任何協助、聲音與動作。

在班上、校內，或是隊伍少的校際比賽，我們建議以鼓勵性質為主，對於學生的主題與規則不要做太嚴格的限制，這樣才能培養學生主動學習與簡報有興趣的中文知識，而隊伍多的校際比賽則必須注重規則，並且最好有一定的主題，然後讓學生在主題範圍內選擇適合自己的題目，這樣裁判比較容易比較跟打分數，比賽完後，主辦人與裁判們應該要提供講評，讓學生知道如何改進。因為這項比賽是全新的，累積這幾年的經驗，以下評分表是我們所建議的：

| 中文表達：20% | 除專有名詞與數字之外，用非中文（包括英文、廣東話與其他語言）來展示、說明、簡報、回答等等，裁判得以依照嚴重程度扣分。這不是演講或朗誦比賽，所以發音標準都不在評分之內，裁判能聽得懂報告內容才是評分重點。 |
|---|---|
| 主題內容：30% | 評分不應該以題目的難易程度為打分數的依據，而應該以裁判是否很容易明瞭學生介紹的內容、學生蒐集與介紹題目相關資料的深度、對於題目的了解程度。學生花多少時間準備也不應該是評分的依據，應該以簡報當場呈現的效果為主。 |
| 臨場反應：20% | 台風穩健、臨場反應機智。裁判所提問的評分以本項為主，就算學生無法回答裁判的問題，也應該要能適當地回應，而不是愣住與不知所措。 |
| 創意美感：20% | 表現方式、美感、效果、整體印象、團體合作。簡報的方式應該以有助於了解內容為主，學生不需要透過耗時與花俏的方式來講解。 |
| 時間掌握：10% | 簡報時間為三分鐘到四分鐘，不足或是超過，每十秒扣一分。每次回答時間如果超過三十秒，將由計時人員中斷，繼續下一個問題或結束比賽。 |

我們鼓勵家長與老師從旁協助與指導學生做作品，但應該要讓學生自己動手做，裁判問的問題應該以學生簡報內容為主，確認學生了解自己所做的簡報是主要目的，問題應該要簡單明瞭，不應該問過於

艱難與離題，問題可以分成以下兩類：

| 一般性 | 為什麼選這個題目、資料來源、花多少時間準備與製作、遇到什麼樣的困難、用了什麼軟體與材料、如何分工合作、指導老師或家長協助的地方、對於這簡報的效果。 |
|---|---|
| 知識性——與簡報內容有關 | 請學生回到某一頁再解釋一次、學生自己的經驗與對主題中的人、事、物看法、日常生活有哪些跟簡報主題與內容有關、對於主題的感想。 |

## 四、案例討論Case Discussion

　　我們分析這幾年來校內專題報告與比賽、校際競賽學生的專題報告與競賽，我們把學生們曾介紹過的題目分為三大類在以下表格中列出。

| 旅遊與娛樂 | 台灣高鐵、台灣旅遊、台灣的偶像劇、台灣夜市、台灣小吃、北京之旅、台北101、上海世博台灣館、台灣購物、台北一日遊、台灣著名的餐廳、遊北京、中國名勝、台灣的旅遊景點、難忘的台灣夏令營 |
|---|---|
| 生活與習俗 | 米飯、台灣小吃、端午節、稻米的世界、包餃子、學中文的好處、十二生肖、華人的偶像、年輕人的開車方式、餛飩、珍珠奶茶、傳統中國節日、麵食、中國奇特的水果、在白人眼中的華裔學生、中國茶、港式點心 |
| 文化與人物 | 祭孔大典、毛的最後舞者——李存信、林書豪、李小龍、鄭和下西洋、鄭和、扯鈴、元宵節、二胡、算盤、長城、少林功夫、滿族對中華文化的影響、中國舞蹈、海外華人、萬里長城、中國紙張發明的影響、中國鶴、秦始皇兵馬俑、京劇、布袋戲、西安兵馬俑、關穎珊、北港朝天、唐詩的貢獻、中國 |

> 傳統新年、香港英國與中國、台灣與中國、中文造字與六書、孔子、書法、舞蹈、四大發明、中國新年特別的食物、曾雅妮高球之路、《西遊記》、中國端午節的故事、農曆新年、周杰倫、人生保值的中國諺語、詩中的長江和黃河

因為大多數傳統班的學生都來自台灣家庭，因此在旅遊與娛樂方面，大多數的題目都跟台灣有關；而且我們可以從學生的簡報中看到他們對於台灣的體驗與喜歡哪些事情，學中文對於他們日常生活上的幫助。經過交叉分析，我們可以發現雙語班（Chinese as Second Language, CSL）的學生所選擇的題目大都以人物、生活與習俗為主，這也展現出他們學習中文的目的是希望能對日常生活有所幫助。雙語班學生因為學中文環境與時間的限制，簡報多以英文為主，我們覺得這在美國中文學校裡是無法避免，畢竟他們所學的中文單字不多，不可能完全用中文簡報，只要學生從活動中有學到一些生活與文化常識，了解如何應用所學的中文單字，有興趣繼續學習中文，這就達到這項比賽的目的。有些題目可能是由老師或家長建議[8]，目的是希望學生能透過這項活動利用網路研究一些課堂上沒有教的中華文化常識，畢竟美國沒有中文環境，大多數英文學校也不會教導中華文化知識，如果老師與家長不要求跟指導學生去研究一些生活上不常會接觸的事項，學生可能永遠也不會接觸跟了解到這些知識，這也是這項活動另一個特點。

在此，我們特別以2012年新澤西中文學校協會多媒體比賽中年級組第一名的現場影片[9]當作範例來討論，這組三位同學的簡報題目是京劇，她們分工合作找資料、影片、照片、打字，在介紹完她們的簡報後，裁判們提出幾個問題與學生互動，有位學生分享曾參加過的京劇夏令營經驗，還現場講解幾個動作，這就是我們在本文中強調的整合式學習。美東中文學校協會在2013年5月26日年會中第二次舉辦中華文化專題簡報比賽，學生的作品圍繞著今年的主題——端午節[10]，以活潑的方式介紹了端午節的由來、各種習俗，並與裁判們互

動，例如：透過表演與詩詞講解屈原投汨羅江的情形，以話劇表演傳
說中的五毒老爺、以投影片介紹當時的楚國地理位置與戰國時代的情
形、用投影片介紹各地方不同的粽子、以影片介紹如何包粽子、用樂
器演奏《離騷》、再以實際的材料介紹粽子與香包，學生們分享自己
所做的研究讓大家學到很多書本上沒有的知識，裁判與學生之間有趣
的互動，讓在場的老師、學生與家長們感受到這競賽的好處，這種溫
馨的教學相長效果獲得現場大多數人的稱讚。

　　以下兩個圖片是不同多媒體簡報比賽的現場情形，學生以投影片
搭配不同的方式介紹他們的主題，如何讓觀眾與裁判對於所介紹的內
容印象深刻是創意美感的一部分。所謂的多媒體不是只限於電腦，而
應該結合現場的表演，有些知識用很多文字都很難形容，甚至講了半
天可能比不上幾個現場的動作與解說來得有效果，例如扯鈴、舞蹈與
國樂等中華文化才藝，透過多媒體簡報並且結合表演與影音呈現的效
果是令人驚嘆的，這就是整合學習的優點，比賽現場的影片也是很好
的中文上課教材。

圖1　學生以投影片介紹中文造　　圖2　學生以投影片介紹台灣高鐵，
　　　字，並且解說何謂形聲字　　　　　　透過照片與文字，解說高鐵與
　　　　　　　　　　　　　　　　　　　各站資料與風景

　　此外，除了推廣透過多媒體簡報比賽學習中文之外，我們也期
盼中文學校老師們多鼓勵與指導學生們利用多媒體方式學習中文，
不論是英文學校的作業與專題、各種競賽、課外活動與社團的專

案，學習中文不應該只限於中文學校的兩個小時語言課，例如，新
澤西州維德中文學的高年級學生以「利用多媒體教中文」（Teaching
Chinese Through Multimedia）作為她女童軍最高榮譽金牌獎的專
案題目，她把多年所學的知識製作了一系列針對非華裔青少年的中
文教學錄影片，以生活對話的方式分成Greetings[11]、Clothes and
Numbers[12]、Food[13]、Family[14]、Holidays[15]等五個短片放在
YouTube網路，只要有網路與電腦，全世界對學習中文有興趣的人都
可以隨時隨地學習並且重複地觀看，這種結合網路、影音、電腦、互
動的語言學習模式是未來的趨勢，我們應該多鼓勵第二代華裔子弟多
做這方面的專題討論，真正做到語言學習社區化的境界。

## 五、結論Conclusion

　　在海外的中文教育應該要語言文字與文化知識並重，而所謂的中
華文化不應只是局限於文化常識比賽的範疇，也不能是限於像扯鈴等
文化才藝，還應該要包括海內外華人過去、現在社會所有的領域與實
際情形，以及適合現代的華人傳統美德。希望讓學生能透過這項學習
方式的訓練，利用現代電腦科技整合聽、說、讀、打字、跟用中文思
考的能力，鼓勵學生主動研究有趣的華人事物，進而活用所學的語言
跟中華文化知識，老師跟同學們更可以交換經驗、學習課本上沒有的
知識，這是學生與老師雙向討論跟學習的最佳方式。我們更希望在各
中文學校推廣這項活潑與多元的競賽，最後建立起校內、區域到全美
國的中文多媒體簡報競賽系統，就像美國的TSA與 NHD比賽方式，
讓全美國有興趣學中文的學生與老師們能透過這項活動相聚在一起切
磋學習，我們甚至期盼僑委會能針對學生在台灣舉辦世界級的中文多
媒體專題簡報競賽與會議，讓來自全世界的優秀學生與台灣本地學生
在台灣相互學習，透過多媒體簡報與各種社區化的作品來相互學習中
文的語言與文化，以交流的方式透過經驗分享來拓展學生與老師們的
視野。

# 參 考 文 獻

Standards for Foreign Language learning http://www.actfl.org/sites/default/files/pdfs/public/StandardsforFLLexecsumm_rev.pdf

Jersey Shore Science Fair (JSSF) http://www.jssf.us/index.htm

Delaware Valley Science Fairs (DVSF) http://www.drexel.edu/dvsf/index.htm

Intel International Science and Engineering Fair (ISEF) http://www.societyforscience.org/isef

National History Day (NHD) http://www.nhd.org/

Technology Student Association (TSA) http://www.tsaweb.org/

Google Translate http://translate.google.com/

2013年維德中文學校校內多媒體簡報比賽，學生簡報主題「中文造字與六書」http://www.youtube.com/watch?v=lp0youD12ew

2012年新澤西中文學校協會多媒體簡報比賽第一名的比賽現場影片 http://www.youtube.com/watch?v=tdxIKw3VpJQ

2013年美東中文學校協會第四十屆年會中華文化專題簡報比賽，http://www.acsusa.org/acs2013/Welcome.html

Grace Huang, Girl Scout Gold Award project, "Teaching Chinese Through Multimedia Episode 1: Greetings," http://youtu.be/dHA5Br1K_6I, 2012

Grace Huang, Girl Scout Gold Award project, "Teaching Chinese Through Multimedia Episode 2: Clothes and Numbers," http://youtu.be/K-y36W5WPjQ, 2012

Grace Huang, Girl Scout Gold Award project, "Teaching Chinese Through Multimedia Episode 3: Food," http://youtu.be/t0Bp9K8NH8w, 2012

Grace Huang, Girl Scout Gold Award project, "Teaching Chinese Through Multimedia Episode 4: Family," http://youtu.be/KEPzwqspEoc, 2012

Grace Huang, Girl Scout Gold Award project, "Teaching Chinese Through Multimedia Episode 5: Holidays," http://youtu.be/52QI-TzMCfY, 2012

# Chinese Multimedia Contest – A New Horizon in Interactive Digital Chinese Language Learning

**Ching-yu Austin Huang**（黃清郁）

Department of Computer Science, Kean University, New Jersey, USA

chuang@kean.edu

**Jing-Chiou Liou**（劉景秋）

Department of Computer Science, Kean University, New Jersey, USA

jliou@kean.edu

## Abstract

In traditional Chinese language education, various Chinese language contests are mostly in the mode of unidirectional communication. In such contests, students usually just demonstrate their language knowledge to the audience without any interaction and feedback and are not able to express their learning experience. Hence, these types of contests lack of the integration of multi-dimension of a language. With the advance in digital learning and information in the Internet, students should go beyond the classroom language instruction, and take the advantage of digital multimedia to gain knowledge in multi-dimension of the Chinese language. In this paper, we propose a new concept in digital interactive Chinese language learning that utilizes digital multimedia contests for students to creatively link current and past Chinese culture and history knowledge into their language skills. This Chinese multimedia contest can help students to think beyond what are taught by the teachers. Moreover, it will also allow a strong interaction between students and audience to exchange ideas on Chinese culture and history knowledge. Both help to build a live experience in Chinese learning.

Keywords: Multimedia instruction、Internet learning、Chinese culture、Standards for foreign language learning、Interactive learning、Heritage Chinese School

# 建構影片為華語文教學的
# 「四、五、六學習空間」

周小玉[1]
台灣亞洲大學幼兒教育學系

劉渼
新加坡南洋理工大學新加坡華文教研中心

## 摘要

　　本文探討影片可以提供哪些面向的華文學習空間。首先，討論影片用來設計聽說讀寫「四」技的學習空間。其次，討論影片可提供「五」Cs目標的溝通、文化、連結、比較、社區之學習空間。再次，除了上述四技外，討論影片用來設計口語互動、書面互動的「六」技學習空間。接著，將上述」四、五、六學習空間」，應用在課堂教學上，學生可以自行觀看影片來學習華語文。最後，本文將說明影片和平臺學習空間的實用性及優點。

關鍵字：影片教學、聽說讀寫、口語互動、書面互動

## 一、前言

　　微電影（micro film）相對於傳統電影敘事的一大優勢，在於僅僅幾分鐘的時間便能夠講述一個情節完整、內容感人且具有思想性的故事。微電影的三個鮮明特徵：一是通過專業團隊製作；二是以電影

---

手法進行故事講述；三是經由網絡等進行傳播。本文所論及的影片具備著類似微電影的特徵，不過是以支持學生的華語學習為目的，都是經過完整策劃和系統製作體系支持的具完整故事情節和語言學習點的「微（超短）時」（3-5分鐘）影片。

影片中的主題內容，提供了二語學習者不同生活情境和文化語境的學習，用影片來學習華語，其目的是將眞實生活情境帶入課堂中，幫助學生再次造訪各種情景語境，以便將來在生活中遇到類似的情況，能夠自然地應用出來。

本文首先探討影片在華語文教學的相關文獻和理論背景；其次，提出設計和製作華語文教學影片的原則和注意事項；接著，探討影片所提供的不同面向的華文學習空間，依次為「四」、「五」、「六」的學習空間。最後說明影片如何應用在課堂教學中。

## 二、影片製作和應用在華語文教學的文獻探討和理論背景

### ㈠文獻探討

姑且不論教師們使用影片的目的為何，近半世紀來影片已是教育現場廣為接受，也是不可或缺的素材，不僅如此，影片的使用同時也是二語和外語教師普遍接受的教學元素。根據Branigan（2005）的觀察，多媒體功能的電腦、低價位的剪輯軟體和網速容量的提升，學校教師競相地將影片做為教學工具。事實上影片作為二語或外語教學的理論和研究並不少見（Altman, 1989），但是應用在英文為二語或外語的學習還是最為普遍（Stempleski, 1987; Canning-Wilson, 2000; McNulty和Lazarevic, 2012）。

影片可用在各式各樣的教學情境中（Burt, 1999）。由於影片的種類眾多，涵蓋面廣，從文獻中可知，學者或教師們對於影片的定義不盡相同，包括了電影、連續劇、情境喜劇（sitcoms）、卡通、紀錄片、訪問、討論、運動節目、脫口秀、遊戲節目、教育性影片、

新聞、天氣報告、各式各樣的廣告、語言教學影片等（Stempleski, 1987; Sherman, 2003）。

　　Stempleski（1987）以製作目的不同作為分類標準，將影片分為兩類：一類是一般人可常常接觸到的真實性影片，另一類則是與目標語教學有關的影片。將真實性影片用在語言教學的用途上，雖然容易，花費也低，但由於影片未能依語言程度來分級，在使用上有其難點。陳立芬（2007）指出，利用電視影片進行華文學習，影片中的文化議題、語用的隱義、場景取境和拍攝手法是學生感興趣的話題，但是學生對影片的理解，往往因為角色的咬字清晰度、劇情對話中所夾雜的熟語、文言等原因，降低了學習者對於內容的理解。Talavan（2007）也不約而同地指出這類型的影片在教學上較難以掌控。至於，強調語言學習的教學影片，製作上的優點是能配合學習者的語言水準和學習目的，如日常會話、商業情境對話、目標語文化、聽力和文法等。Herron, Cole, Corrie和Dubreil（2000）的研究分析發現，初級的外語學習者能借助於教學影片有效地理解目標語的文化實踐。但是，Stempleski（1987）則指出相對於前面提到的真實性影片，語言教學影片內容通常較不真實，或者比較無趣。綜上所述，可知依影片製作目的所分出來的兩大類影片的優缺點互補。

　　Arslanyilmaz（2007）在其博士論文指出，由母語者演出的真實、有字幕、相似任務的影片（Authentic Subtitled Similar Task Videos-ASSTVs），且分配給學習者的任務跟影片內容知識相關，可以提高學習者的語言。這是因為通過反思，比較和連結自己的語言使用經驗，學習者建立了一個近似於母語者的記憶儲存。Arslanyilmaz運用ASSTVs作為一種方法，在網上的第二語言學習環境，使用相似的任務以增強意義協商和語言的產出。他用的影片片段雖然是記錄真實生活的情境背景，但它的腳本卻是預先寫出來給演員的，且演員都是母語者，再加上隨後剪輯的影片片段及配上的字幕，都是為研究目的服務的。

## ㈡ 理論背景

焦點於製作兼具眞實性和教學特點的教學影片開發，我們借用Mehrabian（1971）的溝通模式理論、Dale的金字塔學習理論（1969）和Shedroff（1999）的訊息互動設計理論。

### 1.Mehrabian的溝通模式

Mehrabian的研究指出，當人們收集到的各種資訊不一致時，其總體效果等於7%的言語聯繫（言辭），加38%的聲音聯繫（聲調），加上55%的面部表情和肢體聯繫（見圖1）。由此可知，面部表情和肢體語言非常重要，從眼神、姿勢到距離，拿捏得適當，溝通交流會起到事半功倍的效果。基於上述的研究發現，Mehrabian因此提出「三V公式」的溝通訊息，即口語（Verbal），聲音（Voice）與視覺（Visual）。

根據上述理論，我們認爲三V公式是任何視覺性產品在製作上需要關注的溝通要素。本研究用影片來進行華語文教學，藉由聽到和看到溝通對象所傳達出來的話語、聲音、面部表情和肢體語言等，來幫助學習者有效地溝通交流。我們的焦點仍然在語言的學習，但透過語音、語氣、音調等來增強語言輸入的可理解性，又透過表情等來正面增強學生對語言的理解。

圖1　Mehrabian的溝通模式

## 2.學習金字塔理論

　　「學習金字塔」學習方式的理論，支援了用影片來教學的有效性。「學習金字塔」（Cone of Learning）是美國愛德加‧戴爾（Edger Dale, 1969）《視聽教學法》一書中所提出的，緬因州的國家訓練實驗室（National Training Laboratories）用數字形式形象地顯示採用不同的學習方式，學習者在兩週以後其平均學習保持率，也就是還能記住內容多少的比率（見圖2）。

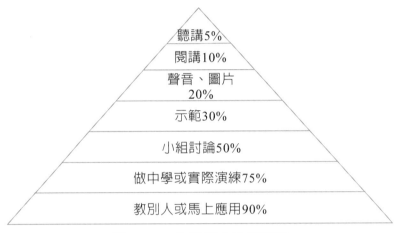

聽講5%

閱講10%

聲音、圖片20%

示範30%

小組討論50%

做中學或實際演練75%

教別人或馬上應用90%

圖2　Dale的學習金字塔理論

　　本研究根據戴爾的學習金字塔理論，在製作層面上把聽講、閱讀、聲音、示範四要素同步呈現在影片上，增加訊息接收的管道，以滿足不同學習風格（多元智慧）者的需求。又透過小組討論、做中學和應用等活動，來鞏固強化其學習，增加學習的愉悅感，以調動其學習動機，並加深其記憶的內化。

　　但在操作時，會注意認知負荷量的問題，所以採取Stempleski（1987）所建議的，選取較短的片段來播放，以減輕學生認知負荷的問題。因為相對於其他藝術來說，影片對時間有著絕對的控制權，它賦予時間一種價值，並且可以隨意地分割、打亂和重新安

排，從而創造出自由的、擺脫外界一切束縛的延續時間。我們利用影片的三種時間：放映時間、劇情時間（故事時間）、心理時間來精心製作較短的影片，並設計華語文的學習活動。

### 3. 訊息互動設計理論

Shedroff（1999）提出訊息互動設計理論框架：即交叉學科的資訊化設計（Information design），交互設計（interaction design）和感官設計（sensorial design）（見圖3）。

圖3　Shedroff的訊息互動設計理論

Shedroff的「資訊設計」指的是出版和圖形設計，也就是說，將數據加以系統的組織和呈現，轉化成有價值的、有意義的資訊。感官設計，簡單地說，就是運用所有的技術，通過視覺和聽覺的感官來和受眾者／學習者溝通。在寫好腳本後，通常最先被認可和採用的是視覺設計技術，如平面設計，錄像，攝影，排版，插圖，攝影。在某些適當的情況下，聲音的設計工程、音樂和人聲，也是非常有用的。Shedroff認爲交互設計的本質，無論在古老的藝術或新媒體技術，都是創造故事和說故事。媒體一直影響著說故事和創作經驗，目前新媒體提供了許多功能和機會，從影像敘事技巧方面來說，打破了線性敘事的習慣，出現菜單式講述故事、關鍵詞式講述故事、資料庫式講述故事等新方式。如何通過互動技術來展示故事的創造和說故事，觀眾

將有什麼樣的要求和興趣，這是交互性產品成功的關鍵步驟。本研究於是根據Shedroff的理論框架，提出設計和製作華語文教學影片的三層面框架（見下節）。

## 三、設計和製作華語文教學影片的要素與原則

教學影片的製作既要具備眞實生活內容，又要有語言學習焦點，且能引起學生的學習動機和興趣。以下根據Shedroff（1999）的訊息互動設計理論，並結合實際製作華語文教學影片的經驗，從資訊處理、感官呈現、互動體驗三方面（見圖4），探討影片在規劃和製作過程中需要關切的要素與原則（見圖5）。

### ㈠ 信息處理

我們認爲對影片資訊的處理原則是：貼近眞實生活、連結學習者的新舊經驗，以促成跨文化理解：

1. 貼近眞實生活：影片中的主題內容的，須從眞實生活中龐雜多元的資訊裡，有目的地選取其中有用的資訊（如話題性、專題性內容），使其近似學生要完成的學習任務；且要加以妥善處理，如針對語能能力較弱的二語學習者，要替換詞彙、簡化語言、放慢語速、誇大表情等，以滿足學習者的興趣、需求，並符合其語言水準。

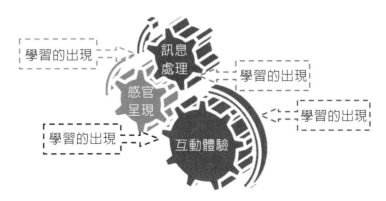

圖4　根據Shedroff（1999）的訊息互動設計的理論框架

圖5　設計和製作華語文教學影片的要素與原則

2. 連結新舊經驗：影片中的情景和對話內容，能喚起學習者的舊經
   驗，且影片中的規範性語言和常見習語要起著示範作用，幫助學
   習者觀摩、模仿、培養語感，且連結到其自身的生活，在生活中
   應用所學到的語言。
3. 促成跨文化理解：影片中人物的行為舉止和言談，提供母語者應
   用語言的環境，促成學習者的跨文化理解。

(二) 感官呈現

　　我們認為影片感官呈現的原則是：利用拍攝和製作等技巧，如用
留白或跳接手法以造成受眾者／學習者視覺上的資訊差，以增加影片
的趣味性、突顯戲劇張力，並發展其推理想像空間：

4. 增加趣味性：影片的多感官觸媒（stimulus）和娛樂性內容，能滿
   足不同學習風格者，享受在不同的感官世界中，以提高其學習興
   趣和動機。
5. 突顯戲劇張力：影片中的戲劇張力，如語音、語調、表情和肢體
   語言等，有助於學習者理解說話者的意圖和隱藏資訊。
6. 發展推理想像：善用拍攝、運鏡和剪輯等技巧，如將畫面留白，
   幫助學習者根據故事情節，以發展其認知推理和想像空間。

## (三) 互動體驗

　　我們認為影片互動體驗的原則是：影片須提供語言習得的鷹架和互動對話的機會，並進行有意義的溝通：

7. 習得的鷹架：影片中嵌入（embedded）語言點，且根據學習者的語言水準來設置對話，以隱性學習（implicit learning）的方式，幫助學習者自然地習得。且影片中的視覺、聽覺和文字元號（如字幕）等要素的單獨存在，或要素點間的交互連結或連鎖推進，形成多感官刺激的習得鷹架。

8. 互動的對話：影片中的互動對話，可作為「明示-推理」的示例，且引起觀賞後的師生或生生互動討論，影片中所運用的互動策略，可幫助學生增強其溝通互動能力。

9. 意義的溝通：影片須提供學習者資訊差、可理解的輸入（Krashen, 1985），幫助其進行意義協商和主動建構知識的機會，使學習者在有意義的情境中學習，並有機會輸出語言。

　　影片作為一個視聽的載體，通過聲、光、影、色再現生活畫面，繼而形成代碼信號，為受眾所解碼並最終產生意義。因此通過影片中的語言和畫面的互相滲透、相輔相成，能夠營造出有助於二語學習的聽、說、讀、寫學習空間，且影片的主題內容，也能營造出溝通、文化、比較、連結、社區的5C學習內容，再加上口語互動和書面互動技能，而影片中的大量對話和疊映效果，能有效地營造出語言六技的學習空間，茲說明如下（見圖6）：

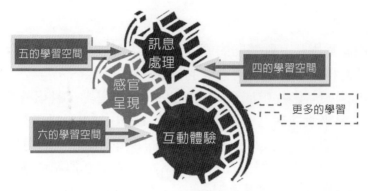

圖6　影片中的「四」、「五」、「六」學習空間

## 四、「四」的學習空間

　　「四」的空間指的是一般語言教師熟悉的聽、說、讀、寫四個能力。以下將先說明影片本身可以營造哪些聽說讀寫的學習空間,並在說明每個技能之後以教學活動舉例說明。

### (一) 聽

　　在聽方面,影片提供了語速快慢、語調高低、語氣輕重、音量大小等的示範。影片中角色使用語音、語調、表情和肢體語言適度地呈現戲劇表現力,這些經過排練的語言和肢體表達,有助於學習者理解說話者的意圖和隱藏資訊。此外,影片也提供有效傾聽的技巧示範,可以讓學習者透過「聽」影片的任務了解傾聽的用詞、傾聽的技能、傾聽的層次和傾聽的禁忌。

　　特意地處理角色的語音表現是基於Mehrabian(1971)提出在溝通訊息時,理解的達成有38%是起於聲音(vocal)的幫助,用這類非語言來傳情達意可包括說話的口吻語氣、語音、語調、語速等條件的充足性。影片製作上進行這樣的處理,同時是希望藉著加強性輸入(Sharwood Smith, 1991)來引起二語學習者對音調的認識和熟悉,在表達時語氣加重,語調改變或轉折,語速放慢,聲音提高等引起其

認知上的注意（noticing）。以下的「聽」影片活動，便是希望藉著二語學習者能了解和注意與人對話時的聲音使用，正因為該元素的使用能協助和增加他們的語言理解力。

「四」的學習空間──「聽」的教學活動：

| 教學目標： |
| --- |
| 1. 學生能藉由聽影片中角色的語音、語調和語氣，了解話輪轉換與承接的例子。<br>2. 學生能使用對話中的詞語：其實、不過、應該、你說得沒錯、雖然是這樣等詞，進行話輪的轉換與承接。 |
| 教學步驟： |
| ⑴ 教師在學生先聽過或看過「誤會」影片中的片段後（對話一），請學生說明所聽到的對話者是誰以及對話內容的大意。<br>⑵ 教師再放該影片片段一次，給予學習任務請學生注意聽志偉和俊浩二人對話時，用了什麼詞語（其實、不過，見對話一黑體字）進行話輪的轉換。<br>⑶ 學生再重複聽同樣的影片片段一次，教師給予學習任務請學生注意聽志偉和俊浩二人對話時，用了什麼詞語（應該、你說得沒錯、雖然是這樣，見對話一黑體字）作為話輪承接之用。<br>⑷ 學生提出話輪中轉換和承接的詞語後，教師可以進行標的詞語的教學或練習。例如，影印對話一的內容讓學生標出影片中的轉換和承接詞語，以結合「讀」的語言學習。此外，也可以將對話一的內容刪掉，只保留轉換和承接的詞語，讓學生創作可能的對話內容，這是結合「寫」的語言教學。 |
| 註：若是教學對象的華語程度較高，教師可以結合步驟二和三的活動任務。 |

對話一：

志偉：過後，我又收到你的短信。我就想，怎麼那麼倒楣，東

西買貴了，朋友又生我的氣。

俊浩：**其實**（話輪轉換），你收到短信後，**應該**（話輪承接）先問清楚的。

志偉：**你說得沒錯**（話輪承接），我**應該**（話輪承接）先問清價錢才對。

俊浩：同樣的，你收到我的短信後，**也應該**（話輪承接）先問清楚的。

志偉：**雖然是這樣**（話輪承接），**不過（可是）**（話輪轉換），我昨天已經沒心情問你了。

俊浩：嗯，下次記得問清楚。

志偉：我會記得的，我可不想再這麼丟臉了（結束話輪）。


## □說

　　在說方面，影片提供了咬字吐音、意圖功能（如清楚地表情達意）、形式功能（如語法正確）、語用功能（如表達得體）等的示範；此外，影片中角色的對話有聲音、表情、肢體語言等副語言的協助，加強了戲劇的表現力外，也提供二語學習者更多的學習刺激，聯繫理解外，也提供學習者認識非語言元素在語言表達的意義和效果，了解口語互動中語言和非語言元素的綜合運用，可用來增加表達看法的能力。

「四」的學習空間——「說」的教學活動：

教學目標：
1. 學生能藉由觀看影片中角色的肢體表達，了解說話時也可運用口語的技巧來補充或加深自己的說明或看法。
2. 學生能藉由觀看「熱帶風情」影片中片段透過角色的對話了解說明事物的方法（數字說明、舉例說明）。

教學步驟：

(1)教師將對話二的內容，用有影像、沒聲音、沒字幕的方式播放，
之後，請同學列出角色所使用的非語言動作，如表情、姿勢、肢
體動作等，之後再根據角色的非語言動作討論二個角色之間的可
能對話內容，並發表。或者教師可在角色明顯使用肢體處以暫停
的方式，讓同學針對影片的定格點，發表角色所使用肢體語言的
可能對話。

　（**非肢體語言的呈現：對話二角色台詞後括弧內的的表演說明，**
**見對話二**）

(2)教師提示觀看影片對話二中的任務，要學生注意角色用來說明事
物的方法，再以有影像、聲音和字幕的方式播放影片。觀看對話
二的影片後將學生分組，進行討論劇中角色用了哪些（數字和舉
例，見對話二黑體字）說明事物的方法，以及說明時提供了哪些
訊息。之後，請同學發表。

(3)教師解釋完畢後，老師發給每組任務單，註明要用數字說明的事
物，如機場、學校的食堂等地方，要學生討論後以數字和描述的
方式來說明所分配到的地方或事物。

註：學生如果華文程度好，步驟三的活動可以結合「寫」的語言學習，要學
　　生寫下所說明的內容。

對話二：

志偉：麗文，等等我。（滿頭大汗、氣喘吁吁的樣子）

麗文：快點，快到了。

志偉：到哪裡？

麗文：碧山公園最高的地方。你看，這邊幾乎可以看到每一個
　　　角落。（把手放在眼睛上遠望四方）

志偉：哦，碧山公園還真大！（表示驚訝）

麗文：對啊！這裡有9個足球場那麼大呢（數字說明）。（用手
　　　比劃其大）

志偉：太大了！今天走不完了，回家吧！

麗文：不行！我們今天來到這裡是要做我們的專題作業的。而
　　　且碧山公園的環境這麼美麗，**一年內就有300萬人來參
　　　觀，不走完太可惜了**（數字說明）。

志偉：為什麼大家喜歡來？

麗文：**第一，交通方便，你看，我們剛才坐地鐵很快就到了**
　　　（舉例說明）。（邊走邊伸出指頭指向地鐵站。或疊印
　　　二人從地鐵站出來的畫面）

志偉：沒錯，真的很方便（點頭）

麗文：**第二，來這裡曬曬太陽，放鬆心情，壓力就沒有那麼大
　　　了**（舉例說明）。（在草地旁停下來，背景是有人在悠
　　　閒地走路，有人在一旁做深呼吸的動作。）

志偉：（開始擦汗，搖頭，做不屑狀）

麗文：**最後，這裡的設備很多，週末的時候大家可以來活動活
　　　動**（舉例說明）。

志偉：這裡又曬又熱。（擦汗）我要去吹冷氣。

麗文：整天吹冷氣，很不環保喔！（指志偉）

志偉：但是很熱。（不耐煩的表情）

麗文：走，我帶你去樹下，那裡比較涼爽。（往前走）

志偉：還要走啊，我想回家了。（哀號不肯跟著走。但是被麗
　　　文拉到公園樹下。）


㈢讀

　　在讀方面，影片不僅提供了文本閱讀的學習，而且也給予學習者
視覺閱讀（visual literacy）、剪輯（montage）等的機會，二者的相
互作用同時能促成理解的深化。

　　以「熱帶風情」的影片為例，在劇中人物舉例說明新加坡之所以漂亮之處時，提出「因為新加坡太陽很大，天氣很熱，雨水很多，花草樹木也多，所以才有漂亮的風景」，這時影片的處理不是只用「說」的方式來點出新加坡風景漂亮的原因，畫面的處理為了增加視覺閱讀的趣味性和理解性，同時用太陽、雨水、花、草四個畫面來強化理解。以字幕取代一般文本的閱讀，逐行出現文本的方式增加閱讀的動感和樂趣，再以視覺畫面的搭配，學習者可以快速連結所提到的風景漂亮的原因。對於二語能力低者，視覺的閱讀深化了該語段的理解。此外，影片的語言學習處理之一是根據學習者的語言水準設置對話，並嵌入語言點，協助華語較弱學習者的學習，因此影片腳本的閱讀可以是一個經常使用，並且可以提升學習者閱讀能力的教學活動。

「四」的學習空間──「讀」的教學活動：

| 教學目標： |
| --- |
| 1. 學生透過真實性影片提供的閱讀經驗，即文字閱讀、字幕閱讀和視覺閱讀，說明自己的閱讀感受和了解自己的閱讀習慣。<br>2. 學生能以不同的閱讀方式理解所播放影片片段的訊息。 |
| 教學步驟： |
| ⑴教師以不同方式播放以下三個影片片段，並逐次請學生發表所理解的內容。<br>　①以定格「真人圖書館」影片中的畫面，並讓學生閱讀影片上的電郵<br>　②以只有字幕的方式閱讀「家有一老」影片中的片段<br>　③以只有影像的方式觀看「熱帶風情」影片中的片段<br>⑵教師再次播放三部影片片段，請學生提出對於所播放影片的閱讀感受。<br>⑶教師請學生以二人一組的方式與同學分享自己偏好哪種或哪些閱讀方式，以及理由。之後，教師請數位同學發表自己偏好的閱讀習慣和理由。 |
| 註：該活動也可以簡單化，只焦點於閱讀其中一影片片斷的理解。 |

## (四) 寫

在寫方面，影片提供了二語學習者寫劇本、對話腳本、電郵、日誌、讀書報告、評論等學習空間。

為了輔助學習者的理解，影片製作過程中特別注意對話的處理和語言點的置入，加上文字和視聽刺激的學習鷹架，目的是激起學習者的動機，願意親近影片中所提供的語言文本、聽覺文本或視覺文本內容，進而產生與影片內容的互動。影片能提供的語言學習活動，文類眾多。除此之外，既可以提供廣大的創意空間，也可以依學習者的華語能力加以的調整到很聚焦的語言點學習。例如看完影片後，可以針對影片的話題或內容寫觀後感，甚至可以自行創作劇本或對話；若是微技巧的寫作可以套用影片內容的句型或架構，進行句子、段落或是整篇作文的書寫。

「四」的學習空間——「寫」的教學活動：

教學目標：
1. 學生能透過與真人圖書館的「書」的對話，了解如何和人交談與發問問題。
2. 學生能夠針對要訪問的人物，擬出至少五個要訪問的問題。

教學步驟：
(1) 教師在觀看影片的片段前，要學生注意人與「書」的對話（見對話三黑體字）內容，觀看完後，學生說出麗文所訪問的問題。
(2) 學生分組討論麗文所訪問問題的目的，如打招呼、讚美、表示興趣等。
(3) 教師提問學生最有興趣訪問的人是誰？如足球明星、總理、校長等，選定要訪問的人後，學生分組討論和擬出要訪問的五個問題。
(4) 老師扮演學生要訪問的人物，學生以集體角色的方式扮演同一個訪問者，向教師所扮演的角色發問。

註：步驟四的活動，受訪者可以由學生擔任。

對話三：

麗文和借的「書」在圖書館一角坐下。

麗文：你好！我是麗文。（打招呼）

演員：你好！我是曾曉芬。

麗文：我看過你演的戲。你演得很好。（讚美）

演員：謝謝你。

麗文：我想聽聽你的故事。（表示興趣）

演員：我很樂意告訴你。

麗文：首先，我想問你為什麼想當演員？（職業選擇）

演員：因為我喜歡表演。除了這個原因之外，我還想讓更多人
　　　認識我。

麗文：你認為當演員難嗎？（工作難易度）

演員：你認為呢？

麗文：我覺得當演員很容易。只要長得好看，就會有很多人喜
　　　歡你。（回應）

演員：其實，當演員不能只是長得好看而已。也要努力學習
　　　的。

麗文：怎麼說呢？（期待解釋）

演員：因為演員要扮演各種角色。如果你不努力學習，就會演
　　　得不好了。

麗文：那你怎麼做？（方法）

演員：我得了解他們的生活、表情、動作，和說話的語氣。

麗文：你用什麼方法去了解呢？（方法）

演員：多和不同的人談天，多觀察人們的生活，讓自己更了解
　　　他們。

麗文：這樣就可以了嗎？（確定）

演員：我還要從電影和電視中，學習別人怎麼演戲。

麗文：真不容易啊。（**反饋**）

演員：對啊！當演員很辛苦的。

麗文：怎麼說呢？（**期待解釋**）

演員：我們常常出外景，外面又熱又沒有地方換衣服、上廁
　　　所。

麗文：那你們怎麼辦？（**方法**）

演員：我們只能忍。

麗文：真的很辛苦。（**反饋**）

演員：對，不過當演員也有好玩的地方。我們可以到不同的國
　　　家去拍電影，也能認識很多新朋友。觀眾喜歡我，我就
　　　會很開心。

麗文：（笑）看來當演員有苦有樂，真不容易啊。（**反饋**）


## 五、「五」的學習空間

　　影片為二語學習者所提供「五」的學習空間，是指美國
外語教學協會（ACTFL）所提出的5Cs（National Standards
in Foreign Language Education Project, 1999），包括溝通
（Communication）、文化（Culture）、連結（Connections）、比
較（Comparisons）和社區（Communities），以下從影片的主題內
容來談其所提供「五」的學習空間：

### ㈠溝通：是指運用中文達到溝通目的

1. 人際交流：指學生以交談方式詢問或提供訊息、交換意見及表達
　 情感。

　　影片中的互動對話，可作為「明示-推理」的示例。在人際交流
方面，最重要的是要意識到，人可以不同意另一個人的想法，但仍
然可以承認對方是從不同角度來看待事情的，也就是說，即使你不同
意對方，不一定要直說「我不同意你的觀點」，而可以換不同的說法

來婉轉表達，如：「我知道你從這個角度來看」、「我非常感謝你的關注」、「這是一個重要的問題」，用這種方式來承認的他人的意圖，卻不一定意味著他們是正確的。這是溝通交際中的「禮貌」原則，所以影片中的對話，要符合此一原則。

　　以「誤會」一片為例，俊浩說：「你收到短信後，應該先問清楚的。」、「同樣的，你收到我的短信後，也應該先問清楚的。」都是學生以交談方式詢問的例子。

2. 理解詮釋：指學生了解並能詮釋各種口語及書面的主題內容

　　人際交流的非語言方面，包括了體態語（肢體語言）、身體的接觸（觸覺）、空間關係、時間因素、保持沉默、某種意象物和身體外表等。Wood（2008）認為口頭話語和非語言溝通之間的最大差異是非語言溝通往往更值得信賴，因為它表達出真實的情感。因此，藉由影片的視覺效果所傳達出的非語言資訊，不但有助於溝通理解，且有助於強化溝通者的互信。

　　在「誤會」一片中，志偉和俊浩在影片一開始就因為短信而有了誤會，所以二人談話一會兒低頭，志偉的身體還稍稍退後，很自然地用身體語言說明瞭二人因為發生的誤會而有了距離，這些都需要老師在課堂上用明顯的教學法指引出來。

3. 表達演示：指學生透過表達方式，將不同理念及內容表達給聽眾或讀者。

　　在影片中沒有提供表達演示的示例，不過老師需要透過活動設計來進行。比如「街頭藝術」就讓學生在學習的最後面，進行上臺的表達演示（詳見七）。

（二）文化：是指體認並了解中華多元文化

1. 文化習俗：指學生能表達對華人社會習俗的了解與認識，並能應對得體。

2. 文化產物：指學生能表達對中華文化、藝術、歷史、文學知識和理解。

　　影片本身就是一種獨特的文化形態：首先，影片是一種物質文化，以科技爲媒介的工業生產；其次，影片也是一種制度、體制文化；最後，影片是一種作爲人類精神產品的藝術。影片也是一種文化傳播媒介，一種視覺符號，承擔著文化傳播功能。影片中的形象體現出文化價值觀，有潛移默化的「文化滲透」作用，其影響力是不容忽視的。以下舉主題內容與文化直接相關的「誤會」一片來說明：

　　在「誤會」一片中，因爲文化用語的不同而造成了誤會。如在二岸三地，打八折是折扣二十巴仙，可是學生很可能用翻譯的方式去理解打八折的意思，以爲是折扣八十巴仙，在價錢上就會有很大的落差：

　　　　*阿姨手拿著廣告傳單，傳單上有電子遊戲
　　　　機打八折的優惠，拿出手機傳短信給志偉。
　　　　志偉在校門口收到阿姨發來的短信：「志　（書面互動）
　　　　偉，阿姨看到最新款式的遊戲機正在打八
　　　　折，限量只有5台，你要買嗎？」
志偉：打八折，這麼便宜一定要買啊。（志偉自
　　　　言自語）
志偉回「阿姨，請你快點幫我買，謝謝。」
短信給
阿姨：
　　　　過了一會兒，阿姨開開心心地提著一個購
　　　　物袋，站在街邊發短信給志偉：「我幫你
　　　　買到了，一共是400元。」
　　　　志偉看到短信上的價錢嚇了一跳，打電話
　　　　給阿姨。
志偉：喂，請問是阿姨嗎？我是志偉。　　　（口語互動）
阿姨：嗨，志偉。

志偉：　阿姨，謝謝你幫我買到了遊戲機。　　　禮貌原則

阿姨：　不客氣，還好你說快點買，那是最後一台了。

志偉：　阿姨，可是，它是400元嗎？　　　　　確認核實

阿姨：　是啊！

志偉：　打八折，八十巴仙，不是100元嗎？　確認核實

阿姨：　哈哈，打八折是折扣二十巴仙。

志偉：　（先沉默想了一想，然後恍然大悟）哦，
　　　　我搞錯了，對不起啊！

## (三) 連結：是指結合並貫連其他學科

影片中將課文中提到的「熱帶風情」三元素：陽光、綠色植物和水，藉由碧山公園來再次呈現出來。影片是有意識地進行拓展性連結：首先是將機場和碧山公園裡的二個地方場景相連結，前者人為的裝置藝術，後者是自然景觀，透過二者的對比呼應，讓學生明白生活元素是來自大自然的。

其次是將「陽光機場」裡所描述的三元素，和學生的生活場域相連結，比如隨處可見的各種透光、水牆、綠牆等的裝飾藝術，讓學生明白「陽光機場」一課所說的「熱帶風情」，不是單一的藝術創作個案，而是一種真實的生活原貌，以培養學生的敏銳的觀察力和豐富的感性經驗，以鞏固其所學。

最後是透過課堂活動，如尋找其他熱帶意象，將學生所學遷移到整個新加坡的代表象徵物。

所以「陽光機場」的課文雖然較長，詞語較難，但學生只要學習到核心概念，透過幅射式的向外連結，就很容易理解課文，鞏固所學和遷移學習，以加深其理解和應用的能力。

## (四) 比較：是指領悟並比較不同語言與文化的特性

1.比較語言：指學生比較華文及其母語而促進對語文本質的了解。

2. 比較文化：指學生比較中華文化與其本國文化而達成對文化本質的了解。

　　比較的議題在影片中處處可見，生活方面，如「草莓族」一片中比較了二位中學生，一位因爲輸球而不想打球了，因而引起了草莓族之譏和反思，另一位則因爲腳受傷還練習投球，因而激勵了同伴。在「眞人圖書館」中比較了做演員的苦與樂。在「街頭藝術」中比較了亂畫和街頭藝術的不同。

　　但是比較對於二語學習者來說，其眞正的意義就是進行跨文化的比較，如「誤會」一片中文化用語的比較，老師在課堂上還用了更多的例子來比較跨文化的不同，如土豆在中國是馬鈴薯，在台灣是花生，又如伸出大姆指和食指的手勢，在中國是數字八的意思，在新加坡和台灣則代表數字七。上述的比較都有助於學生對跨文化差異的理解。

㈤ 社區：是指應用於社區與國際多元社會

1. 學以致用：指學生可以在校內校外運用中文。
2. 學無止境：指學生將中華語言文化溶於日常生活，成爲終身學習者。

　　在「街頭藝術」一片中，以社會創意團體爲例，其在社區裡號召組屋區的居民一起創作壁畫，來說明社區人士宜彼此扶持，共同創造美好的社區生活。

　　影片中談到畫壁畫的人，「這些人有的四、五歲，有的七、八十歲。」充分舉出了終身學習的實例，二位中學生後來也參與了該社團，一起加入終身學習的行列。

# 六、「六」的學習空間

　　新加坡2010年母語教育檢討委員會報告書中強調母語學習的「六」技，也就是在語言四技外，加上了基於語言四技的口語互動和書面互動，語言四技見「四」的學習空間，以下僅針對口語互動和書

面互動來談：

## (一) 口語互動

在口語互動方面，影片的規範性語言和習慣用語起著示範性的作用，而觀看影片時，其中對話的互動技巧，有助於學生潛移默化地習得它，至於觀看影片後的師生、生生等活動設計，則是通過互動技能和意義協商過程的顯性教學，來鞏固學生的學習，並遷移到生活的應用中（詳見七）。

### 1.影片中的示範性作用

以「家有一老」為例，應用了許多的話語標記，以培養學生互動時的技巧和語感，如：

*他們剛好走過斜坡設計的走道。

美華：（指了指走道）這個也是嗎？

媽媽：對啊，有了這個走道，輪椅就可以推上去。

美華：除了輪椅，還可以讓嬰兒車推上去。

媽媽：說得沒錯。

美華：這樣阿公就可以自己幫自己了。

媽媽：雖然是這樣，不過阿公還是需要很多生活上的幫助。

「對啊。」是話輪承接的話語標記。「說得沒錯。」也是話輪承接的話語標記，起到回應上一話輪觀點的作用，是肯定性銜接成分。

### 2.強調互動技能和意義協商過程

以「真人圖書館」為例，麗文借書的片段中，圖書館管理員和麗文的對話如下：

麗文：　你好，我要借這本書。　　　　　　互動技能和意義協商過程

　　　　管理員辦好借閱手續之後把書拿
　　　　給麗文。

管理員：我們有「真人書」可以借哦！　　觸發語（Trigger）

麗文：　「真人書」？什麼是「真人書」　示意語（Indicator）
　　　　　　　　　　　　　　　　　　　　澄清請求

管理員：「真人書」是一個活生生的人。應答語（Response）
　　　　我們「看」書的方法就是和這本
　　　　「真人書」說話。

麗文：　原來如此，真有趣。我想看看。　對應答語的回應
　　　　　　　　　　　　　　　　　　　（Reaction to the
　　　　　　　　　　　　　　　　　　　Response）

　　影片中根據Long（1983）的互動假設（Interaction Hypothesis）
和互動調整的方式，設計了大量應用澄清請求、確認核實、理解核實
等常見調整策略的對話。又根據Varonis和Gass（1985）的意義協商
模式，發展成意義協商過程，作為互動學習的示例（見上述對話和表
1的說明）。

㈡ 書面互動

　　在書面互動方面，影片中也設計了電子郵件和短信等，如「誤
會」：

| | 阿姨手拿著廣告傳單，傳單上有電子遊戲機打八折的優惠，拿出手機傳短信給志偉。 |
| --- | --- |
| 志偉在校門口收到阿姨發來的短信： | 志偉，阿姨看到最新款式的遊戲機正在打八折，限量只有5台，你要買嗎？ |

| 志偉： | 打八折，這麼便宜一定要買啊。（志偉自言自語） |
|---|---|
| 志偉回短信給阿姨： | 阿姨，請你快點幫我買，謝謝。 |
| 過了一會兒，阿姨開開心心地我幫你買到了，一共是400元。提著一個購物袋，站在街邊發短信給志偉： | |
| | 志偉看到短信上的價錢嚇了一跳，打電話給阿姨。 |

### 2.影片的超時空蒙太奇手法和旁白配音

由於影片可以製作出超時空的蒙太奇手法，以及用並置、互換等技巧來增強書面即時互動的效果，且書面文字如短信、電子郵件加上了旁白配音，又增強了其可讀性和可理解性。也可以善用拍攝、運鏡和剪輯等技巧，將畫面留白，幫助學習者根據故事情節，以發展其認知推理和想像空間。如「眞人圖書館」中美寶和麗文的電子郵件往來，在影片的畫面中二者是同步進行、穿插呈現的，頗有臨場感。

## 七、課堂學習空間

本研究通過自製的影片，根據華語文教學的「四、五、六學習空間」來設計適合學生的任務型活動。

互動對語言習得起著至關重要的作用。生生之間、師生之間的互動能為學生提供相互合作、意義協商，以及共同解決問題的機會。本研究為幫助語言水準較低的學生的語言可理解輸入和輸出，增加師生互動、生生互動和人機互動的機會，乃設計「互動轉換模式」（Interactive Rotation Model，見圖6）的混成式學習。下面舉《街頭藝術》的課堂教學實例來說明之。並且採用內容分析法，從交流、合作和意義磋商這三個方面對數據進行了質的分析。

　　交流（Interpersonal Communication）屬社交型互動，指學生之間或師生之間面對面進行情感交流，這可從話輪總數得知其交流情形。合作（Collaboration）是指學生之間相互幫助、分享資訊或共同解決問題，這可從小組討論得知其合作情形。意義協商（Negotiation of Meaning）是指學習者與其對話者預測、覺察或在理解困難時對話語進行的修改和重構，這可從意義協商的分析中得知。

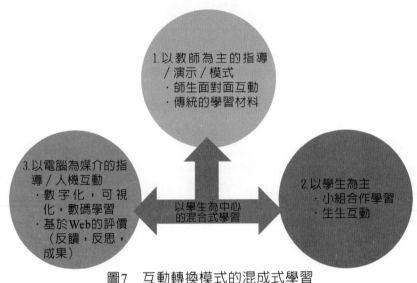

圖7　互動轉換模式的混成式學習

## ㈠ 以教師為主的指導／演示／模式

　　在課堂上進行觀賞影片和師生互動的活動，是互動轉換模式的方式之一。

### 1.播放全片，初步討論

　　上課時，老師首先進行暖身活動，如「街頭藝術」的學習點是時間（如早上十點、中午過後、晚上）和空間（如左上方、右下方、中間），老師用有本班同學參與的檳城羽球賽活動照片，來說明該次比賽的早上出發時間，中午抵達時間和晚上的活動等。

暖身活動之後，老師就運用顯性教學，在播放前請學生注意影片中的學習點，然後播放影片（約3-5分鐘）。

接著由老師主導，針對影片中的主題內容或名稱進行面對面的師生互動，以引發學生回應。在師生互動過程中，老師運用了促使注意（push notice）、重覆、語碼轉換、反饋等策略，來提供學生可理解性輸入和語言輸出的機會。

### 2. 播放影片片段，深化討論

雖然在觀賞影片後有師生互動，但由於學生受限於語言水準，往往只能回應較簡單的問題，所以老師需要再以片段播放的方式，有針對性地對影片片段中的細節或互動策略／對話技巧等進行更加深化的討論，以引發學生對主題內容、語言知識和技能的理解，並以意義協商的方式，幫助學生主動建構知識。

當第二次片段播放後，老師再次詢問影片的名稱，學生都能很快地回應。且學生能說出「**他們要學**」的故事情節重點，老師則用了反饋和補足策略（「嗯，**他們要學藝術**」）來幫助學生說出完整的一句話。

### (二) 以學生為主的小組合作學習和生生互動

小組合作學習和生生互動是互動轉換模式的方式之一，所以在觀賞影片全部和片段，以及師生互動之後，需要進行二人一組的對話或討論，以提供生生互動的機會。

我們發現在生生互動中大量出現意義協商。Varonis和Gass（1985）將意義協商分成四個階段：即觸發語（Trigger）、示意語（Indicator）、應答語（Response）、對應答語的回應（Reaction to the Response）。下表舉例說明之：

表1　生生互動中意義協商的實例

| 意義協商的階段 | 話輪順序 | |
| --- | --- | --- |
| | 學生A | 學生B |
| 觸發語（T） | 背景介紹，我剛才說了。 | |
| 示意語（I） | | 什麼？ |
| 應答語（R） | 背景介紹。沒有表情，emotion。 | |
| 對應答語的回應（RR） | | 沒有表情哦？ |

　　在這段意義協商的過程中，學生B提出了澄清請求，學生A回應了他，但當學生B對應答語的回應後，學生A不知道如何再回應，所以轉而向老師提出澄清請求：

學生A：「老師，emotionless講的是？」
老師：「沒有表情，面無表情，或者他看起來目無表情，很多說法。」

　　由此可知，對學生來說，生生互動中還經常需要插入師生互動，以幫助其持續話輪。
　　表1所舉的實例是小組中比較成功的案例，對於大部分說華語缺乏自信的學生來說，有上述的表現已經相當可圈可點了。有研究指出當意義協商得以實現時，互動學習就到達了知識構建的最高層面。可見以影片作為觸媒來引起學生的學習興趣和動機，再加上討論活動的設計，學生在意義協商中主動建構語言知識，有助於學生的語言輸出和提升其口語互動能力。

## 八、小結

　　當前華語文教師應用真實性影片來教學，教學方法相當多元，有

的僅作為學習之後的獎賞，有的用來塡補課堂時間，有的作為華語教學過程的輔助教材，有的是純粹欣賞，有的則會將影片提升到教學法的位置，作為主導教學的工具。然而，實際上屬於後者的運用還是很少，可能的原因之一是少見兼具眞實生活和課堂學習點的教學影片的開發。本文藉著此一系列教學影片的製作，探討如何用影片來開發學生的「四」、「五」、「六」語言學習空間，希望藉本文提醒有意開發華語文教學影片者該注意的製作原則，並希望能引起華文教師們的共鳴，嘗試和願意將影片作為主導華語文教學的方法之一。

## 參考文獻

Altman, R. (1989). *The Video Connection: Integrating Video into Language Teaching.* Boston: Houghton Mifflin Company.

Arslanyilmaz, A. (2007). *Using Similar Tasks to Increase Negotiation of Meaning And Language Production in An Online Second Language Learning Environment.* Unpublished doctoral dissertation, Texas A & M University.

Branigan, C. (2005). Video Goes to School. *eSchool News*, Vol. 8. No. 4. pp.25-29.

Burt, M. (1999). *Using Video with Adult English Language Learners.* ERIC Digest.

Canning-Wilson, C. (2000). Practical Aspects of Using Video in the Foreign Language Classroom. In *The Internet TESL Journal*, Vol.4, No.11.

Dale, E. (1969). *Audio-visual Methods in Teaching.*(3rd Ed.) (pp. 37-51). New York: Dryden Press.

Herron, C., Cole, S. P., Corrie, C., & Dubreil, S. (2000. Using Instructional Video to Teach Culture to Beginning Foreign Language Students. *The Computer Assisted Language Instruction Consortium*

*Journal.* Vol. 17 No. 3. pp.395-429.

Krashen, S. D. (1985). *The Input Hypothesis: Issues and Implications.* New York: Longman.

Long, M. (1983). Native Speaker/Non-Native Speaker Conversation and the Negotiation of Comprehensible Input. *Applied Linguistics*, Vol.4. No. 2. pp.126-141.

McNulty, A. & Lazarevic, B. (2012). Best Practices in Using Video Technology to Promote Second Language Acquisition. In *Teaching English with Technology*, Issue 3. pp.49-61.

Mehrabian, A. (1971). Silent Messages(1$^{st}$ Ed.). Belmont, CA: Wadsworth.

National Standards in Foreign Language Education Project. (1999). *Standards for Foreign Language Learning in The 21st Century.* Lawrence, KS: Allen Press.

Sharwood Smith, M. (1991). Speaking to Many Minds: On the Relevance of Different Types of Language Information for the L2 Learner. *Second Language Research*, Vol. 7. No.2. pp.118-132.

Shedroff, N. (1999). Information Interaction Design: A Unified Field Theory of Design. In *Information Design.* Jacobson, R.(Ed.). Massachussets: MIT Press. pp.267-292.

Sherman, J. (2003). *Using Authentic Video in the Language Classroom.* Cambridge: Cambridge University Press.

Singapore Mother Tongue Languages Review Committee. (2011). *Nurturing Active Learners and proficient Users: 2010 Mother Tongue Languages Review Committee Report.* Singapore: Singapore Ministry of Education.

Staker, H. & Horn, M. B. (2012). *Classifying K-12 Blended Learning.* CA, USA: Innosight Institute.

Stempleski, S. (1987). Short Takes: Using Authentic Video in the English Class. *Paper presented at the Annual Meeting of the International*

*Association of Teachers of English as a Foreign Language*. Westende: Belgium.

Talavan, N. (2007). Learning Vocabulary through Authentic Video and Subtitles. In *TESOL-SPAIN Newsletter*, Vol.31 pp. 5-8.

Varonis, E. M. & Gass, S. (1985) Non-Native/Non-Native Conversations: Model for Negotiation of Meaning. *Applied Linguistics*, Vol. 1. pp.71-87.

Julia T. Wood, J. T.(2008). *Communication in Our Lives*. Boston, MA: Cengage Advantage Books.

陳立芬（2007）。從影片欣賞到華語教學的課程設計與實驗。第5屆全球華文網路教育研討會。頁331-337。台灣：中華民國僑務委員會。

陳姮良（2012）。數位學習科技在K-12華語文教育上的實施與應用。中文教學現代化學報第一卷第一期。頁18-26。北京：中文教育現代化協會。

# 跨文化交際與華語文文化教學
## ——《僑教雙週刊》網路資源運用與教學設計

陳品

國立暨南大學中國語文學系博士班

vivi@tcis.ac.th

## 摘要

　　網路科技日新月異，文化融合與借鑑更爲顯著，舉凡電影、戲劇、新聞、廣告、服飾、食品、文學作品、翻譯文本、語言學習以及科技網路等，無一不是跨文化交際（intercultural communication）之產物。對外華語文教學，是第二語言、外語、文化教學，其任務是架設跨文化交際橋樑，培養跨文化交際能力。跨文化交際的核心，在於文化最底層、穩定的價值觀。文化即交際（culture is communication），無論語言或非語言交際，都受到文化制約。語言承載文化，文化是歷史的饋贈，語言教學必置於人類之文化系統中，才能培養文化感知（culture perception）達到溝通任務。一般文化教材與教學，多聚焦於節慶習俗認識與傳統技藝養成，極易忽略語言表達與文化理解。多媒體、數位化、虛擬、遠距、社群與科技網路融入教學，不僅改變訊息傳遞模式、加速知識傳播，也顛覆語言教學形態。網路資源與多媒體教材整合視覺與聽覺管道，與認知活動關聯密切（Mayer, 2001），可快速建構認知網絡，彌補教材與教法之偏頗與缺失，是實踐跨文化交際教學之捷徑。本文〈跨文化交際網路華語文教與學〉是泰國中華國際學校文化教學實務，以《僑教雙週刊》2012年至2013年網路互動期刊爲教學設計，透過心智圖軟體（mind mapping, X mind 2012）分析文化模式（cultural patterns）。《僑教雙週刊》系列期刊之延續性與實用性，跳脫褊狹之文化教學議題；心智網絡圖反映認知活動，協助教學者與學習者快速掌握語言知識與文化模式。網際網路、數位多媒體與雲端教學平台等教學模式入主華語文教學現場，華語教師媒體素養、網路資源運用與數位技能養成，是網路華語文教學設計前提，亦是提高跨文化交際教學效能之關鍵。

關鍵詞：跨文化交際、文化感知、心智圖、僑教雙週刊

# 一、前言

　　網路科技日新月異，國際交流日漸頻繁，文化融合與借鑑更為顯著，舉凡電影、戲劇、新聞、廣告、服飾、食品、文學作品、翻譯文本、語言學習與科技網路等，無一不是跨文化交際[1]（intercultural communication）之產物。人與人之間語言交際與表達方式，即是跨文化交際（intercultural communication）之最佳印證。

　　網際網路普及與多媒體工具發達，帶動數位學習（e-learning）之風潮。多媒體、數位化、虛擬、遠距與社群、科技網路等融入教學，不僅改變訊息傳遞模式、加速知識傳播，也顛覆語言教學形態。相較於傳統語言教學，數位化教學之資源分享與知識共享之概念，構築多元化、網路化、趣味性的學習空間，雖無絕對性之教學優勢，卻具高度交際效能。網路教學運用科技、數位化資源或網站等與世界互動，傳遞訊息與建構知識的歷程，即是跨文化交際能力的體現，或雙向同步，或非同步訊息傳遞，改變訊息傳遞與接收模式，更衝擊教學現場教師之角色，然教師之角色不能全然被數位科技取

---

[1] 何道寬譯，《無聲的語言》（北京：北京大學出版社，2010）導論，頁2。Hall（1959）提出跨文化交際一詞（intercultural communication, cross-cultural communication），被視為跨文化交際學奠基者。

代，舉凡課程規劃、教學設計、教材使用以及教學活動等，皆需要教學者引導說明，尤以語言教學更為顯著。

　　「國際化」與「多元化」發展趨勢，華人（overseas Chinese）概念泛化，文化認同覆蓋政治意識，擴大華語文教學場域與教學對象，海外華文教學由「華僑教育」、「華文教育」轉向「國際語言教育」之對外華語文教學（teaching Chinese as a second/foreign language），大大提升華語之經濟效能，也開啟全球華語文教學契機。對外華語文教學，是第二語言教學、外語教學、文化教學，亦是跨文化交際教學，其任務是架設跨文化交際橋樑，培養跨文化交際能力[2]。跨文化交際的核心在於文化最深層、穩定的價值觀[3]，跨文化交際能力，即是透過語言理解與文化感知（culture perception）來完成溝通之任務。

　　霍爾（Hall, 1976）以高、低語境分析文化多樣性，中國、日本、泰國等文化屬高語境（high context cultures），歐美西方文化為低語境（low context cultures）[4]。綜觀第二語言與文化教學之研究，多著重於高、低語境語言與文化差異之對比分析[5]，極易產生相似或鄰近語境教學不存在文化衝擊或誤解的迷思[6]。對比分析是華語

---

[2]　畢繼萬，《跨文化交際與第二語言教學》（2009），頁15-21。

[3]　胡文仲，《跨文化交際概論》（北京：北京大學出版社，1999），頁136-137。

[4]　同註1，頁86。霍爾：「高語境交流或高語境訊息大都存於物質環境中，經過編碼後，傳輸出來的資訊卻非常之少，低語境交流正與之相反。」。

[5]　林俊宏、李延輝、羅雲廷、賴慈芸譯，《第二語教學最高指導原則》（第五版）（台北：東華書局股份有限公司，2013），頁294-295。對比分析假設（Contrastive Analysis Hypothesis, CAH）是Robert Lado（1957）提出，此假說是以行為主義和結構方法論為基礎，主張第二語言習得的主要障礙來自第一語言系統干擾第二語言系統，將第二語言學習錯誤歸因於母語到外語的負面轉移。

[6]　畢繼萬，〈跨文化交際研究與第二語言教學〉，《語言教學與研究》1998年第1期，頁10-24。畢繼萬：「東方文化屬高語境文化，在交際中注重依賴語境，其交際行為的特點是婉轉而又含蓄，注重禮貌卻不真誠；而屬於低語境文化的美、德和北歐諸國人則坦誠和直率，其

文教學研究重要策略之一，豐碩之高低語境之對比研究成果[7]，並不表示同為高語境文化，如中日或中泰等，其語言與文化之學習不具困難。實際上，相似語境教學困難，並不亞於高低語境的教學，對比分析或能客觀顯示兩種語言之語音、詞彙與句法與表層文化之差異，卻未必能辨析學習者的理解能力與溝通能力，更無法提升學習成效。成功的語言教學需置身於文化語境中，穿越表層文化象徵，進入更深層之文化系統，才能協助學習者建構語言知識、培養文化感知，發展跨文化交際能力。跨文化交際能力當如何養成？交際能力，是語言學習成功的關鍵。華語文教學與理論研究，多關注於語言形式之掌握，忽略學習者交際能力之體現。本文希冀藉由網路資源融入語言教學之主題教學設計，強化學習者交際話語結構之正確性以及交際話語在特定文化語境中的可行性與得體性。

　　語言是文化的符號，文化是語言的管軌，不同文化語境中，人際關係模式、交際策略以及價值觀念等差異，都會影響思維運作與言語行為表現。一般文化教學與教材編寫，多聚焦於節慶習俗認識與傳統技藝養成，容易忽略語言表達與文化感知能力之養成。網路科技融入語言教學，最大優點是營造影音、圖像雙軌學習管道與虛擬化語境，數位化的互動學習模式，如何幫助學習者建構語言知識與文化認知，提升交際能力？科技網路教學能否完全取代教學者之角色？網路

---

資訊的傳遞溢於言表而很少依賴語境。」。

[7] 例如王志明，〈中西文化交流中顏色詞「紅」與「白」的象徵意義〉，《濮陽職業技術學院學報》（2008），1，84-85；朱恕平，《漢德顏色詞文化語義對比研究─以黑、白與紅為例》，輔仁大學碩士論文，2012年；吳彬、趙平，〈淺析顏色詞在中英文化中的差異〉，《江西農業大學學報（社會科學版）》（2003），2，128-131；李菁菁，〈漢語動詞與形容詞重疊式之量性對比分析〉《清華學報》（2009）新39卷第4期，567-613；曹逢甫，〈對比分析與錯誤分析──以中英文句子總體結構的異同為例談兩者的關係〉《英語教學》（1987），12, 2: 46-53; 12,3: 37-49；鍾榮富、司秋雪，〈從發音與聲學的對比分析探討美國學生的華語擦音〉，《華語文教學研究》（2009）6卷2期，頁129-162。

教學提供一個想像空間與世界互動，學習環境從教室走向網路，學習者由被動轉為主動，學習內容由靜態而動態，網路多元資源不僅擴大知識網脈，也使得語言教學與文化教學更為緊密、融合，學習者主動建構的知識，是語言能力與文化理解的表現，是培養跨文化交際意識的基礎。科技網路融入教學，讓教室「炫」起來，使教材「活」起來，卻無法令教學設計自己「動」起來。換言之，網路教學能提供豐富資源、自由彈性的教學模式，無法取代教學者在教學現場穿針引線的引導角色。

　　本文〈跨文化交際與華語文文化教學──僑教雙週刊網路資源運用與教學設計〉是泰國中華國際學校（Thai-Chinese International School，簡稱TCIS）文化教學實務，以《僑教雙週刊》2012年至2013年網路版期刊為網路資源，輔以心智圖軟體（mind mapping, Xmind 2012）分析文化模式（cultural patterns），期以提升TCIS學童華語交際能力與文化理解。《僑教雙週刊》迄今已發行六百八十期[8]，具平面刊物與多媒體網路教材[9]兩種形態，歷經多次改版，基本上可分為語言認知、文化知識、對話溝通與閱讀教材等四大類型，是海外華裔子弟學習華語及認識台灣多元文化之平台，也是華語教師文化教學的輔助資源。網際網絡資源分享概念下，《僑教雙週刊》閱讀對象不再局限於華僑、華裔，逐漸擴及至全球對華語文化認同的人士。《僑教雙週刊》是系列期刊，其編寫概念環繞華人語言與文化知識，涵蓋語言、文字、社會、習俗、藝術、文學等面向，具延續性與

---

[8]　《僑教雙週刊》期刊數，乃依據本文教學實務與完稿日期出版的期數。

[9]　僑委會《僑教雙週刊》，自2005年8月1日起發行數位僑教專刊（含平面版及網路版），包括《全球華文網路教育中心導覽》（由芝加哥易學中文網路學校石鴻珍校長執筆）、《數位台灣藝文》（由大漢技術學院李芝瑩講師執筆）、《數位台灣華語》（由元智大學羅鳳珠教授執筆）及《師資交流園地》（由淡江大學楊明玉副教授執筆）等四個版面。2012年版面包括文化篇、兒童篇、我會說華語；2013年單數週版面為字的故事、幼兒專刊、閱讀專刊，雙數週版面為字的故事、兒童華語、我會說華語。

實用性兩大特性：心智網絡圖反映學習者之認知歷程，是學習者語言能力產出，也是文化感知之體現，可協助教學者檢驗學習者理認知與教學成效。網路資源融入語言教學是跨文化交際趨勢，跨文化交際是雙向互動的，是兩種語言與兩種文化激盪的結果，對教學者而言，是教學資源與策略的運用，對學習者而言，是語言認知與交際能力養成途徑，是體現跨文化交際「教」與「學」雙效能的捷徑。

## 二、文獻探討

全球化發展趨勢，跨文化交際無所不在，無論是科技文明或精神文明，皆是跨文化交際交融的痕跡。跨文化交際障礙，在於文化融合與跨越之間的混淆，一種對新、舊與熟悉、陌生之文化的包容度或排斥感。網路科技與數位媒體融入語言教學，是跨文化交際趨勢，不僅改變知識傳播與接收模式，也成為語言教學與文化教學相互滲透、互動與借鑒之平台。

㈠ 跨文化交際

跨文化交際（intercultural communication, cross cultural communication）或譯為跨文化溝通、跨文化交流。胡文仲（1999）將跨文化交際定義為不同文化背景的人從事交際的過程[10]；畢繼萬（2004）認為跨文化交際原指旅居海外美國人和當地人之交際，而後擴展到指稱來自不同文化的人之間的交際[11]。[12]人類交際經歷語言的產生、文字的使用、印刷術的發明、近百年交通工具的進步和通訊手段的迅速發展以及跨文化交際等五個階段，說明跨文化交際與語言

---

[10] 同註3，頁1。

[11] 同註2，頁7-8。

[12] 方麗娜，《華人社會與文化》（台北：正中書局，2009），頁172。

的產生同等重要、相互影響[13]。跨文化交際，是多元文化在一定時間與空間發生碰撞、接觸、學習與融合，不斷發展的一種文化現象。

　　語言，是一種世界觀，不同民族的語言稜鏡折射不同的世界。語言認知是語言使用者對文化的了解，這種獨特的經驗，是文化賦予的本能。文化即是交際（culture is communication），文化傳播主要藉由貿易活動、人類遷徙和教育三種途徑[14]，教育是跨文化交際最直接、最有效的手段。文明是符號世界，任何交際都是符號編碼與解碼的歷程。無論語言或非語言交際，都受到文化制約，這種制約來自文化最底層、最穩定的價值觀。價值觀是人類行為表現判斷標準[15]，是文化發展的基石，是個人或群體交際模式的度量衡；價值觀差異是跨文化交際障礙與衝突之源頭，也是語言教學無法融入文化教學之癥結。

　　從跨文化交際視角審視文化，文化無所不在、是動態發展的。文化接觸多以自己文化為出發點而出現文化衝擊（culture shock，文化休克）。Brown認為：「第二語言學習者不僅讓兩種語言互相碰撞，讓兩種文化彼此影響，此時會出現社會文化變數。此外，就某方面來看，學習第二種語言時，也必須同時學習第二種文化。」[16]第二語言學習，是第二文化學習，意味著新文化身分的建立與文化適應能力的養成。跨文化交際研究，即是揭示文化差異與文化衝擊，提高學習者

---

[13]　同註3，頁2。

[14]　同註12，頁5。

[15]　同註3，頁165-166。Hofstede（1980）發表《文化的後果》（*Culture's Consequences*）一書，提出個體主義—集體主義（individual-collectivism）、權力距離的態度（power distance、對不確定因素的迴避程度（uncertainly avoidance）以及男性—女性（masculinity-femininity）四個衡量價值觀之尺度，爾後參照Michael Bond對中國價值觀研究，1991年*Cultures and Organizations: Software of the Mind*書中增列長期觀/短期觀（long/short term orientation）第五個尺度。

[16]　同註5，頁178。

文化差異的敏感性，增強目的語文化的適應能力[17]。

　　對外華語文教學是第二語言教學、文化教學，是一種跨文化交際教學。跨文化交際現場，教學對象是異質的、語言是多元的，文化是動態的，課程標準、教材教法、測驗評量以及師資等教學環節也會隨之波動而產生變化。這些跨文化交際教學的潛在困境，即是對外華語文教學發展之障礙。跨文化交際教學觀，以提高跨文化交際意識爲前提，透過文化價值觀的認識、觀察與接觸體驗，有助於消減學習者對標的語之語言與文化信息超載（information overload），進而降低語用失誤、促進交際效能。

## (二) 網路教學

　　科技教育之實用性、便捷性與創造性，爲語言教育帶來新氣象。網路教學主要是運用多媒體、網路資源或網站等與世界互動，或雙向同步、或非同步訊息接收傳遞，構築動態、虛擬的數位學習環境。Mayer（2001）將多媒體定義爲文字（words）及圖片（pictures）：文字指語文形式（verbal form），包含書寫視覺文字（printed words）以及口語表達文字（spoken words）；圖片指的是圖像形式（pictorial form），涵蓋靜態（如插圖、座標圖、圖解、照片、地圖）與動態（動畫、影片）二種圖。多媒體教學，是雙碼學習（dual-code learning）、雙種管道學習（dual-channel learning），透過視覺與聽覺管道互動建構知識能力的認知活動。多媒體教學運用圖、文焦點轉移的閱讀歷程，本質上是一種主體（figure）與背景（ground）交替的動態認知歷程。「主體／背景分離」（figure/ground segregation）的現象，是基於突顯原則（prominence）和分離原則（segregation）的空間認知對語言資訊理解與詮釋[18]。多媒體

---

17　李曉琪，《對外漢語文化教學研究》（北京：商務印書館，2006），頁40-41。

18　弗里德里希‧溫格瑞爾（Ungerer. F.）、漢斯尤格‧施密特（Schmid. H. J.）著，彭利貞、許

融入教學，具有強化認知以及促進對訊息理解與詮釋的效能。

　　科技網路發達，知識建構與傳播更為便捷。媒體科技輔助教學，主要功能在於擴大知識網脈及活絡教學現場，而非取代教學現場資源與人力。網路教材教法的選擇與運用，更涉及教學專業、資源設備以及實際需要等議題。為數位而數位化，只是表演性的教學形態；為交際而數位化，是任務性的教學模式。網路資源融入教學活動，除數位化、多元化、趣味性與教育性的特色外，最重要的是在跨文化交際和第二語言教學之間提供一個相對應的、互動的文化語境，強化語言教學與文化教學之間的融合度與滲透力。

## (三) 心智圖（mind map）

　　心智圖，1970年代由英國Tony Buzan提出的一種輔助思考工具[19]。心智圖的複雜網絡，如腦神經般放射狀傳遞訊息，逐步連結相關符號，擴大語義網狀結構（Semantic network），在教學上具有筆記、重點提要與訊息整合歸納等功能，是語言和文字邏輯性與空間化的表現形態。心智工具軟體運用於語言教學，可引導學生開放性思考，強化認知，建構語言能力。Xmind 2012心智軟體，具文字與圖像視覺化功能，提供流程圖、樹狀圖、組織圖等圖表範本，操作簡易，可運用於華語詞彙教學、閱讀摘要、故事分析、寫作指導以及漢字教學等。心智圖繪製過程，反映學習認知思維過程，是「做中學」的學習策略。

---

國萍、趙微譯，《認知語言學導讀第二版》（2009），頁186。Rubin（1921）以「人臉／花瓶幻覺」圖說明人臉與杯子無法在同一時間看見，此現象稱為「主體／背景分」（figure/ground segregation）。

[19]　心智圖Mind Maps，是由英國Buzan於1970年代提出的一種輔助思考工具。心智圖通過在平面上的一個主題出發畫出相關聯的對象，像一個心臟及其周邊的血管圖，故稱為「心智圖」。

## 三、跨文化交際教學

　　文化內涵豐富深遠，定義不勝枚舉。《周易‧賁卦‧象傳》：「觀乎天文以察時變文；觀乎人文，以化成天下。」《教育部重編國語辭典》，文化：「人類在歷史發展過程中創造的總成果。包括宗教、道德、藝術、科學等各方面。」英國人類學家泰勒文化之定義：「文化或文明，就其廣泛的民族學意義來講，是一複合整體，包括知識、信仰、藝術、道德、法律、習俗以及作爲一個社會成員的人所習得的其他一切能力和習慣。」Brown將文化定義爲：「文化是一種生活方式。我們都在文化的架構下生存、思考、感知，並與他人相處。文化可說是一種黏著劑，使特定的一群人緊緊相繫。」[20]無論是人文教化、文明或生活方式等定義，在在說明文化反映人們的生活方式與交際模式。

　　第二語言教學，本質上是一種語境導向（contextual orientation）的教學形態。無論是語言或非語言交際，都是建立於文化語境中。第二語言學習，是第二文化學習，必須置身於第二文化之語境中才能進行有效的交際任務。傳統文化是歷史餽贈、民族財富，也可能是跨文化交際之包袱或障礙。跨文化交際教學，是探索交際過程中語言軌跡所蘊含的文化知識，如何在教材編寫、課程設計與教學策略中體現，如何幫助學習者掌握第二語言知識與文化模式，提高語言交際之流利度與正確性。文化廣博精深，文化教學範疇實難以規範，無論是語言課程中的文化教學，或專門學科之文化教學，都須將文化教學視爲一個主體，而非附加的教學活動，才能掌握第二語言知識與文化精髓。

　　本文〈跨文化交際與華語文文化教學〉，是以《僑教雙週刊》網路教材爲教學資源，運用心智圖軟體（mind mapping, X mind 2012）分析文化模式，藉由平面教材、電子教材與網路資源爲互

---

[20]　同註6，頁222。

文性（intertextuality）教學文本，擴大語言與文化教學面向，學習者透過多元化管道學習，可提升語言與文化的理解力，降低語用失誤，促進交際能力。

## ㈠ 泰國中華際學校華語文教學

　　泰國中華國際學校（โรงเรียนนานาชาติ ไทย-จีน，Thai-Chinese International School，簡稱TCIS），成立於1995年，位於曼谷地區近郊之北欖縣（Samut Prakarn），是一所K-12十五年一貫中、英、泰三語教學之國際學校。TCIS原為海外四國六校之一[21]，2006年脫離海外台北學校之列，回歸海外僑校。從「台北學校」到「國際學校」，是「華文教育」轉向「國際教育」之印證、更是跨文化交際之產物，在華教政策、華文教育、僑務推展以及對外華語文教學等，都具有指標性的意義。TCIS目前學校之定位是海外僑校，僑委會每年提供華語教材、刊物與活動經費等各項補助。TCIS中、小學使用之華語文教材，包括南一版國小國語、五百字說華語、千字說華語、生活華與以及泰編版兒童華語教材等。TCIS中文分班是以國籍區分，包括以台籍學生為主之母語班以及非台籍（泰籍、日籍、韓籍等）學生之外語班，母語班使用與台灣同步教材，如南一版教材；外語班使用僑委會編審之教材。數位化教學是TCIS課程發展方向，科技網路融入中文教學，擴大語言與文化教學面向，使語言教學與文化教學更為緊密、融合。除課堂語言教學外，校內活動諸如中文卡拉OK比賽、中文字打以及中文電影比賽等，皆是網路數位化教學運用。

## ㈡ 《僑教雙週刊》網路資源運用與教學設計

　　交際文化不僅受到語境制約，也會因學習者背景差異而產生誤解，學習者套用母語之文化概念模式是干擾第二語言學習的主要因

---

[21] 四國六校包括：馬來西亞檳城台灣學校、吉隆坡中華台北學校、印尼雅加達台北學校、泗水台北學校、泰國中華國際學校及越南胡志明市台北學校。資料來源：中華民國教育部。

素。中、英、泰三語教學是TCIS語言教學特色，三語相互干擾情況極爲普遍，涵蓋語音、詞彙和語法等偏誤，除語內遷移、語際遷移、學習風格以及溝通策略外[22]，另一項影響交際因素是學習者不能辨識華語詞彙的內在意涵和語用規則。

　　本文以TCIS五、六年級泰籍學生爲研究對象，學習華語平均年齡約3.6年[23]，由於學生的語言知識和交際能力並沒有對等，常常說出不得體的用語，諸如「我喜歡戴綠（色的）帽子」、「他是一個可愛的小人（小孩）」等。此類偏誤主要在於華語文化認知不足導致語用偏誤。中、泰同屬高語境文化，問候語或感謝語都強調禮貌與尊敬，然表現方式也極爲不同，以泰語之語尾敬語「ka/krab」爲例，表達你好「sawatdee」時，女性使用「sawatdeeka」，男性使用「sawatdeekrab」，因此泰籍學習者以中、英文表達感謝時，常會說出「謝謝Ka」、「Thank you Ka」等雙語混用的偏誤來表示禮貌。學習者對標的語語言知識與文化感知混淆或偏離，是導致偏誤並影響交際的關鍵。

　　本文教學設計目的，除配合TCIS數位化教學目標，另一個任務是協助學習者掌握華語文化意涵，提升交際能力。一般體驗式或技能性的文化教學，固然能提高學習興趣，然僅是物質文明的文化接觸，而非語言與文化的認識與感知，學習者接觸的是表層、且沒有系

---

[22] 同註6，頁315-316。Brown將學習者語言錯誤區分爲語際轉移（Interlingua transfer）、語內轉移、學習情境（context of learning）與溝通策略四類。語際轉移是第二語言初學階段，學習者還不熟悉第二語言系統，受到母語的語際轉移或干擾造成的錯誤；語內轉移，則是學習者懂得新語言系統的一些部分後，學習者的第二語言能力越進步，將先前的經驗與先前習得的知識擴展應用到整個目標語裡，是一種過度類化；學習情境，指教學環境中，教師與教材可能導致學習者對語言做出錯誤假設；溝通策略學與學習風格相關，學習者爲了增進訊息傳遞效果，所採用的策略，幽幽默感、新創的字詞和套用句型的句子，都可能是錯誤來源。

[23] 2012至2013年，TCIS五、六年級外語班學生共六十六位，學習華語六年以上有（K3-6）十二位，五年十四位，四年有十三位，三年有七位，二年有九位，一年有六位，一年以下有六位，平均學習爲3.6年。

統的文化知識，一旦脫離文化課程，交際能力便下降，甚至逐步喪失。文化教學不能脫離文化系統運作，琳瑯滿目的文化教材與網路資源，當如何選取？如何運用？本文以僑委會提供之泰編版教材為文本，《僑教雙週刊》網路資源為輔助教材，是非同步教學設計，運用紙本、電子書以及網路資源，多元文本相互指涉可強化學習者語言認知與文化感知，多元主題貫串、相互連結的教學設計，可視作互文性（intertextuality）之語篇閱讀。圖1是跨文化交際華文化教學總覽圖。

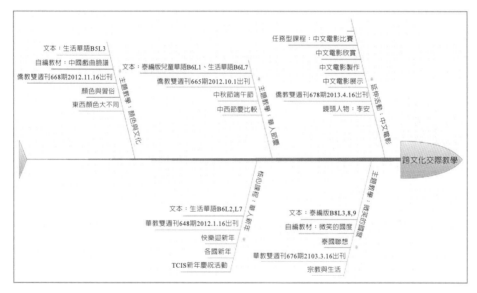

圖1　跨文化交際華語文文化教學總覽圖

　　《僑教雙週刊》是系列期刊，涉及多元文化議題，編寫團隊為文化面向把關；《僑教雙週刊》網路版提供離線下載，可避免網路連結或網頁下載速度所產生的問題。跨文化交際文化教學模式，是以平面文本教材開展教學主題，以「華人新年慶典」為核心課程，以中文電影製作為教學任務，從2012年12月到2013年4月，歷時約四個月，共選取《僑教雙週刊》668期、665期、648期、678期與676期等五期期

刊，並搭配自編教材、學習單與網路資源等完成系列主題教學。從顏色、新年、華人節慶、認識泰國到中文電影製作等，每個教學主題雖各自獨立運作卻環環相扣、關係緊密，是極具延展性與連續性的教學模式。圖2是《僑教雙週刊》文化教學流程圖。

圖2　《僑教雙週刊》文化教學流程圖

　　《僑教雙週刊》文化教學步驟，以教材讀本導入主題，是暖身活動，包括泰編版兒童華語、生活華語以及自編教材等，著重於基礎語言與文化知識；《僑教雙週刊》網路版教材影音教學，可強化學習者認知、激發學習興趣，是延伸課程；《僑教雙週刊》紙本或PDF檔，是閱讀與互動教學的資源；心智圖繪製，是學習者理解能力的表現與教學回饋。文化滲透（cultural infiltration）是一股不可忽略的意識強流，文化滲透保留同質性，卻也突顯差異的存在。關注於語言教學與文化教學之融合與滲透，即是跨文化交際意識的養成。

## 四、《僑教雙週刊》教學實務

　　《僑教雙週刊》網路資源，是視覺與聽覺雙管道學習，可刺激學習者的認知，也能活絡教學現場。《僑教雙週刊》紙本教材提供注音、拼音兩種標音系統，符合不同學習對象需求，作為閱讀與中文打字練習詞彙庫，具有詞彙、閱讀、複習與提示的功能。心智軟體（X mind）是邏輯化與圖像化學習策略，可強化記憶與理解；教學者繪製之心智圖表，是教學綱要統整；學習者繪製之心智圖，是語言與文化認知之表現[24]。

---

[24] 本文心智圖分析，主要是以華語平均學習年齡三年者為主，不涉及個案研究，選取兩年與六

## (一) 顏色與習俗教學

　　顏色與習俗，是文化教學中普遍且重要的教學主題。跨文化交際文化教學從顏色教學開展，以生活華語教材第五冊文本〈小丑〉導入主題，再搭配自編教材【中國戲曲臉譜】進行顏色解析與文化比較，輔以《僑教雙週刊》668期[25]紅色、黃色、黑色與白色顏色意義，導引華人社會中顏色象徵與喜好，藉由中、西顏色比較，認識中西方顏色的喜好與習俗，反映華人之價值觀與審美觀。

　　語言與文化既存在對應空缺，便會產生矛盾性，這種矛盾性源自於不同的文化語境。東、西方紅色都有熱情、溫暖與熱鬧的象徵，是一致性，卻又蘊含暴力、死亡的聯想，是矛盾性；黃色在華人社會中是尊貴與榮耀之象徵，傳統戲曲中，黃色臉譜具有暴力意涵[26]，是矛盾性；華人社會中，白色表悲傷，在傳統戲曲中，白色臉譜象徵狡猾人物，白色在西方社會表純潔、和平，是矛盾性。黑色在華人社會象徵權力（烏紗帽），在傳統戲曲臉譜表示勇敢與智慧，西方社會則具有恐怖、黑暗的涵義，是矛盾性。從主題課程到延伸課程，多元文本相互指涉，可引導學習者發現差異與矛盾，逐步掌握文化圖式（cultural schemata）[27]。圖3是《僑教雙週刊》文化教學設計概念圖。

---

年之心智圖，是突顯初級學習者與中高級學習者在語言輸出的差異。單一圖表雖未能概括解釋所有學習者語言能力與輸出，對於普遍學習者心智活動與認知建構歷程能提供相當程度的解釋力與預測力。

[25] 可參考《僑教雙週刊》668期「紅色」文化教材文本。http://edu.ocac.gov.tw/biweekly/668/welcome.htm

[26] 本文戲曲人物臉譜顏色象徵，依據劉會復（1990）著，《京劇臉譜圖說》，北京：燕山出版社。

[27] 何自然、冉永平（2013），頁251。

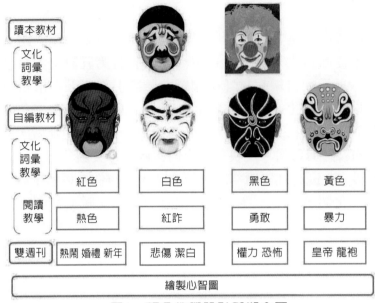

圖3　顏色教學設計與概念圖

　　心智圖繪製，是詞彙教學、文化教學，可藉以審視學習者語言理解與文化感知，作為教學者修正或調整教學策略的依據，是一種總結性的教學評量與教學回饋。《僑教雙週刊》是TCIS學童繪製心智圖的詞彙庫。圖4是學習華語兩年之學童A所繪製紅色之心智圖。TCIS初級學習者在詞彙量不足的情況下，多會以母語（泰文）或英文來呈現。第一環心智圖，反映學習者從教學文本或《僑教雙週刊》獲得之基礎文化知識；第二環心智圖，除顯示學習者詞彙能力外，也是學習者創造力的表現。心智網絡反映學習者的認知理解，學習者A繪製的圖表中出現新年活動、紅包、錢、龍等相關詞彙，即使非以標的語來表述，顯示學習者已能掌握華人社會中紅色之基本文化意涵。

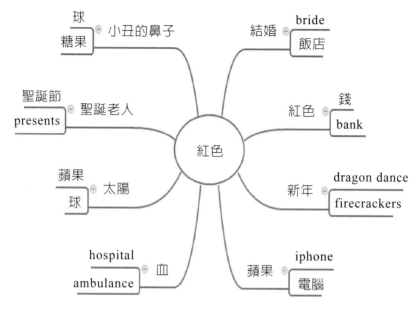

圖4　紅色心智圖（繪製者A：學習華語兩年）

## ㈡ 新年活動與華人節慶

　　中國新年是TCIS最重要的教學活動，也是校內華語教學成果。《僑教雙週刊》648期【快樂迎新年】介紹華人新年習俗、故事、年節食物以及各國新年比較，跨文化比較可補足教材讀本不足之處。以顏色導入新年活動，相同主題反覆出現，具有強化文化感知之效能。圖5是學習華語三年學童B繪製的新年心智圖。

　　心智圖反映學習者的認知歷程，學習者B學習華語已三年，語彙能力已具有相當的基礎，此心智圖之開展雖無明顯層級區分，然詞彙極為豐富且呈現短語形態，例如「吃東西」、「穿新衣服」等，能清楚表述華人新年的食物、習俗與慶典活動，說明學習者具備語言知識與交際能力，反映學習者的文化感知。實際上，泰國華人社會保留許多傳統中華文化，諸如紅包、舞龍舞獅與放鞭炮等，說明中國新年活動在泰國是一個極易掌握、不須特別教導的主題，顯示新年活動在泰

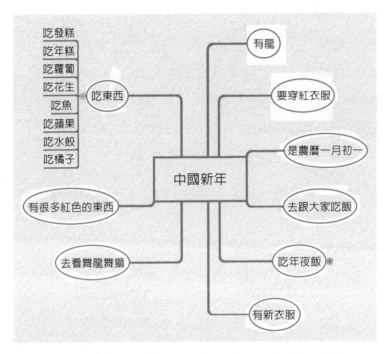

圖5　華人新年心智圖（繪製者B：學習華語三年）

國非異國文化，而是跨文化交際的產物，華人新年文化早已滲透、融合於泰國社會。

　　節慶教學最能顯現華人文化內涵。以中秋節為例，泰編版兒童華語教材著重於語言形式與習俗介紹，其設定之教學對象為海外華裔，因此詞彙較為晦澀、難懂；生活華語以童謠、韻文方式呈現，淺顯易懂，然文本「聲口」不符TCIS五、六年級學習者心智年齡與認知，亦無助於跨文化交際能力之養成。《僑教雙週刊》665期【月圓人團圓——中秋節】，介紹中秋節習俗、慶典食物與外國人過中秋等，是生活化與趣味化的文本，可引導學習者以跨文化視角認識中秋節。圖6是學習華語六年學童C繪製之中秋節心智圖。

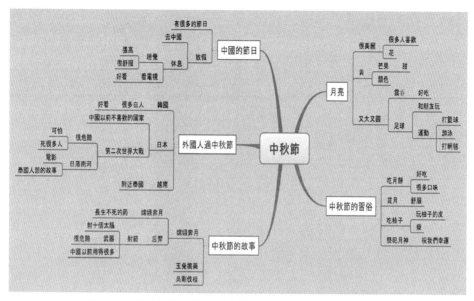

圖6　中秋節心智圖（繪製者C：學習華語六年）

　　中秋節是華人三大節慶之一，象徵闔家團圓，有關中秋節的習俗與故事非常多，諸如嫦娥奔月、后羿射日以及台灣獨特的烤肉文化等，要完整、系統化呈現，必須具備完備及流利的語言能力和文化知識。學習者C已學習華語六年，心智圖呈現系統性、多層次的網絡，不僅能依據文本進行分類、歸納，且能運用大量詞彙、短語和句式，顯示學習者不僅已掌握詞彙意義與文本內容，也能將中秋節概念具體化、知識化呈現。

## (三) 綜合性文化教學

　　跨文化溝通（交際）已是當今世界的一個重要特徵，而注重雙文化教育，甚至多元文化教育，更是文化多樣性發展的動力所在[28]。跨文化交際必基於「國際化」與「在地化」思維，透過自我文化反思

---

[28]　同註12，頁172。

與世界互動。綜合性文化主題教學，涵蓋【微笑的國度】與【中文電影製作】兩個任務型教學。【微笑的國度】是TCIS泰國新年（宋干節）教學活動，以《僑教雙週刊》648期中、泰新年文化比較以及676期【不同宗教一樣情】三大宗教為知識主體。如圖7、圖8所示。

　　無論從習俗、食物或宗教聯想，學習者D與E所繪製之心智圖，雖具層級性與系統性，且能依據性質開展心智活動，然大量的英文詞彙，顯示學習者對於自我文化認識不足與詞彙對應空缺的現象，反映學習者欠缺表述自己文化特性的能力，同時揭示華語文化教學教材與教法之偏頗與缺失。外語教學，應關注本族文化與目的語（標的語）文化的互動；教材編寫者必須具備全球化的思維，省思在地化文化和全球在地化的交互影響，引導學習者從全球文化角度理解與反思自己的文化[29]。無論是網路資源或平面教材，當以學習者文化為基

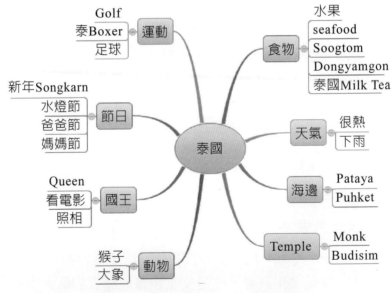

圖7　泰國心智圖（繪製者D：學習華語三年）

---

[29] 方麗娜，〈對外華語文化教材的設計與編寫研究──全球教育的視角〉《中原華語文學報》（2010），6，101-123。

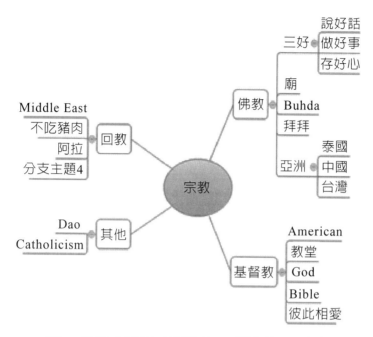

圖8　宗教心智圖（繪製者E：學習華語三年）

礎；所謂互動教學，非僅是視覺與聽覺的刺激，須提供符合學習者文化語境的教材與教法，才能體現跨文化交際教學任務。

《僑教雙週刊》678期兒童專刊主題【愛我家鄉愛我家】，鏡頭人物介紹國際知名導演李安，是「在地化」與「國際化」編寫理念，是TCIS中學部中文電影製作的暖身課程。圖9是中文電影《朋友》心智圖，是由八位五年級學生共同完成，學生以心智圖介紹影片內容，並以6W（Who, Where, When, What, Why, How）說明電影人物、時間、地點、主題與情節等。從教材讀本、《僑教雙週刊》網路教學到心智圖表繪製，目的是培養學習者腳本書寫的能力與溝通表述能力。中文電影製作是綜合性的學習活動，也是TCIS中學部年度任務型教學成果與評量。

圖9　中文電影心智圖（小組繪製：五年級8位學生，平均學習華語三年）

　　本文運用心智圖軟體（mind mapping, X mind 2012）分析文化模式，學習者繪製新年、節慶、顏色、宗教以及朋友等心智圖是其文化認知之體現，這些文化認知相互聯繫，形成華人注重家庭倫理、祭拜祖先、愛國、助人與誠信等文化模式，此文化模反映華人生活方式與社會價值標準。綜觀《僑教雙週刊》文化教材內容，雖然橫、縱之間並沒有明確的連結性，但著重於東、西文化差異對比分析，如東、西顏色喜好、飲食習慣與節慶習俗比較等，可作為跨文化交際教學之教材。中、泰文化同屬高語境文化，語言與文化差異在對比模式下未必可洞悉二者真正的差異性或相似性。語言教學必置於人類之文化系統中，文化教學須透過多元化教材引導，促發學習者對標的語文化的興趣與探索，以深入跨文化交際核心，對兩種文化思想與價值觀進行剖析，才能培養文化感知，進而提升語言交際能力，此即本文運用多元素材於文化教學之理由。

## 五、結語

　　對外華語文教學課程是一個中外語言文化接觸、衝擊和碰撞的典

型場域，文化的特徵會在這個場域裡表現出來，而外國學生就是在跨文化溝通（交際）的環境下習得華語溝通能力[30]。對外華語文教學是跨文化交際教學，任務是培養學習者跨文化交際能力。華語熱，是跨文化交際產物，要成功推廣華語教學，必須洞悉華語熱背後的學習動機與文化意識，無論是基於文化認同或語言工具性考量，最終目標在於溝通能力之養成。語言與文化相互融合與滲透之教學，是培養跨文化交際能力的根本。

　　本文〈跨文化交際與華語文文化教學 —— 僑教雙週刊網路資源運用與教學設計〉，是以《僑教雙週刊》為文化知識核心，運用心智圖軟體分析文化模式，《僑教雙週刊》系列期刊之延續性與實用性，跳脫褊狹之文化教學議題；心智網絡圖反映認知活動，協助學者與學習者快速連結並掌握文化蘊涵。平面、電子教材與網路資源共構的互文性文本閱讀與教學，對教學者而言，是文化教學資源與教學策略；對學習者而言，是語言與文化閱讀文本，是認知理解邏輯化與空間化的表現。

　　中、泰同屬高語境文化，對比分析教學能夠辨析語音、詞彙、具法以及表層文化的差異，卻無法透析學習者語言理解與交際能力。網路資源與多媒體教材整合視覺與聽覺管道，透過圖像、文字與影音等多管道互動強化認知，是培養跨文化交際能力最直接、快速的途徑。心智圖軟體（mind mapping, X mind 2012）概念分析，是學習者心智邏輯化與空間化的表現方式，反映學習者語言認知與文化感知，是教學者檢驗學習成效與教學回饋的重要參照。網路教學除數位化、多元化、趣味性與教育性的特色外，最重要的是在跨文化交際和第二語言教學之間提供一個相對應的、互動的文化語境，可強化語言教學與文化教學之間的融合度與滲透力，彌補教材與教法之偏頗與缺失。

---

[30] 同註12，頁217。

　　科技網路融入華語文教學是跨文化交際趨勢，網際網路、數位多媒體與雲端教學平台等教學模式入主華語文教學現場，改變華語教學模式，也衝擊華語教師的角色。媒體科技輔助教學，主要功能在於擴大知識網脈及活絡教學現場，而非取代教學現場的資源與人力。無論教材如何多元、網路資源多麼豐富，交際障礙依舊存在，語言與文化對應空缺無法全部倚靠科技媒體或網路資源來填補、替換，科技網路融入教學，讓教室「炫」起來，使教材「活」起來，卻無法令教學設計自己「動」起來。網路教學能提供豐富資源、自由彈性的教學模式，仍無法取代教學者在教學現場穿針引線的引導角色。華語教師媒體素養、網路資源運用與數位技能養成，是網路華語文教學設計前提，亦是提高跨文化交際教學效能之關鍵。

# 參考文獻

方麗娜（2009）。華人社會與文化，台北：正中書局。

方麗娜（2010）。對外華語文化教材的設計與編寫研究──全球教育的視角，中原華語文學報，6，101-123。

王振亞（2005）。以跨文化交往為目的的外語教學──系統功能語法與外語教學，北京：北京語言大學出版社。

冉永平、張新紅（2007）。語用學縱橫，北京：高等教育出版社。

朱我芯（2013）。對外華語文化教學實證研究──以跨文化溝通與第二文化習得為導向，台北：師大出版中心。

何兆熊主編（2000）。新編語用學概論，上海：上海外語教育出版社。

何自然主編（2008）。語用學研究，北京：高等教育出版社。

何道寬譯（2010a）。無聲的語言，北京：北京大學出版社。

何道寬譯（2010b）。超越文化，北京：北京大學出版社。

余光雄譯（2005）。第二語言教學最高指導原則，台北：朗文出版社。

李泉（2005）。對外漢語教學理論思考，北京：教育科學出版社。

李泉（2011）。文化教學定位與教學內容取向，國際漢語，1，14-19。

李曉琪（2006）。對外漢語文化教學研究，北京：商務印書館。

周思源主編（1997）。對外漢語教學與文化，北京：北京語言文化大學出版社。

林俊宏、李延輝、羅雲廷、賴慈芸等（譯）（2013）。H. D. Brown著，第二語教學最高指導原則（第五版），台北：東華書局股份有限公司。

施玉惠、楊懿麗、梁彩玲譯（2003）。原則導向教學法，台北：朗文出版社。

胡文仲（1999）。跨文化交際學概論，北京：外語教學與研究出版社。

胡文仲、高一虹（1997）。外語教學與文化，長沙：湖南教育出版社。

張德鑫（1996）。中外語言文化漫談，北京：華語出版社。

畢繼萬（1998）。語言教學與研究跨文化交際研究與第二語言教學，1，10-24。

畢繼萬（2009）。跨文化交際與第二語言教學，北京：北京語言大學出版社。

彭利真、許國萍、趙薇譯（2009）。認知語言學導論第二版，北京：復旦大學出版社。

彭增安（2007）。跨文化的語言傳通，上海：學林出版社。

溫曉虹（2008）。漢語作為外語的習得研究，北京：北京大學出版社。

賈玉新（1997）。跨文化交際學，上海：上海外語教育出版社。

劉會復（1990）。京劇臉譜圖說，北京：燕山出版社。

潘文國（2004）。對外漢語教學的跨文化視角，上海：華東師範大學出版社。

蔡承志譯（2010）。Tony Buzan著，超高效心智圖學習法，台北：商周出版社。

Hall, E. T. (1959). *The Silent Language*, Garden City, N.Y: Doubleday.

Hall, E. T. (1976). *Beyond Culture*, New York: Doubleday.

Hofstede, G. (1983). *National Cultures in Four Dimensions: A Research-Based Theory of Cultural Differences Among Nations. International Studies of*

*Management & Organization*, 13(1, 2), 46. Retrieved October 31, 2010, from ABI/INFORM Global. (Document ID: 1142450).

Hofstede, G. (1984) *Culture's Consequences: International Differences in Work-Related Values*, Beverly Hills CA: Sage Publications.

Hofstede, G. (2001). *Culture's Consequences: Comparing Values, Behaviors, Institutions, and Organizations Across Nation*, Thousand Oaks, California: Sage.

Levinson, S. C. (1983). *Pragmatics*, Cambridge: Cambridge University Press.

Mayer, R. E. (2001). *Multimedia Learning*. Cambridge, UK: Cambridge University Press.

Nunan, D., & Bailey, K. M. (2010). *Exploring Second Language Classroom Research: A Comprehensive Guide*. Beijing: Foreign Language Teaching and Research Press.

Samovar, L. A. & Porter, R. E. (1997). *Communication Between Cultures* (3rd. ed.). Boston, MA: Wadsworth, Cengage Learning.

Samovar, L. A., Porter, R. E. & McDaniel, E. R. (Eds.) (2006). *InterCultural Communication: A Reader* (11th ed.). Belmont, California: Thomson/Wadsworth.

Tylor, E. B. (1920). *Primitive Culture: Researches Into the Development of Mythology, Philosophy, Religion, Language, Art, and Custom*. London: J. Murray.

教育部重編國語辭典修訂版　　http://140.111.34.46/dict/
僑教雙週刊　　　　　　　　　http://edu.ocac.gov.tw/culture/
　　　　　　　　　　　　　　biweekly/index.htm
泰國中華國際學校　　　　　　http://web.tcis.ac.th/

# 電子白板融入華語教學之個案研究

胡瑞雪

銘傳大學華語文教學學系

bonneige@gmail.com

## 摘要

　　華語已經成爲了世界強勢的語言之一，華語學習者的年齡層日趨下降，針對美國AP的華語文教材研發已有豐碩的成果，但是以兒童華語爲主的教材則是有待開發。儘管目前市面上有了少量的相關教材，然而除了書面教材之外，要如何讓母語非華語且專注力較低的兒童華語學習者快速且輕鬆地學會華語？多媒體教材的設計與應用於是就顯得更爲重要。

　　本研究把電子白板融入《兒童華語教材第一冊》之課本內容，結合動畫與遊戲，試圖研究出專門爲兒童華語學習者所設計的一套多媒體輔助教材。本教材將透過此課本內容，運用電子白板製作成動畫與互動遊戲來呈現，使兒童華語學習者專注力更集中、提升其學習華語的動機。電子白板呈現的功能在於趣味性和生動性，藉由互動式教學提高兒童華語學習者的學習意願與成效，也期望電子白板教學和華語學習的相輔相成之下，使兒童華語學習者更能將所學靈活運用於日常生活中。

　　本研究除了探討電子白板相關的教學理論、參考文獻的蒐集和分析，並從兒童華語學習者的角度出發，思考兒童華語教育發展的模式，希望能對國內外兒童華語教學推廣提供一些參考。

　　本論文架構如下：(一)研究動機與目的、研究方法與流程。(二)國內外有關本研究之重要參考文獻評述，內容包括電子白板的教學觀、教學精神和教學原則。(三)結果與討論包含根據電子白板相關教

學理論及精神而設計的教學實驗步驟、學習者學習歷程的分析、課室觀察心得、學生問卷回饋及回饋問卷分析。㈣融入電子白板教學的優缺點比較、應善用電子白板作為結論。

關鍵詞：兒童華語、電子白板、多媒體教材設計

## 壹、緒論

　　由於中國經濟的崛起，帶動全球華語文學習的風潮，亦造成對華語學習資源的大量需求。然而，又隨著資訊科技的發達，有關華語教學、閱讀、寫作教學等等網站陸續在近幾年大量地成立，運用電腦來輔助華語教學也越來越多元化。我僑務委員會建置「全球華文網路教育中心」，以統整相關教材，同時也提供華語文學習者的需要；顯然，華語文教學及教材的數位化將是未來的趨勢。

　　世界各地除了華語文學習者的人數日漸激增，其年齡層也日趨下降。如此，以華語為官方語言的地區如台灣，即連帶受到關於開發兒童華語文教材的刺激，但如何讓母語非華語且較易分心的兒童華語學習者快速學會華語，教材的設計於是更能突顯其重要性。

　　相關學者證實兒童從圖畫書中的探索，對口語發展與知識是有效的動機（Mol et al., 2009），而許多研究中學者們也主張孩子可利用動畫的設計，從生活用語開始而逐漸加深認識字彙（Medwell, 1992）。陳淑琦（1984）的研究觀點指出，利用圖畫書進行教學能啟發兒童的語言能力，以及培養兒童的閱讀興趣和發展兒童的思考與想像能力等。但就國內兒童華語教材目前仍以較傳統的紙本圖書為主，僅少有針對學習內容設計，著手去研究如何運用電子白板互動功能之華語教材。儘管近幾年大量成立相關華語教學網站，但大都還是以靜態的網頁文字為主。因此，部分學者開始投入電子白板的研究並指出：運用電子白板來實施語文教學的華語教材，並搭配多媒體技術融入相關的教育領域中，不僅能與兒童的生活經驗做結合，增加教

學的多元化，更能提升兒童學習興趣，達到最佳的學習成效（葉德明，1999）。有鑑於此，本研究旨在探討兒童華語教材以電子白板來呈現學習內容，以及實際應用於兒童華語教學與傳統紙本教學之比較分析，並針對電子白板教材內容與傳統紙本教材內容做比較。

　　本研究將透過電子白板和教材內容結合成一系列的動畫及遊戲，試圖設計出專門針對兒童華語學習者的一套實驗性參考教材。教學者以《兒童華語教材第一冊》為教學內容，運用電子白板製作動畫及互動式遊戲來呈現，使學習者更專注且更能提升其學習興趣。

　　本研究除了探討電子白板相關的教學理論、文獻的蒐集和分析，並從兒童華語學習者的角度出發，思考華語教育發展的方式與空間，希望能對國內外兒童華語教學推廣提供一些參考。

　　本論文架構如下：㈠研究動機與目的、研究方法與流程。㈡國內外有關本研究之重要參考文獻評述，內容包括電子白板的教學觀、教學精神和教學原則。㈢結果與討論包含根據電子白板相關教學理論及精神而設計的教學實驗步驟、學習者學習歷程的分析、課室觀察心得、學生問卷回饋及回饋問卷分析。㈣融入電子白板教學的優缺點比較、應善用電子白板作為結論。

## 貳、文獻探討

### 一、電子白板的特色

　　電子白板如其他像手機、平板電腦、提款機等觸控式面板的相關產品，其最大的特色在於提供容易操作的人性化介面。我們可以用手指頭在電腦螢幕上直接翻頁；與畫面裡的人事物進行互動；甚至可以藉由手指旋轉進入不同角度的立體畫面中。在教育界裡，也有一些學者提出電子白板應用在教學上的例子，如小學中文科、常識科等教學的應用[1]。

---

[1]　莊護林、李肖蘭（2006）。〈在小學中文科及常識科應用互動電子白板的策略〉，《粉

　　而香港教育統籌局於2004年起於中小學推行互動式電子白板的
試教計畫，為這種創新的課堂學習工具於課堂的應用策略及學生的學
習成效進行研究[2]。相對於傳統的黑板，作為學習工具的互動式電子
白板則更具功能性及展示性。教師在教學的過程中，可以一邊操作電
子白板，同時也可以有效率地演示教學內容及記錄教學過程的相關訊
息，而學習者在學習過程中也能有更多的參與及互動機會。

　　互動式電子白板是一個大尺寸的觸控式屏幕，只要用手指或滑鼠
筆，就可以輕觸這個大屏幕，互動式電子白板是由電子感應白板及感
應筆等附件與操作系統所組合而成的。它融合了電腦技術、微電子技
術與電子通信技術，使電腦具有輸入以及輸出的特性，既是白板又是
電腦螢幕。螢幕上所顯示的內容可隨意圈點、操作、注釋、修改，並
可儲存和列印。請見網奕資訊（2006），互動式電子白板示意圖。

　　http://www.habook.com.tw/habook_epaper/2006/950731_
IWB/950731_IWB.htm

　　互動式電子白板是一種優良的展演示輔助工具，其優點如下：

㈠ 改變學習者在觸覺、視覺和聽覺三方面的學習方式

　　教師在教學過程中利用手指或是滑鼠筆在白板上直接進行操控
和書寫，減少在課堂上因轉換介面的不便以及促進教學過程的連貫
性。電子白板也是一種色彩化、形象化的學習工具。教師在課堂教學
上將有關的學習重點或要學生留意的地方，能透過白板筆把相關的資
料以特別的顏色或圖形即時標示。而且，電子白板有許多富有變化的
學習模式。例如：我們可以在白板中書寫或標示資料，也可以把白板
上的訊息轉為圖像化的訊息，更可以將音樂或是語音檔案融合入教材

---

　　嶺公立學校：資訊科技教育論文集》，亞太教育研究國際會議，http://www.flp.edu.hk/coe/
Publications/Ses-6.pdf。

[2]　同上。

裡。藉由電子白板的多樣化功能，使我們在學習過程中，能夠改變學習者在觸覺、視覺和聽覺三方面的學習方式，讓學習過程更加有趣富有變化性。

## ㈡ 互動式教學提升教師與學生之間互動的機會

能夠進一步改善電腦化的教學情境，增加多元互動。對於電腦教室的學習模式或單以簡報的教學模式而言，互動電子白板教學模式可更能提升教師與學生之間互動的機會。透過電子白板的輔助，教師能有效率地依據成本效益去運用教學資源。相對於建立一個電腦室的成本來說，電子白板可以大大地節省成本。互動電子白板在也不需要清理，對於教師與學生的呼吸系統的影響比傳統的黑板較低。

老師的教學技巧中，特別是鼓勵學生加強「互動」將影響到學生的學習成就。若課堂中師生之間沒有明顯的互動，學生就容易分心或誤解老師的意思。互動式教學顧名思義就是要有「互動」，有教師與學生之間的互動、學生與教學媒介（電子白板）之間的互動，或是學生之間的互動，如圖1。此圖顯示出「互動」是雙向的，而不是只有單向的輸出（output）或輸入（input），只有達到雙向的滿足才稱為「互動」。當可以透過聽覺、視覺、動覺這三種感官來接收與表達時，透過多重感官的途徑來學習，可以更加深印象而更有助於長期記憶。也可以利用音效或栩栩如生的圖片和兒童互動，待兒童接收到這些訊息之後，也可以喚回記憶（游乾桂，2002）。以下三種互動結合了聽覺、視覺以及動覺三種感官來刺激兒童的學習，不僅提升了兒童的學習動機，更可以讓他們發揮自己的想像力。

## 1. 教師與學生之間的互動

教師在台上講故事時，不時地會針對教學內容向台下的學生問問題，或是讓學生思考、推測一些開放性的問題。教師在講述時的表情、語氣以及肢體動作都是提供給學生的訊息，而學生就可以憑著這些訊息開始天馬行空地想像，想像著如果自己是課文情境裡的

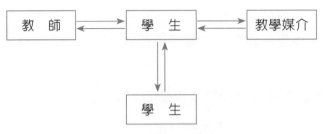

圖1　互動式教學模型

角色：想像著如果自己遇到了課文情境中的其他角色，又要如何反應？在師生間的互動中，教師扮演著引導的角色，將學生引導至課文情境中，才可以激發學生的想像力。「頭腦像是個蹺蹺板，往返於可能與真實之間」（游乾桂，2002），對孩童而言更是如此，就是因為沒有辦法很明確地分清楚真實與虛幻，所以可以想像的空間就更大了。幾乎每課課文中的情境都可以拿來作為人際關係的討論或行為動機的題材，有技巧的教師在帶活動的時候都可以成功地將重點導引出來，把所討論的重心放在每個人都會發生的普遍行為。在討論情境裡各種角色的過程中，每位學生都可以把所看到、聽到的問題作為借鏡，就可以了解到自己或其他小孩的行為。如果沒有辦法找到和學生生活相關的情境，教師也可以自己編纂故事[3]。在進行說故事教學的同時，也要考慮到孩子的年紀。年紀比較小的孩子會比較不容易安靜地坐著聽故事，他們可能會邊聽故事邊做些其他的事情。說故事最重要的就是氣氛，所以教師沒有必要太過嚴格要求他們，強迫他們時，他們會覺得不被環境所接納，反而會更反抗[4]。

## 2.學生與教學媒體之間的互動

教學媒體有很多種，繪本、故事書、電子白板及投影簡報方式來

---

[3] 原文「Dreikurs, Rudolf; Grunwald, Bernice Bronia; Pepper, Floy C.（曾端真、曾玲珉譯，2002）。《班級經營與兒童輔導》。台北：天馬文化。頁224-261。」

[4] 同上。

說故事。學生要如何跟教學媒體有所互動呢？依上段所提及到的以教師作爲引導的媒介，在此是以教學媒體爲主要的關鍵。以電子白板爲例，首先有圖片呈現，且圖片的大小可以依照我們的需求縮放，但應該比課本或講義還要清楚才是。有了圖片，還可以再加上生動有趣的音樂或聲響來吸引學生的注意，因此對學生而言，就有視覺以及聽覺上的刺激，受到刺激之後，更可以激發學生的想像力及創造力。這時教師也需要在旁提問，主要是看學生有沒有把教學內容吸收進去。

### 3.學生之間的互動

在上完教學內容之後，教師可安排一些課室活動，如角色扮演等充滿趣味性的互動式活動。教師在此爲輔助角色，首先將學生引導至課文情境中，讓學生動腦筋應該如何詮釋課文情境中的角色。在角色扮演的過程中，學生不僅可以體會當中的趣味，還可以思考在故事中是如何描述該角色。學生之間的互動主要是以動覺爲主，將自己融入情境中，一舉一動都是在重新詮釋故事。學生在這當中更可以發揮自己無限大的想像力，並將此轉換成動作、表情甚至是聲音以重新呈現課文相關情境。

### (三) 提高學生學習成效

互動式電子白板在進行教學時能直接透過系統的錄製功能把整個互動電子白板上的教學過程及教師的音訊資料記錄下來，不用像以前一樣，利用錄影機或是錄音機輔助。教師或學生若希望重新複習之前的教學活動，只要開啓之前的檔案，便能重新複習教學內容。因此，對於整個教學的複習不但可以省時，更可以詳細地記錄每一次的教學過程。而教師也能透過相關的教學網站去下載更多學習資源，使教學內容更爲豐富。電子白板的好處相當多，若能將其應用於本研究，必能提高學生學習華語在聽、說、讀、寫甚至是溝通方面的成效。

## 二、電子白板的探討

### ㈠ 電子白板的教學觀

　　華語的教學方式越來越多元化，但大都是以靜態的文字爲主，較少有互動學習的機會，對於年齡較低的學生來說，他們的注意力比較不集中，在學習上也顯得較被動。區別於其他媒體，電子白板具備能操控自如的互動功能，能生動地展示知識，運用知識的情景和模擬需要，我們可以利用它的資源多樣性、內容生動性等的優勢來輔助兒童華語教學。

　　隨著資訊技術在教育中的普及應用，越來越多的學校開始嘗試使用電子白板進行教學，將其視爲變革課堂教學方式的動力。隨著基於互動式電子白板教學研究的不斷深入探討，互動式電子白板與具體學科課堂教學的深入整合問題越來越受到關注。

### ㈡ 電子白板的教學精神

　　電子白板的介入，使課堂教學輕鬆地從過去以傳授知識爲核心轉化到以培養學生自發性的學習與求知爲重點的模式。教師再也不是權威的知識傳授者，而是引導、啓發學生學習的朋友（孫金田，2011）。老師和學生在課程中要能夠適應群體合作參與課程；學生在過程中適合主動參與，老師透過教學過程加強彼此之間的凝聚力，同時讓學生兼顧個性化。兒童以形象思維爲主，需要有圖像的表達及生動的教學方式吸引他們的注意力。電子白板不但能即時呈現書寫的文字，還能展示任何數位化的教材，符合教育兒童應具備的高度互動性的教學精神[5]。

---

[5]　高苗，〈基於互動式電子白板的小學英語教學設計研究〉，頁6-8（2012年11月23日），取自http://jiaoyu.139.com。

## (三) 電子白板教學原則

　　針對學生，我們可以把文字資訊轉化爲具體情景，化抽象爲形象[6]。舉例：席慕蓉〈一棵會開花的樹〉：「如何讓你遇見我，在我最美麗的時刻；爲這，我已在佛前求了五百年，求祂讓我們結一段塵緣。」，這樣的一首詩，可透過電子白板模擬情境來播放，把學生帶入詩文所敘述的情景中，從而更能感受詩裡少女懷春的內涵。互動式電子白板儘管兼具傳統的黑板和多媒體教學的雙重優勢，但在課堂教學使用中還是要注意合理運用，把握尺度。教師在使用互動式電子白板的時候，不僅要將其做展示教學內容的工具，而且要將電子白板與課程做深度的整合，讓教學內容和電子白板能夠發揮最好的效果。

## (四) 電子白板教學步驟

1. 在同學剛上課時，教學者用聊天的方式，循序漸進地將主題導入。這種生活化的方式可以引起同學的注意力進而帶入課文。
2. 導入主題後，教師先帶學生將課文讀一遍，在這當中會遇到不會的生字，再用英文解釋一遍讓學生初步了解課文大意，接著再重複朗誦課文一次。運用電子白板高度互動性讓學生多加練習，此方法可以幫助學生加深印象和提高學習效率。
3. 學生對課文大致了解後，教師開始解釋課文單字和句型。解釋完後用設計好的小遊戲讓學生練習單字，接著可以分成小組讓學生上台實際演練句型。此種方式不但具趣味性，也能讓學生更熟悉學習內容。
4. 最後運用電子白板互動的特性帶領學生複習，其趣味性比一般教學方式更高，使學生在課堂上樂於吸收知識，並提高學習效率。

---

[6]　儲文茹，〈電子白板為語文教學錦上添花〉，頁24-25（2012年11月23日），取自http://www.douban.com/note/175234723/。

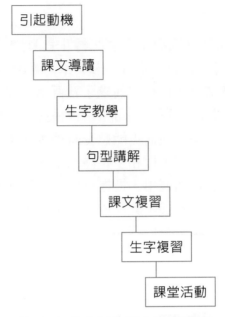

圖2 電子白板教學流程示意圖

## 參、研究方法

　　本研究採用實驗調查法以及問卷調查法。由於兒童華語文能力測驗（Children's Chinese Competence Certification, CCCC）是適合七至十二歲母語非華語兒童的華語能力檢定[7]，故研究者以通過此測驗為目標，將研究對象設定為台灣北部七至十二歲且母語為非華語的兒童七名，以中華民國僑務委員會印行的兒童華語第一冊（共四課）作為紙本參考教材，並且將課本內容運用電子白板設計成華語課程進行教學，過程採全程錄影，以觀察學生對電子白板互動功能的反應。待

---

[7]　兒童華語文能力測驗—簡介http://cccc.sc-top.org.tw/ch/overview.html。

教學結束後，再發放中英雙語版本的開放式問卷[8]，由受試者填寫，為時半小時。問卷內容將針對課程學習之後的感想為主，問卷題目共四題，採用簡答題方式回答。

　　本研究流程如下：

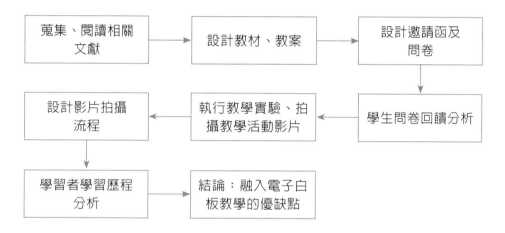

## 肆、研究結果與討論

## 一、教學實驗步驟

### (一) 學生學習背景的基本概況

　　研究對象由3位男生及4位女生組合而成，平均年齡9歲半，學生來自美、英、法、日等國家，皆就讀台灣雙語小學雙語部，具有基礎的華語能力。

---

8　本論文礙於篇幅的緣故，問卷題目内容僅以中文版本呈現。

表1：學生學習背景基本概況分析表[9]

| 名字 | 國籍 | 年齡 | 性別 |
|---|---|---|---|
| Jennifer | 美國 | 8 | 女 |
| Emily | 美國 | 10 | 女 |
| Jessica | 法國 | 11 | 女 |
| Gina | 英國 | 11 | 女 |
| Daniel | 日本 | 9 | 男 |
| Tony | 美國 | 9 | 男 |
| Ian | 英國 | 9 | 男 |

資料來源：葉君琪、邵勻同學協助整理

## (二) 引起動機

1. 老師先行自我介紹。
2. 請學生分別自我介紹、來自哪些國家。
3. 進入課文前，老師問學生早上起床後如何向父母打招呼？

## (三) 課文導讀

1. 請學生跟著老師將電子白板上播放的課文逐字唸出來。
2. 唸完之後，老師問學生課文標題「早」用其母語將如何表達？
3. 課文講授之後，老師用英文解釋課文大意。
4. 為了讓學生對課文加深印象，老師將班上同學分成兩組藉由角色扮演來練習課文，接著兩兩一組實際演練，在進行演練時老師適時糾正學生發音。

---

[9] 本教學實驗地點：江亦帆數位音樂中心（租借教室）

時間：2012年3月18日（13:30-16:30）

教學內容：參照《兒童華語教材第一冊》第一課

㈣ 生字講解

1. 老師先帶學生唸一遍生字，讓學生自己唸一遍，並適時糾正錯誤的發音。
2. 為了讓學生更明白生字的涵義，先請學生用自己所知道的意思去表達，老師再解釋生字。
3. 為了增加學生的專注力，進行小遊戲時間。當老師唸出生字，請學生使用教學棒在電子白板上找出正確答案，答案正確便給予小獎勵，以提升學生的自信心。

㈤ 句型講解

1. 老師播放句型請學生跟著唸一遍。
2. 請學生更換稱謂來造句，例如：「爸爸早」、「姊姊早」。
3. 請學生解釋「早」和「好」的不同。
4. 請學生分別練習「我的名字叫＿＿＿＿」和「我姓＿＿＿，名字叫＿＿＿」有什麼差別。老師再用英文進行說明。
5. 請學生先更換稱謂，再練習造句，例如：「老師再見」、「叔叔再見」。

㈥ 複習課文

1. 老師利用電子白板帶學生把課文複習一遍。
2. 請三位學生上台角色扮演，看著電子白板上的課文進行練習。

㈦ 複習生字

1. 老師利用電子白板讓學生複習一遍生字。
2. 進行教學活動，老師使用教學棒指著電子白板上的生字讓學生搶答。

㈧ 課堂活動

1. 遊戲一：老師請學生上台，請學生使用教學棒點選電子白板上的

選項，聽到選項聲音後找出正確的答案。

2. 遊戲二：句型重組，請學生把遊戲框框內的文字組合成一個完整的句子。

3. 兩種遊戲皆答對者，即可獲得精美小禮物當作獎勵。

## 二、學習歷程研究分析

### ㈠ 課堂前

1. 七位學生一開始因為互不認識，彼此感到陌生，所以不太敢開口說話，但是對於電子白板教室的環境很感興趣。

2. 為了讓學生放鬆心情，老師播放輕音樂。

3. 課前先告訴學生此次上課的內容，並做簡單的操作，例如：電子白板可以直接觸控等等，讓學生對電子白板有基本的認識，也讓老師能夠順利進行教學。

### ㈡ 課堂中

1. 教學過程中，學生都能踴躍回答問題，配合度非常高。

2. 在課堂中，如果學生有發音上的問題，老師適時糾正，讓學生及時改進。

3. 進行課堂活動時，學生利用電子白板複習上課內容，讓學生認識電子白板豐富的功能，體驗電子白板的功能和互動性。

4. 在課堂的尾聲，學生已熟悉整個教學環境，因此參與度愈趨踴躍。

### ㈢ 課堂後

1. 課後讓學生填寫回饋問卷，每位學生皆對本次課程有極度的好感。

2. 學生在問卷中，電子白板結合兒童華語是一項非常有吸引力的教學，在活潑的課程中理解得更快。

3. 學生認為老師新鮮且生動的教學方式，使整個課堂的互動相當融
　洽，讓他們在較無壓力的環境下輕鬆學習。

## 三、課室觀察心得

　　現今台灣普遍的教學方式，多數仍是黑板和課本，即使學校備有
電子白板，使用機率仍然鮮少。因此，用電子白板來輔助學習，對於
小朋友來說是一種很新鮮的學習方式。此次實驗教學不同以往，小朋
友對於與電子白板的互動感到相當好奇，搭配邊玩遊戲邊上課的方
式，小朋友回答問題的情況相當踴躍，各個等待上台的機會，以便小
試一番，而非以往一上台唸課文因感到害羞而卻步。透過這樣的方
式，不但讓他們能夠快速學習華語，亦能提升其學習動機。

## 四、學生問卷回饋

(一) 你覺得今天上課好玩嗎？

表2　學生問卷問題一之回饋表

| 名字 | 國籍 | 年齡 | 性別 | 回饋 |
|---|---|---|---|---|
| Jennifer | 美國 | 8 | 女 | Very good |
| Emily | 美國 | 10 | 女 | Yes |
| Jessica | 法國 | 11 | 女 | I think it is fun |
| Gina | 英國 | 11 | 女 | 好玩 |
| Daniel | 日本 | 9 | 男 | Yes |
| Tony | 美國 | 9 | 男 | 好玩 |
| Ian | 英國 | 9 | 男 | Good |

資料來源：葉君琪、邵勻同學協助整理

　　根據以上表2，100%的學習者皆有正面的回饋，認為融入電子白
板的華語教學是有趣且好玩的。

㈡ 你覺得今天上課最有趣的地方是什麼？為什麼？

表3　學生問卷問題二之回饋表

| 名字 | 國籍 | 年齡 | 性別 | 回饋 |
|---|---|---|---|---|
| Jennifer | 美國 | 8 | 女 | Game |
| Emily | 美國 | 10 | 女 | When we play a game, because we can play with the computer. |
| Jessica | 法國 | 11 | 女 | 生字最好玩了！因為有新的字可以學！ |
| Gina | 英國 | 11 | 女 | 玩遊戲，因為遊戲很新奇 |
| Daniel | 日本 | 9 | 男 | No |
| Tony | 美國 | 9 | 男 | 玩遊戲因為很好玩 |
| Ian | 英國 | 9 | 男 | 沒有 |

資料來源：葉君琪、邵勻同學協助整理

　　根據以上表3，約71%的學習者皆有正面的回饋，認為融入電子白板的華語教學中所設計的生字學習及遊戲等活動是有趣的。而其中兩位男生（Daniel和Ian）所呈現的回饋跟以上表2中的回饋結果是互相衝突的：兩位都認為上課好玩，卻表示上課沒有趣味。

㈢ 你覺得今天的上課和平常的上課有什麼不同呢？

表4　學生問卷問題三之回饋表

| 名字 | 國籍 | 年齡 | 性別 | 回饋 |
|---|---|---|---|---|
| Jennifer | 美國 | 8 | 女 | 可以摸的白板 |
| Emily | 美國 | 10 | 女 | We can sit on very comfortable chairs. |
| Jessica | 法國 | 11 | 女 | 一個是English一個是中文 |
| Gina | 英國 | 11 | 女 | 平常上課只是唸課文 |
| Daniel | 日本 | 9 | 男 | Fun! Happy |
| Tony | 美國 | 9 | 男 | 不用寫功課 |
| Ian | 英國 | 9 | 男 | 沒有什麼不同 |

資料來源：葉君琪、邵勻同學協助整理

　　根據以上表4，只有一位學習者直接提到和平常的上課不同的是電子白板的使用。Gina認為平常上課只是唸課文，或許她應該想表達本次融入電子白板的華語教學讓她更樂於學習。另一位學習者Daniel表示和平常的上課不同的是快樂、有趣，跟以上表3的回饋結果亦有互相衝突的情況。而Ian則回答：沒有什麼不同，也跟以上表2的回饋同樣有互相衝突的情況。

㈣ 和平常上課的課本比起來你比較喜歡課本還是電子白板？為什麼？

表5　學生問卷問題四之回饋表

| 名字 | 國籍 | 年齡 | 性別 | 回饋 |
|---|---|---|---|---|
| Jennifer | 美國 | 8 | 女 | 電子白板 |
| Emily | 美國 | 10 | 女 | I like electronic interactive because it is more fun. |
| Jessica | 法國 | 11 | 女 | 電子白板，因為可以自己操作 |
| Gina | 英國 | 11 | 女 | 電子白板比較有立體感 |
| Daniel | 日本 | 9 | 男 | Whiteboard, because is convenience |
| Tony | 美國 | 9 | 男 | 電子白板，因為可以畫在上面 |
| Ian | 英國 | 9 | 男 | 電子白板比較好玩 |

資料來源：葉君琪、邵勻同學協助整理

　　根據以上表5，100%的學習者對融入電子白板的華語教學皆有正面的回饋，和平常上課的課本比起來，較喜歡電子白板。

## 五、回饋問卷分析

　　透過這些學生的回饋問卷，我們可以發現學生對於電子白板感到新鮮有趣。相較於傳統黑板，他們覺得電子白板可以自己操控，而且畫面有立體感和色彩豐富的特點，更能吸引小朋友學習華語。但是對於年紀較小的學生，在操控電子白板時，則需要老師的輔助。

# 伍、結論

## 一、融入電子白板教學的優缺點

　　經過文獻蒐集以及實驗教學拍攝成影片後，整理出電子白板在兒童華語教學應用上的優缺點，細列如下：

(一) 優點

　　互動性質較傳統教學方式高。

1. 生動活潑的教學性質，容易吸引學生注意。
2. 以學生為主角，讓學生能積極參與課程，培養學生主動積極的學習態度。
3. 有別於傳統黑板教學，電子白板創造了綠色教學環境。使用電子白板不需用到粉筆或白板筆，降低環境污染，也降低碳粉對老師身體上的傷害。
4. 豐富的功能使教學更具便利性。
5. 增加師生間的互動性。
6. 可直接在白板上操作，適當調整教學內容，讓教學更加流暢。
7. 可即時將白板上操作的內容記錄和保存下來。

(二) 缺點

1. 觸控螢幕有時候會接觸不良，還是需要配合電腦操控。
2. 成本過高。因電子白板所花費的成本較其他多媒體教材高，所以不是每所學校都能夠有電子白板的設備。
3. 不適合大班教學。因為人數太多，造成部分學生無法操控到電子白板，導致師生之間的互動性降低。
4. 易使眼睛疲勞及視力減退[10]。

---

[10] 根據教育部2012年9月20日（星期四）舉辦之「研商視力篩檢工具視標及視力保健成效指標

## 二、應善用電子白板

　　總之，本研究建立在如何將電子白板應用於兒童華語教學，並試圖改變一般的課室學習和多媒體教學，為兒童華語教學帶來不同的教學模式。從本研究和探索過程中發現電子白板應用於兒童華語教學上的確是可行的，有別於傳統的課室教學，我們可以把文字資訊化為情景，化抽象為形象，易於把學生引領到學習內容所敘述的情景當中，感受作者想表達的情境。研究者發現電子白板可以激發學生的學習興趣，增加師生的互動性，改變了傳統以老師為主的教學模式。也因為教師和學生都可以操作電子白板，上課的氣氛非常融洽，可以帶領學生進入較無壓力的學習環境。

　　本文所探討的是電子白板融入華語教學，透過電子白板的輔助，可以增加學生對於學習華語的興趣，也提供師生合作的機會。電子白板的出現並不意味著要捨棄傳統的教學手段，我們可以利用電子白板的優勢，達到最理想的教師教學效果和學生學習成效。

　　縱使電子白板在兒童華語的應用還是有很多地方值得更深入地探討，希望本論文能提供未來投入相關研究的人員作為參考的依據，進而把電子白板推展成更普及、完善的教學輔助工具，也可以為兒童華語教學帶來革新。

## 參考文獻

中華語言研習所編輯小組（1998）。兒童華語課本，台灣：行政院僑務
　　委員會。

---

中華語言研習所編輯小組（1998）。兒童華語課本—教師手冊，台灣：
　　行政院僑務委員會。

兒童華語文能力測驗—簡介（2012年11月23日）。取自http://cccc.sc-
　　top.org.tw/ch/overview.html。

孟麗蓉、張俊（2011）。淺談電子白板在英語課堂教學中的運
　　用，（2012年11月23日）取自http://www.cnki.com.cn/Article/
　　CJFDTotal-XKZX201106147.htm。

邱凡芸、邱泊寰、孫劍秋（2011）。觸控式面板觸動繪本融入初級
　　華語習得教學之研究：以量詞教學為例，第七屆「全球華文網路
　　教育研討會」（2012年11月23日），取自http://ocac.go2school.
　　com.tw/icice/PDF_Full-lenght-Article/Industrial-Thesis/Industrial-
　　Thesis_102.pdf。

孫金田（2011）。互動式電子白板促成了語文教學理念和學習方式的變
　　革，中國現代教育裝備，14期，頁31-33。

高苗。基於互動式電子白板的小學英語教學設計研究，頁6-8（2012年
　　11月23日），取自http://jiaoyu.139.com。

莊護林、李肖蘭（2006）。在小學中文科及常識科應用互動電子白板的
　　策略，粉嶺公立學校：資訊科技教育論文集，亞太教育研究國際會
　　議。

國民小學使用電子白板注意事項（2013年5月21日），取自http://jweb.
　　kl.edu.tw/userfiles/537/document/14434_%E7%82%BA%E7%B6%A
　　D%E8%AD%B7%E8%A6%96%E5%8A%9B%E9%9B%BB%E5%A
　　D%90%E7%99%BD%E6%9D%BF%E4%BD%BF%E7%94%A8%E8
　　%A6%8F%E5%AE%9A.pdf。

陳淑琦（1984）。故事呈現方式與故事結構對學前及學齡兒童故事回
　　憶與理解之影響，中國文化大學兒童福利學系研究所碩士論文，台
　　北，頁22。

張良民（2006）。全球華語學習熱潮與僑教發展，研習資訊，第二十三
　　卷第二期。

游乾桂（2002）。激發孩子學習熱忱，台北：生命潛能文化。頁129、153。

葉德明（1999）。華語文教學規範與理論基礎，台北：師大書苑，頁60。

網奕資訊（2006）。互動式電子白板示意圖（2013年5月21日），取自http://www.habook.com.tw/habook_epaper/2006/950731_IWB/950731_IWB.htm。

劉春燕、張龍革、吳筱萌、張麗麗（2011）。基於交互電子白板的數學課堂教學優化策略研究，現代教育技術，第二十一卷第五期。

儲文茹。電子白板為語文教學錦上添花，頁24-25（2012年11月23日），取自http://www.douban.com/note/175234723/。

Rudolf Dreikurs, Bernice Bronia Grunwald, Floy C. Pepper著，曾端真，曾玲珉譯，班級經營與兒童輔導，台北：天馬文化，2002，頁224-261。

Medwell, J. "A school policy for reading". *Reading*, 26(1), 3-7,1992.

Mol, S.E., Bus, A. G., & De Jong, M. T.(2009). "Interactive Book Reading in Early Education: A Tool to Stimulate Print Knowledge as Well as Oral Language", *Review of Educational Research*, 79(2), 979-1007.

*Note*

*Note*

國家圖書館出版品預行編目資料

華語教學與電腦輔助運用／陳俊光，謝佳玲
主編. 一一初版. 一一臺北市：五南，
2016.07
　面；　公分
ISBN 978-957-11-8187-5（平裝）

1.漢語教學　2.數位學習　3.文集

802.03　　　　　　　　　　104011460

1X4Z 五南當代學術叢刊 021

# 華語教學與電腦輔助運用
## Chinese Language Teaching and Computer Usages

總 策 畫 ― 信世昌教授　國立臺灣師範大學華語文教學
　　　　　　研究所（470）

主　　編 ― 陳俊光　謝佳玲　國立臺灣師範大學華語文
　　　　　　教學研究所

編輯助理 ― 張閔婷　陳翊綺

發 行 人 ― 楊榮川

總 編 輯 ― 王翠華

企劃主編 ― 黃惠娟

責任編輯 ― 蔡佳伶

封面設計 ― 陳翰陞

出 版 者 ― 五南圖書出版股份有限公司

地　　址：106台北市大安區和平東路二段339號4樓

電　　話：(02)2705-5066　　傳　真：(02)2706-6100

網　　址：http://www.wunan.com.tw

電子郵件：wunan@wunan.com.tw

劃撥帳號：01068953

戶　　名：五南圖書出版股份有限公司

法律顧問　林勝安律師事務所　林勝安律師

出版日期　2016年7月初版一刷

定　　價　新臺幣400元